THE pretty SMART GIRLS SERIES

Fearless

SHAE ROSS

Entangled Publishing, LLC
2614 South Timberline Road
Suite 109
Fort Collins, CO 80525
Visit our website at www.entangledpublishing.com.

Embrace is an imprint of Entangled Publishing, LLC.

Edited by Candace Havens
Cover design by L.J. Anderson and Heather Howland
Cover art from 123rf

Manufactured in the United States of America

First Edition July 2015

embrace

For my Mom, Laura Smith Vinton
*I have always known the kind of woman I wanted to be
because I have watched you. Thank you for teaching me the
value of love and kindness.*

Chapter One

BEN

I'm standing on stage watching her strut in front of me with a beauty queen swagger. Her dark hair is bouncing above the curve of her ass, drawing me in like the swing of a bull-fighter's cape.

We met earlier today, and my head is spinning think-ing about what happened. She has every right to be pissed at me—and I should definitely be pissed at her. What I did was a mistake, but what she did was intentional. As soon as I get off this stage, I'm going to track her down, man up, and apologize. We'll see how that goes.

I remove my gaze from her ass and try to concentrate on our host as he introduces her. She's part of the team we'll be competing against this week in the ACE's—Association of College Entrepreneur's competition. Her name echoes over the sound system, ringing in my ears. "Devin Dalton." She flips a backward glance, dips her chin, and casts a knowing smile. It hits me like a spotlight. She told me her name was Daisy, and I fell for the whole act.

For the benefit of the audience, I stand composed and solid next to my teammates, but in my mind I'm shaking my head and covering my mouth with an "I can't believe I said that" hand. My mind tumbles into the replay of my epic college boy fail.

We mistook her and her team for part of the travel coordination staff. It could have been the way they were dressed that had me confused—matching black skirts and white shirts. More likely though, it was the fact that we were still working off the fog of partying like rock stars last night—celebrating my twenty-first birthday. Rather than our competitors, we thought they were our escorts—three smoking-hot girls from Michigan State. They were more than willing to flirt with us, which led to our bragging about how confident we were that we would beat the other team. Everyone knows the only thing Michigan State is known for is beautiful, *easy* women. Yep, that's what I said. A palm-to-forehead moment.

Our host finishes introducing the two teams. Team Jett: me and my two buddies, Jett Trebuchet and Vaughn Jung, and Team Ryan: Ryan Rose, Devin Dalton, and Jade Song. The audience applauds and begins to disperse into the Great Hall of the Metropolitan Museum of Modern Art—the Met. Jett lets out a low exhale, and he and Vaughn huddle around my shoulders. "I honestly did not think we were going to make it," Vaughn says.

We may have insulted Team Ryan, but they struck back *hard*. They jacked with our flight itinerary—had the limo we were traveling in drop us at the wrong airport terminal. We missed the flight and barely made it onto this stage.

"We might have to step up our game," I say, stretching my neck to loosen my collar.

"One thing's for sure," Jett says, "We are not going to be beat by three beauty queens from Michigan State. We'd never hear the end of that."

Our attention turns to the girls as they exit the stage, passing in single file. The blonde, Ryan, has her nose in the air, ignoring us. Jade follows close behind, shifting an uneasy glance, but Devin—also known by her stage name, "Daisy" —is taking her sweet time.

She's the tallest of the three, with full curves and a face worthy of an encore. Her bright hazel eyes dance with a lively spark as she pans a confident gaze that lingers on me. Whistle calls erupt in my head and everything in my body expands. "Beautiful, dumb, and easy." Well, I'm confident now only one of those is right. She flashes a quick raise of dark brows. I return her bold smile, and she winks at me. *I like this girl.*

Jett's hand smacks my chest, "Focus, Ben," he says.

"We should apologize and try to get things back on track," I say, lowering my head back into the huddle.

"I'll consider that after I hear their apology," he says. We discuss a quick game plan as we watch the girls working their way into the audience of well-wishers with the grace of seasoned socialites. Jett nods and his eyes glow with intensity—the after effect of Team Ryan's strike back smacked all over his face. He does not like to lose. "Let's get in the game, and we can talk strategy later."

We step into the crowd of Manhattan business professionals and start to work the room. I don't like to lose either but unlike Jett, I don't run all of my decisions through the "how will it affect the win" filter. Insulting women is high on my list of offenses. Team Jett may not be ready to apologize, but I sure as hell am, and I'm going to.

Dozens of handshakes later I'm shouldering my way through a sea of custom suits and cocktail dresses—smiling, nodding, and searching. A flip of glossy hair draws my attention. I follow the outline of her silhouette, appearing in shadowed bursts between laughing couples and small groups. She stops at the edge of the hall, craning her neck left and right, holding a cell phone to her ear. Her legs stride, moving in long strokes toward the exit. Perfect.

I snag two glasses of champagne from the tray of a passing waiter and follow her into a wide corridor, passing several wandering couples. I'm ten paces behind, closing the distance with each step.

Her assertive voice alternates beats with the strike of her heels as she enters a gallery of Greek artifacts. I hold back a pace, leaning a shoulder against a massive stone column and watching her move gracefully through the maze of statues. She finishes the conversation, tucks the phone into her clutch, and raises her focus to the carved marble form in front of her depicting a warrior goddess. With a look of admiration, she circles slowly, inspecting a wound exposed by the drape of a clinging gown. Her gaze shifts abruptly and lands on me. A moment passes and she smiles.

I move forward, offering the champagne. Her touch curls over my fingers, taking the flute without hesitation, and our glasses raise in toast. A high-pitched chime rings into the air. We drink, studying each other. Her expression mirrors what I'm feeling—challenge mixed with amusement. I clear my throat and ease closer.

"So, I'm wondering who thinks I'm a bigger ass; me, or you?"

She swallows, lowering her glass and tilting her head. "Hmmmm. Pretty sure it's me," she says. But there's a glimmer in her eyes that tells me I'm not out of this game.

I shift my stance watching her red lips draw another slow sip. "I didn't really think your name was Daisy," I say.

"And I didn't really think you were an asshole." She returns the slow smile I feel spreading.

"Well, it was an asshole moment, and I'm sorry I said it."

I take another drink and she raises an appraising look. "A Wolverine apologizing to a Spartan, that's impressive," she says, "You must be trying to get laid."

It's all I can do not to choke on the champagne in my mouth. I gulp down the bubbly swallow. Of course I'm trying to get laid, but I can't really admit that to her. Can I? For the third time today, this girl has me speechless; first, when I sat next to her in that limo, next, when I realized who she really was, and now.

Guilty laughter erupts from my chest. To my relief, she laughs, too, a rich, sweet sound that echoes and fades. But our smiles remain, and I'm still speechless. I am definitely going to have to step up my game this week or this girl is going to kick my ass. It's written all over her face.

She touches her glass to mine and steps past me. I turn and follow the swaying line of her hips, moving farther away. A deflating feeling hollows my chest, as if the air in the room were retracting right along with her.

"So that's it? You're not going to apologize?" I ask, amusement and disappointment evident in my voice.

She stops and holds her position a moment, as if she's considering my complaint. She turns, sauntering slowly back to me. Her tongue darts over her top lip as she steps close, so close I have to angle my head down to maintain eye contact. Dark lashes flutter, and her focus lowers to my mouth.

"If I kissed you, would you forgive me?"

I tilt my head to the opposite angle. My body is screaming "hell yes," but I manage to answer in a cool tone. "Depends on the kind of kiss."

She lifts a hand to the side of my face, and I feel the heat from her body as she raises onto her toes. Warm, full lips meet mine, slanting softly. Instinctively, my hand moves to the small of her back. Gripping the champagne glass, I press her closer. My chest and thighs ache, anticipating the feel of her curves. She leans in, and air returns to the room full-force.

Her mouth opens against mine, the slightest invitation. I deepen the kiss and feel her soft moan down the length of my body in a wave of sensations. I shift, tightening my arm around her, moving my free hand toward her face. She raises a palm to my chest, fingers drum and then press. Her neck arches and she draws back, holding her face inches from mine. Her lips are wet and open, and she looks as breathless as I feel—but it's more than just my breath that's gone. Her confident look falters. She blinks and it recovers in an instant, but the chemistry between us is undeniable. The sparks we've been throwing at each other all day have just ignited.

"Forgiven," I say, whispering in a deep voice. We stare a long beat. She slides a step back and tips her glass to mine.

"Who's the easy one now?" she purrs.

The force of her turn feathers dark hair over my knuckles. Hot breath releases from my chest and a slow smile spreads. I'm as riled as a bull after the first missed pass of the cape. I *really* like this girl. I throw back the rest of my champagne and follow her out.

Chapter Two

DEVIN GRACE

SIX MONTHS LATER

I'm rifling through my purse. I clutch the bottom and dump the contents onto the kitchen table. My fingers fumble over my makeup bag, gum, wallet, keys, tweezers—everything you could possibly need to win on *Let's Make A Deal* except no envelope. *Shit!* I press a hand over my mouth and watch my lipstick flip off the edge of the table. The tortoise shell case of Fearless Red clicks across white-speckled linoleum with a taunting echo. *How could I have lost an envelope holding the entire balance of my savings account in less than two hours!* I am so screwed.

Fourteen hundred dollars, and I need every single penny of it to move into the New York apartment Ryan and I are sub-leasing. I glance at the plastic clock above the fridge.

It's 11:08 p.m. My friends will be here any minute for our all-night road trip. I let out a deflated breath and drop to my knees to retrieve the lipstick. *Think, Devin, think!*

I retrace my steps for the third time. I went to the bank before work, withdrew the money, and locked the envelope in my glove compartment. At ten I left my waitressing job at El Azteco with $180 in tip money. I added it to the bank envelope, shoved it in my purse, and drove straight home. I got in the shower to wash my hair so I wouldn't smell like margarita salt and fried chips for the road trip, got dressed, and packed the rest of my cosmetics.

I've checked my car twice, searched my empty room, the bathroom, and every inch of the main floor. *What am I going to do?* A pit of nausea swirls in my empty stomach as I crawl across the kitchen floor.

Just as I'm about to curl my fingers around the tube, a black Converse shoe descends and kicks it aside. It spins across the floor and crashes into baseboard.

"Whoops," he says, walking past me.

"Asshole," I mutter, pushing myself up onto my knees. This is just what I need. The troll that lives in our basement—also known as my brother, Josh—has slithered up from his cave. His deadbeat friend's car was in our driveway when I got home. Either he came upstairs to see him out or to forage for sustenance. Too bad he has to eat, otherwise I could pour concrete over the seam of the door leading to the basement and entomb him so my mom and I wouldn't have to deal with his messed-up shit.

An image snaps together in my mind of his hunched frame walking down the hallway. He was a few steps past my room when I came out of the bathroom. I sit back on my ankles watching him as his teeth lay into the corner of a bag of Sun Chips, tearing it open.

He stole my money. I know he did. The nausea swirling in my stomach reverses direction and threatens to erupt. I push down a breath and speak slowly. "I need that money back, Josh." He turns and gives me that stupid, jaunty, the whole-world-owes-me something smirk. God, I hate that look.

"What money?"

I slap greasy crumbs off my hands and stand. The familiar feeling of adrenaline pours into my veins—it's the typical reaction to any dialogue I have with Josh that lasts more than one sentence.

"The money you stole from me," I say.

The doorbell rings. I press my eyes closed. Great. The last thing I need is to have a throw down with Josh in front of my friends. We packed Ben's truck earlier today. I should have told them I'd meet them at Ryan's house instead of having them pick me up, but I wanted to work my last shift for the tip money. Now every cent of it is gone. My mind is whirling. I don't even know what to do.

"Hey Devi." Ryan's singsong voice rings through the house. "You ready?"

"I'm in the kitchen," I yell, glaring at Josh.

"Hey," Ryan says as she turns the corner, but her voice and face lose their happy when she sees us facing off. Ben and Jett step in behind her, and a moment of awkward silence hangs in the air as my friends acquaint themselves with the reality of my home life.

"What's going on here?" Ben asks, his usual chipper tone dented a notch with concern. I can't even look at him

I'm so embarrassed.

"Josh stole all the money I had set aside for my rent and security deposit." I bite my lip to steady it and look at Ryan. She's the only one of my friends that knows the extent of the problems my mom and I have with my brother.

"I need that money, Josh." I curse inwardly at the sound of my wobbly voice.

He flips his head, making an effort to move his stringy black hair to the side of his face. "You blame me for everything! I didn't steal your money, you stupid bitch!" From the corner of my eye I see Ben and Jett draw back, as if a foul odor just hit them in the face. Heat washes up my entire body, a flush of humiliation and rage. I point my finger at Josh and attempt to take a giant step but Ryan reaches out and grabs my forearm.

Her voice is abrupt with panic. "I've already got the certified check for first month's rent and deposit, Devi. You can borrow what you need and just pay me back. I'm sure your money will turn up."

I contemplate her words, staring hard at my brother's cloudy dark eyes as they shift from Ryan to me. What good will it do to stand here and argue with him? He won't give me my money back—his junkie friend probably walked out the door with it. *Fuck!* How could I be so stupid?

"I'm sure Josh will find it after you've left, and he can send it out to you, right?" Ryan urges. He stares at her as if he doesn't know her, even though she's been to our house at least a hundred times.

"I'll spend my whole day looking for it, blondie."

Jett makes a deep, low sound and takes a solid step forward, but Ryan grabs his forearm, too. Like a safety guard controlling pedestrian traffic, she's holding onto both of us trying desperately to keep the situation from escalating.

"No," she says, her voice halfway between a shout and a command. She grips my arm tighter. "Let's go, Devi. Come on."

"I can't go. I don't have any other money." My voice breaks, and out of the corner of my eye I see Ben's stance shift. This is a disaster. "If I walk out that door I won't have a dime to my name, Ryan."

"I don't need the money right away," she says. "You can pay me back over time, after you find a job."

I'm staring hard at Josh, trying to come up with some other solution. My mom doesn't have the money. It's all she can do to pay the electric bill. I suppose I should have expected a last parting shot from my baby brother.

"Devi, you can't stay here," Ryan says, and I feel the truth of her words in my gut. I let out a breath, grab my purse and shove everything back in. Tears burn and I use every ounce of willpower I have not to cry. *You are not a crier. You are not a crier! Hold it together.* Ryan reaches to help. Through a blurry haze I mouth out the word, "*Sorry.*" Her pale blue eyes wilt with a mix of sympathy and tenderness, and she squeezes my arm. I press my purse against my T-shirt and take one last look at my baby brother—nothing but a waste of air.

Ben touches my lower back. He has the straps of my cosmetic bag wrapped around one big hand.

"This all you got, Dev?"

"Yeah," I mutter, still avoiding his gaze.

"I'll walk you to the truck." His voice is low and close to my ear. I stare at my feet as he leads me to the front door and down the cracked, uneven pavement of our driveway. I'm sure Ben lives in a mansion, and here I am, trapped in a Jerry Springer episode. I release the breath I've been holding in my chest. A small shudder escapes into the night air and Ben's fingers tighten and move against my lower back. The whole thing is mortifying. I don't even know what to say to him. Well, at least now he understands why I can't date him. When we met last spring at the entrepreneur competition, we hit it off, and I had an absolute blast with him, but I knew then what I know now—it would never work. Everything about my life would be completely out of place in his world.

He opens the door of his truck and pauses. "Hey," he says, waiting for me to look at him. "You all right, Dev?"

I glance at the two-bedroom ranch house I've lived in since my mom left my stepdad. The roof slopes and there's a huge branch jammed under our satellite dish that's been there for at least a year now. Patches of peeling mint-green paint have been there twice as long. Every block has one house that always looks like hell. That's my house—even in the moonlight you can see the disrepair. As bad as it looks on the outside, it's so much worse on the inside.

I hope I'm doing the right thing leaving my mom alone with Josh. But I can't help him, and right now I feel like I have to help myself. If I stay in this house, I will just end up fighting with him about going to rehab, about helping Mom more, and about not having his loser friends in our house.

I drop my forehead and rub my temples. Ben's feet are planted firmly in front of me. "I'm fine. I'll be fine," I say, raising my eyes slowly, over his flip-flops, past the flash of soft blond hair on his shins, up strong thighs, and over the rest of his powerful body. He's wearing navy cargo shorts, and his gray T-shirt hangs loose on his waist, pressing closer over the broad expanse of his chest. Ben's larger than most guys I know, and so is his state of constant happiness. Even after walking into a scene like that, he's calm, unfazed. Our eyes connect, and a slow smile melts over his features.

Moonlight frames his handsome face, catching the edges of his dark blond hair. I stare at the curling ends, recalling the feel of the smooth strands, just long enough to slide through my fingers. He looks tanner than when I last saw him. But it's his eyes that always pull me in—that pale green shade you see when the sun shines through ocean water. It's impossible for me not to smile when I look at him…and I've tried.

We stare at each other for a soft minute, and he skims my face with a smile that's both sensual and soothing. I've missed him. Badly.

"It's good to see you, Dev."

"It's good to see you too, Ben."

Ryan's voice interrupts our tender reunion. "Want to ride in the back with me, Devi?"

"Yeah," I say lifting a beaded sandal onto the running board of the truck. I freeze mid-step. "Shit. I've got to go back in for my lipstick, it's still on the floor," I say, backing up.

"I'll get it." Ben's voice carries in the still night air. "I left my keys on the kitchen table," he calls, and he's already walking up the driveway.

"It's under the cupboard, brown tube."

"I'm on it," he says, pointing a finger into the air. He opens the screen door, ducks his large frame, and disappears. God, I hope Josh is back in the basement by now.

Chapter Three

BEN

The screen door clicks into place, and I listen. I hear paper tearing—a box being opened and the sucking sound of the refrigerator seal pulling away from its base. I step into the small kitchen and stare at Devi's train-wreck of a brother. Gangly legs and arms dominate his tall frame, and I watch him twist the cap off a plastic jug of milk and tip it to his face. He catches sight of me mid-swallow.

"You lost or something?" Milk drips down the corner of his mouth, and he wipes the back of his arm over his chin.

I walk slowly toward him, somewhat shocked this kid doesn't realize he's about to get his ass kicked. My fingertips push the fridge door shut. He stumbles to avoid it and glares at me, still not getting it. My forearm connects with his neck, and I walk-shove him until his shoulder blades hit the wall. He drops the jug, and it barfs white liquid over the bottom half of his black jeans. I lean in, pressing my nose against his until all I can see is the alarmed look in his murky brown stare. Now he's starting to get it.

My voice holds a sinister warning. "If you ever talk to your sister that way again, I'm going to make sure you regret it for a long time."

"Tough guy," he says.

Nope. Still not getting it. I palm the base of his neck with my hand, squeezing.

"All right. All right," he wheezes.

"And you're going to find your sister's money, right?"

"I don't have—"

I squeeze harder, feeling the veins in his neck pulse under my fingers.

"All right, I'll find it," he says, gasping between words.

After a prolonged beat and another shake, I open my fingers, and let him drop. He sinks, braces his hands on his knees, and sucks air.

I smack his back as he hacks, "There ya go. Now see, I bet you feel better about yourself. Deep cleansing breaths… deep cleansing breaths." I demonstrate the technique with gusto and wait for him to look at me. When he does, I let a smile replace my madder than hell features, step back and hold my hand out. "Ben Winslow."

With a look of disbelief he closes a weak grip. "Sorry about the mess," I say, nodding to the floor. I pick up the keys that I purposely dropped when I heard the word "bitch" fly out of his mouth, swipe up Devi's lipstick and head out.

When I was growing up, there were times I felt awkward about my size—always wearing clothes three sizes ahead of my classmates, being questioned by the coach of every opposing team, to find out if I'd been held back. At some point that all shifted, and on days like today—when someone deserves to get their ass handed to them—I'm glad I'm me.

"Everybody ready?" I say, tucking in behind the steering wheel and handing Devi her lipstick.

"Thanks," she says, turning back to the window. I look at Jett, nod a confirmation of the deed done, and throw the truck in reverse.

"Start spreadin' the news..." My voice washes over my friends, and before the first bar has echoed they're moaning in unison.

"Ahhh Ben, come on. You're not seriously going to start singing before we're even out of the driveway."

I raise my voice and ignore them, "We're leavin' today—"

Two hours later we've crossed the border out of Michigan, and the girls are slumped against each other sleeping in the back seat. Another text pings through on my cell—the fourth one in half an hour. "C'mon on, what now?"

"Your sisters are relentless," Jett says. He's been my buddy since high school and is familiar with the constant drama that swirls around the Winslow household.

"Can you read this and tell me what's going on?" I say, handing him my phone. "Start with the first one."

"It's from Chloe, and she says, *'Cate's not home yet, and I have been covering for her but Mom totally busted me. What should I do?'*

"And the next text is from your Mom, and it says, *'Ben, Cate is not home and it's 1:00 in the morning. I know she's out with that construction worker. Will you please, please, please talk to her!'*

"And the next one is from Cate. *'Chloe is such a bitch. She ratted me out to Mom, and Mom is freaking out. Can you talk to her tomorrow? Will you be home next weekend? Love and miss you already.'*

"And, the last one from Priscilla. *'Cate and Chloe just smacked each other and Mom's crying. When can I come visit you in New York?'*"

I hold an open palm off the steering wheel and shake my head. "I don't know what they expect me to do hundreds of miles away."

"They'll figure it out," Jett says.

"Not without driving me crazy first. Text them a group message and tell them to go to bed. I'll call tomorrow."

By two a.m. we're in Pennsylvania, and my shift is officially over. I pull into the Trott to Market station and ease up beside the pump. Trott Markets are owned by the Fortune 500 Company that Jett and I start working for on Monday. We won the entrepreneur competition sponsored by Trott back in the spring and employment contracts were part of the award.

"I'll take the next shift," Jett says. "Do what you need to do, girls. Bus leaves in fifteen minutes." I pull the leather seat forward and reach a hand back for Devi.

"Hey, it's a Trott Market," Ryan says.

Devi crosses her arms and looks up at the glowing turquoise and yellow logo. The double t's are offset from the other letters in the word "Trott," forming two boots to represent their tag line, "Trott to Market."

"I've never been in a real Trott Market," Devi says resting an index finger on her cheek and arching a brow to me. "Do you think they'll have your picture on the wall?"

"Only if they want to draw in women by selling raw male sex appeal."

She rolls her eyes, and I wink at her as she and Ryan head into the store.

I fill the tank and meet Jett inside holding a paper cup under the Slushee machine. I grab one from the stacks, set the plastic dome on top, and twist the handle until an ooze of glowing yellow flows.

"Hey," he says, tilting his dark hair above the machines. Staring down at us is a picture of our new employers, Robert and Elizabeth Trott, their son Robert, and their daughter, Jillian. "Monday morning those four sets of eyes are going to have souls behind them, and they're gonna begin the process of slowly sucking the life out of us."

"So long, good life," I say. What made me think stopping here was good idea? I'd rather enjoy the last few hours of my freedom without thinking about the Trotts, especially Jillian. After what happened between us last month, I've avoided thinking about her all together.

The girls come out of the bathroom laughing and Devi gives my bicep a playful squeeze as she passes. They weave through the aisles and approach the cashier. We step behind the girls, and I reach above their heads, handing my credit card to the clerk. "Gas on eight and the rest of this," I say, nodding to the junk food they've piled on the counter.

Devi pulls a plastic baggie of oversized coins from her purse. "Here," she says. "I can pay. I forgot I have seventeen Sacagawea dollars that the parking garage token machine spit back at me when I parked for work."

"Thanks Ben," Ryan says, plucking the bags of Fritos and Skittles from the counter. I pick up Devi's Smart Water and Twizzlers, ignoring her outstretched hand and guide her to the door.

"Ben, you don't have to buy me stuff."

I stop outside and rip the Twizzler package with my teeth. "I bought it for me. I'm sharing with you." I peel two tacky strips and hand her one. Hazel eyes narrow with speculation as I twist the cap and tip the bottle. Her fingertips land on my wrist.

"Hey, I don't know where those lips have been."

I raise a brow and step as close as I can without actually touching her, daring her not to pull away. She angles her face and watches me with amusement. I raise three fingers to the side of her cheek and kiss her mouth. Dark lashes flicker with surprise. She starts to "mmmm" in protest, but her lips are smiling against mine. I end the kiss and step back.

"Shouldn't matter now," I say, drinking and handing the bottle back.

She grabs the water and Twizzler package and starts for the truck.

"Looks like we're on backseat duty together," I say, smiling and watching her hair skim over her ass as she walks in front of me.

"Why do I get the feeling that means something entirely different to you than it does to me?" she says, stretching her words through a yawn. "All I want to do is go back to sleep, as long as you don't mind me using you as a pillow."

"We might be able to arrange something." I take her hand and help her into the truck, resisting the urge to let loose a playful smack.

Twenty minutes later she's arranging her head on my thigh, and I'm sucking in a deep breath, trying not to get hard while she gets comfortable. She stops moving and within minutes she's asleep. Thank God. I stare down at her profile in my lap. Long wisps of brown hair curl around her ear and fan out over her shoulder. Her lips rest open, looking full and dark in the shadows of the backseat space. I smile thinking about the kiss I stole. I can't feel the imprint on my lips anymore but I sure as hell feel it in my heart.

After the competition ended last spring, I wanted to start a relationship with Devi—a real relationship, more than just the aggressive flirting we exchange whenever we're together. I put the hard press on for a commitment. We had a few make out sessions, but she always came back to holding her line of just wanting to be friends, even though we have never acted like "just friends." When she showed up at Ryan's graduation party with an old boyfriend, I backed off. I will do just about anything for Devi, except be her chump.

She nuzzles deeper into my lap, and I dismiss the memory before it starts to burn a hole in my stomach. Her shoulder turns, and she settles into an angle that reveals more cleavage than shirt. The glow of highway lights burst and dim through the rear window, flashing the spotlight on everything I want so badly it hurts.

Backing off last summer was the right move, but what I did after that was not. When Jett, Vaughn, and I flew back to New York for employee training in July, I had too much to drink one night and made the mistake of letting Jillian Trott lick my wounds. Big Mistake. Now I'm really hoping things won't be awkward between Jillian and me when I start work next week.

I have every intention of getting things back on track with Devi. When Jett told me Ryan was moving to New York to attend NYU law school and Devi was going to be her roommate, I felt like a million bucks had just dropped from the sky into my lap. Our employment contracts granted each of us a subsidized apartment in the building Trott owns. Jett ask me if I wanted to sublease one of the apartments to the girls at the discounted rate and I was all over that idea. Devi living three doors down from me fits perfectly into my plan.

I stare down at her sleeping face, grazing her cheek softly with the back of my knuckles. A shuddering breath feathers over my thigh. Based on what we saw tonight, her home life is tougher than I suspected. Watching her interact with her brother may have been my first glimpse into figuring out the beautifully complicated picture of Devi. I've always known there's more to her resistance—something she isn't telling me. This time I'm committed to figuring it out—no matter what roadblocks she puts in front of me.

Chapter Four

DEVIN GRACE

My cell chirps, and I read the message from Ryan. *Where are you?*

I turn my shoulder to avoid a group of businessmen and again for a woman pushing a stroller loaded with kids. I raise my head and spin, looking for a street sign in the middle of Manhattan's lunch-hour congestion.

It's Wednesday, and I've been dropping off resumes since nine a.m. — my third day in a row pounding the pavement. I wasn't planning on eating out, but by ten a.m. I had finished the apple and bag of pretzels that was supposed to be lunch. The only thing I have left is a yogurt that's the size of a thimble considering my appetite.

I'm at Bleecker and Sixth. You? I lean against the window of a storefront and wait for Ryan to respond. An unlit half-off shooters sign reflects in the glass, taunting me. I was really hoping to find a real job, but I'm down to four Sa-cageweas. Tomorrow I'm going to lower my hopes and start applying at the bars and restaurants for a waitressing gig. By next Monday, I'm going to have a job, even if I have to wear an apron and smile at drunks. My cell chirps.

There's a hot dog place at MacDougal and Bleecker. The Pound. Meet you there in 5?

On my way.

Five minutes later I'm turning the corner onto MacDou-gal. Ryan's sitting on a low bench with her backpack tucked between her legs. A red "Dogs" sign hangs above her, and she's leaning against the brick scrolling a finger over the screen of her phone. "Hey," I call to her.

"Hi!" she says, grabbing her backpack and looping her arm through mine. We head into the small diner and step to the counter. I search the hanging chalkboard for the cheap-est hot dog—which doesn't exist.

"I'm just going to eat my yogurt. I'll find us a seat," I whisper to Ryan, taking the backpack off her shoulder.

"Devi, let me buy you a hot dog."

"I'm fine," I say, walking away. The tables in the diner are all video games—the kind you have to sit behind to play—covered with glass tops. I pull a chair out at the Pac-Man table and wait as the heavy smell of fry grease wafts around me.

Ryan sits and pushes a huge basket of tater tots to the middle of the table.

"Oh my God, I love tater tots. You're the best."

"Eat," she says.

"How was class?" I peel the foil off my strawberry yogurt and lick the lid.

"Good. I feel like I have a ton to do already, but I'm starting to get a schedule lined up, and I met a couple girls this week who asked me to form a study group with them." She tucks a slice of avocado into the bun of her hot dog and tilts her head. "So did it work?" she asks, staring at me as she bites.

"Did what work?" I say, dipping a tator tot in my yogurt.

"Your summer strategy of booting Ben from your life so you could forget about him? Is it any easier for you to be around him now?"

Even if she is my best friend, it's annoying that she knows me so well. "No," I say letting out a deflated breath. "Do you know he kissed me when we were at the gas station?"

"I know you were all over him in the backseat on the way here."

I lean forward, smiling. "I just love his body. His arms are so solid, and he's always so warm. When he hugs me, I just want to roll up in him. He's the greatest sleeping bag ever."

"What would it be like if you just gave in and tried to date him instead of just flirting with him?" she asks.

"I don't even know that he still wants that."

"Yeah right," she says, looking at me as if I'm a moron.

"Seriously, after seeing my house and my brother."

"So he saw it. Now he knows. Has he been acting differently toward you? I know that bothers you, but I doubt that bothers Ben."

"Well, it should," I say, flicking salt off my fingers and picking up my yogurt.

A black-shirted waitress with a thick stripe of purple hair approaches our table. "Uh, miss, you can't have food from the outside in here," she says, pointing the dirty dishrag she's holding toward my yogurt. "It's against health code."

"Oh, really?" I say faking a concerned tone. I pick it up and inspect the label. "This has live cultures," I say, shoving a heaping spoonful in my mouth. "I'm sure it passes the health code," I say, talking through another bite. "Tastes totally healthy." I hand her the container with an innocent expression. "I'm done anyhow. Thank you." She lets out an annoyed huff and carries it to the trash.

Ryan stops mid-bite. "You know what's so funny about you, Dev? You are completely fearless when it comes to everything in life except your relationships." I raise an "oh, really" brow. "Seriously, think about it. Are you ever scared to confront anyone?" She tilts her head toward the waitress.

"What? That?" I say. "That's just being a smartass."

"Yeah, but there's more to it than that. You have no respect for authority." I glance over at the waitress who's standing by the garbage picking her teeth.

"Authority, really?"

"If that had been a police officer busting you out, you would have done the same thing. Am I right? Admit it."

I laugh. She is right. I would have.

"So my point is, you're never afraid to speak your mind, to tell someone off."

"Well, neither are you, Miss Queen of the Comeback."

"Yeah, but I would never punch anyone, Devi. I would point my finger in their face, rip off a bunch of insults, and then run like hell. Not you though. You're not afraid of anything. You're fearless."

"That's not true," I counter. "With the exception of babies, I'm afraid of anything that crawls. Especially those skinny things with pinchers on top of their heads that hide under pots in the summer and eat your brains."

"Earwigs."

"Yeah, earwigs." I shudder. "I'm afraid of those."

"And relationships," she says. "And when I say relationships, I *am* talking about Ben here. You're scared to have a relationship with him because you're scared of what 'might' happen, the unknown. So here's my thought: whatever it is that makes you fearless in those other areas of life—the areas where most people aren't fearless—you need to tap into that and apply it to Ben."

I raise an elbow onto the glass and brace my chin in my palm. My mind turns on each word, searching for an out, but I'm boxed in by the truth. I know I'm a tough girl. I always have been, and I have my own theory on where that comes from. I cast a downward glance, thinking. Ryan is the only person I would discuss this with, and knowing Ryan she's probably already figured it out. "You know what happened when I was four, with my mom and my real dad?"

Her chewing slows, and she swallows. "How much of that do you remember, Dev?" she asks, her expression growing serious.

"I remember him choking her. I remember the sound of the gun going off—like an explosion in my brain, and the sound of his body falling—like a bag of rocks. And I remember the smell of hot smoke." Ryan reaches her hand to my forearm and I continue. "I think I'm not afraid to confront anything physically because I've seen the worst happen."

"And you saw it happen to the person of authority in your life," she says.

"I'm sure there's a connection with all of that. Honestly, I'd rather just let people think I'm a complete badass without the baggage."

"We all have baggage."

"Yeah, but some of us have nice Louis Vuitton baggage. I have the kind you see going round the airport conveyer belt looking like it's been through a tornado." I swirl a hand over the table. "Dirty—with socks and bras hanging out, wrapped in Saran wrap and duct tape."

She raises a triumphant finger. "Yes, but you survived the tornado! And in some areas of your life it's made you so much stronger. We've figured out what makes you fearless; now we just have to figure out how to apply that to what you're scared of."

I scratch my head. "Am I going to owe you anything for this counseling session? Because I only have four Sacage-weas left. Besides, I thought you were going to law school, not psych school."

"I'm pretty sure it's the same thing—just four hundred dollars more per credit."

"Have you heard from the guys today?" I ask her.

"Just briefly," she says, scrunching her brow and checking her phone. "That was Jett texting when you walked up. He said he had a shitty morning, but Ben's was worse. I don't know what that means, but I'm sure we'll find out."

"Ben asked me to go to some amateur cage fight tomor-row, are you guys going?"

"Yeah, Jett said he wants to see Ben."

"See Ben?" My voice mimics the alarm going off in my head. "Is he in it?" I stare at her trying to process the thought of Ben in a cage fight. Goosebumps prickle the back of my skin.

"I think that's what Jett said, I told him I'd go but hon-estly, I kind of tuned him out after he said cage fight—not really my thing. I could be wrong, I'll ask Jett," she says. We stand up and clear the table and I make a mental note to talk Ben out of getting his ass kicked.

"I'm going back to campus to study, but I'll walk with you to the subway. Jett's meeting me here after work. We signed up for a fencing class together."

"That sounds competitive," I say. We tip the contents of our red baskets into the garbage, add the baskets to the stack on top of the trashcan, and head out into the September sunshine. Ryan walks beside me, demonstrating her fencing skills with intermittent lunges and jabs, discussing her strategy for beating Jett. I don't have the heart to puke on her dreams and remind her Jett's a foot taller and has a huge reach advantage. I keep listening, but my mind zones and I think about what Ryan said in the diner and about my big bad handsome fantasy man.

It was a rough summer with Josh, and there were so many nights that I lay in bed regretting pushing Ben away. It has felt so good to see Ben and be near him again. Although that Twizzler kiss only lasted a couple of seconds, the memory of it haunts my senses, along with the thought that keeps creeping into my mind. I am fighting a losing battle with myself—for no good reason.

I walk out of the elevator onto our floor, wondering if Ryan's home from the fencing lesson to have dinner with me.

"Hey," Ben says, as I turn into our hallway. He's in the process of opening his door. "How was your day?"

"Pretty good, but my feet are killing me. I dropped off

resumes all day."

"Well, I see you've worn your sensible shoes," he says, lifting a smile.

"I have got to take these off. Will you help me?" He holds a forearm out. I grip for balance and lift a foot. The pump flips off and drops to the floor with a small thud. The blood rushes into my foot and I gasp. "Oh, my God, that's so much better. It feels like I've been walking on pegs for the last two hours." I swap hands on his forearm and prepare to free the other foot.

"Hey are you planning on fighting in that cage fight tomorrow night?" I ask. He opens his mouth and pauses, leaning back and staring beyond me.

Ryan and Jett have turned into the hallway. They're arguing about something and Ryan does *not* look happy. The corners of her mouth are turned down, and she's walking fast, three paces in front of Jett. His arms are spread, palms open. "Oh, come on, Ryan," he says. Ben and I exchange eyebrow raised glances and move against the wall, clearing plenty of space for them. "Are you seriously going to be mad at me because you lost?" Jett says.

"I don't mind the fact that I lost Jett, I mind the way that you won. No one else in that entire fencing class scored points by repeatedly tagging their partner on the ass!"

I press my lips tight to stifle a laugh, and Ben covers his mouth with his hand. She marches past us, blond hair swishing hard against her shoulders with each forceful step.

"Christ, Ryan, it was a joke."

She turns and flips a firm index finger into the air. "Not funny, Jett. You have no consider-fucker-ation for my feelings!" She steps through the door and slams it in his face ruffling his dark hair. He slumps against the wall crossing his arms. His frustrated expression lifts as he sees our amused faces.

Ben shakes his head. "Wow, Treb. I've never had a girl get so mad at me she actually put a swear word between syllables. That's a strong program you're running."

"You're two of the most competitive people I know," I say. "Messing with her when she's losing is never gonna go well for you."

He thinks a moment and rubs a hand over his chest. "You're right," he says. He looks back at her door and flashes a sinful smile. "But I can only be so good for so long, and it really was pretty funny." He lets out a deflated breath and pushes off the wall. "I might have gotten a little carried away," he says, moving to his apartment door.

"Looks like the girls aren't going to be interested in having dinner with us tonight, Ben. Want to order pizza?" Ben throws a wounded expression my way and mouths out "*What*?" I pat his cheek and leave him standing in the hall.

Ryan looks up from the mail she's sorting on the kitchen island as I walk in. "He can be such an asshole," she says, shaking her head. "I'm never fencing with him again."

"I think he feels bad," I say.

"No, he doesn't," she snaps, blowing out a frustrated breath. "I'm starving. You want to go?"

"Sure. Let me just get a different pair of shoes."

When I come out of my bedroom her small form is pressed against our front door, peeking through the sliver of a crack into the hallway.

"What are you doing?"

She jumps and turns. "Making sure they're not still out

there." She opens the door another inch, and I lean over her shoulder. "We should totally prank them when we get back," she whispers. "We haven't done anything remotely sneaky in way too long."

"Oh, you're so right. I'm totally in," I say. The thought sends a bubble of nervous laughter into my stomach. "What are you thinking?"

"Let's talk about it at dinner."

We duck into Dos Diablos, a Mexican café on our block and brainstorm over margaritas and a plate of three cheese nachos. After dinner we head to the drugstore to shop for supplies.

"What are we looking for?" I ask Ryan. I take the shopping basket she hands me and follow her down the first aisle.

"Something I saw the other day," she says, glancing left and right.

She stops behind a clerk hanging small bags of white fangs onto metal pegs.

"Halloween stuff already," she murmurs, stopping abruptly. She raises a French-manicured finger and traces the plastic blade of a medieval dagger. "This isn't what I'm looking for but it might come in handy." She pulls it from the wall and drops it in her basket. "Grab some of those fangs too," she says, moving on.

"Here!" she says, stopping in front of two oversized Super Soaker water guns. We pile the counter with duct tape, bungee cords, bandanas and our guns. The clerk behind the counter is a twenty-something guy with shoulder length black hair that looks like it hasn't been washed since July. He aims the gray register gun at the duct tape and flips us a sarcastic look. The laser hits the bar code and beeps. "You ladies having a *Fifty Shades* party or something?"

"Oh, have you seen it?" Ryan asks, busting him out.

"No," he says, in a defensive tone.

"You must have read the books then." I wink at him and he smirks and shakes his head.

We head home carrying our arsenal in plastic bags. The guys have left their door cracked open and we sneak past with the stealth of a SWAT team. Inside the safety of our apartment we load up our guns and review our plot. A giddy, weightless feeling invades my stomach as we inch our door open and peer out.

"Clear," Ryan says. We step lightly with our guns pressed against our legs, trying not to laugh. I spring across the span of their open door and take position. We're flanking the sides, pressing our heads to the wall. I nod at Ryan, she inches the door open and we peek into the room. Ben's laying on the couch with his ankles crossed, tossing a football in the air. Jett is sitting with his elbows on his knees grumbling about a play on the big screen.

"Go Green!" she whispers.

"Go White!" I respond.

"Jett! Jett!" She yells, slapping her hand twice against the wall. "Can you guys help us?"

"Ben, will you come too? Come quick! Come quick!"

We hear them standing and shuffling to the door. We turn and walk back to our open door, holding our guns in front of us.

Ryan starts the count down. "Five. Four. Three. Two."

"What's going on?" Jett asks.

"One!" Ryan screams. We turn, flip our guns to our shoulders and unload the Super Soakers. Two solid streams of icy water shoot through the air and pelt their chests. Ryan moves her stream up to Jett's face, and I move mine down to Ben's crotch. They stumble back a pace, hiss out a series of curses, and start to scramble toward us. Jett slides on the wet floor, and Ben knocks into his back. We dive into our apartment and slam the door. My fingers fumble to flip the dead bolt as Ryan slides down the door laughing hysterically.

"Oh, my God, I totally got Jett right in the face!" she gasps.

I drop to my knees and join her trying to draw a breath between wails of laughter.

"I got Ben in the crotch. It looked like he peed his pants." Fits of laughter wash over us as we compare notes on the expressions on their faces. I retrieve a roll of paper towels, and we wind them onto our hands and crawl around to mop up the residue, still laughing. "These are awesome!" I say. "This was all we really needed. Why did we buy all that other stuff?"

"All that other stuff's for defense, when they start to retaliate," she says.

"Let the games begin," I say, and we laugh.

"What do you think they're doing now?" she asks.

"I don't know. It's awfully quiet out there."

"Well, there's no way we're opening the door."

"Nope. Good thing we just ate, we're stuck in here until tomorrow morning." I pick up our guns and set them in the sink. We flop on the couches and Ryan clicks on the TV as I pull the ponytail holder out of my hair.

"I feel better," she says.

"Yeah, me too," I say, lying back on the couch.

"Is *Game of Thrones* on tonight?" In the pause of our conversation, our front door clicks.

Chapter Five

Jett smacks their door with a wet palm. "You can't stay in there forever!" he growls, but they're laughing so hard on the other side, I doubt they hear him.

I flick water off my hands and smirk. "We've got to get ourselves some of those."

Jett's head snaps up. "Hey, I just remembered something. We have a key," he says with a menacing smile.

"Oh, that's beautiful," I say, running my hands over my hair, feeling drips on my shoulders. Jett steps back into our apartment and returns with a self-satisfied smile. The key slides in and clicks. We walk into the foyer of the girls' apartment like we own it.

"Hi, honey, I'm home," Jett says staring at Ryan with a wide grin.

The girls flinch and reach instinctively for each other's

arms. They sit up from their slouched positions on the couch and rise slowly to a stand. Their focus shifts down to the dark wet star patterns on our T-shirts. Shock changes to amusement, and they look like they're trying not to laugh.

"Well, look what the cat dragged in," Ryan says, but there's an edge of anxiety behind her smile, and Devi lets out a quick laugh.

Jett takes a step forward. "You must have forgotten, I have a key to your apartment, Rose." He tosses it casually into the air, catching it with a predatory smile pinned on her. "You think you're funny?" he asks, moving toward her with slow stalking steps. A muffled laugh escapes from both of them.

"Yes, in fact, I do think we're funny," Ryan says. Jett lunges. She shrieks and bolts for her bedroom. His long legs overtake her in the hallway. "Game over, Ryan," He says, catching her around the waist and carrying her into her bedroom, leaving me exactly where I want to be, alone with Devi.

"Well, now," I say, stepping forward with my hands on my hips.

She smiles and slides sideways a foot. "It was Ryan's idea."

I shake my head and continue a slow stalking advance. "You've been a bad, bad girl," I say, watching her eyes search the arm's length perimeter. "You know what happens to bad girls?" She snatches a candlestick from the coffee table and holds it out in front of her like a saber.

"They get tattoos and have all the fun," she questions in a playful tone.

I tilt my head and raise half a smile. "What else?"

"They ride Harleys and date guys named Butch."

"Last guess."

She straightens and drops her hands on her hips. "They beat the ass of guys who think they're going to spank them."

"Wrong!" I shout and dive for her. She's fast, twirling just in time to scramble to the other side of the kitchen island. She reaches behind her into the sink and grabs one of the Super Soakers. She aims, and another blast of icy water connects against my chest. I suck in a breath and ignore the pelting steam, press fingers on the marble island and vault, sending mail and newspapers airborne. She ducks and moves left, but I've got the reach on her, and I catch her waist and scoop her onto my shoulder. "Ha! Gotcha!" She kicks and squirms, and I swat her backside.

"Ouch!" she yells. Her fingers fumble over a passing door jam and hook. I reach up, pull them off, and carry her the rest of the way to the bedroom, closing the door with my bare foot. I let her down, and she scrambles across the small room landing in a boxer's stance with her hands up and feet parted. I lean against the door and cross my arms. "You don't really think you can out fight me, do you, Dev?"

She raises a brow and mimics my tone. "You don't really think you're going to spank me, do you, Ben?"

"Perhaps we could negotiate a deal?"

She adjusts her stance and raises her chin. "Like what?"

"Well, I figure if I were going to spank you, I'd get in ten good strokes before I started to feel bad." I raise my hand and swipe air. "So I'll trade you—ten for ten. One, you say you're sorry, and two, you kiss me—like you mean it. We'll see where things go from there."

"Hmm," she says, pressing her index finger to her lips.

I raise my hand and swat it back and forth in front of my waist.

"We stop at ten," she says, looking for confirmation.

I hold up two fingers, "Boy Scouts honor."

She catwalks forward, cups my face, and kisses my mouth, long and slow. I wrap my arms around her and pull her in.

She gasps a small breath and whispers, "Your shirt is cold." I reach one hand behind my neck to the edge of the collar, pull it off and toss it aside.

"Now yours," I say, nodding a slow gaze over her.

She cocks her head, steps back and crosses her arms, lifting the hem. Rich brown hair bounces and settles around her shoulders as her shirt drops off her fingertips onto the floor. "Two," she says, and I'm mesmerized. She's wearing a black bra, full cleavage pressing against a deep V of lace.

"Come here now."

"Three," she whispers, moving against me.

I wrap my arms around her and kiss her neck as my hands move over the soft warmth of her back. I flick the strap of her bra gently off my finger and it ticks against her skin. "This next," I say moving my mouth back to hers. She returns the kiss, tugging at my bottom lip with her teeth and nods her permission. I twist thumb and index finger and the clasp of springs open. My fingers spread, moving to touch the tops of her shoulders. I slide the thin lace down.

"Four," she murmurs, tightening her arms around my back, and pressing closer. She's not going to let me see. Not yet. I bend my knees, tighten my hold and pick her up. "Five," she murmurs, still kissing me as I walk to the bed. I lower our bodies onto the soft quilt. "Six," she says.

The weight of my body presses into her soft curves while she trails a slow touch over my back and down my ass gripping me tighter. I roll, moving her on top of me, holding the back of her head with one hand and sliding the other into her jeans and over her ass. Her hand is moving up my thigh. She finds the bulge under my zipper and strokes. I groan and kiss her harder. I'm rock hard, feeling as if I could burst under her touch.

"Ben," she whispers through the kiss, "I lost count. What number are we on?"

"Three," I say, in a definitive voice. "We're on three."

"No, we're not," she says, laughing. "So much for your Boy Scouts honor. I'll give you one more."

"I want to look at you, babe, sit up."

"I knew you were going to say that," she murmurs. Her thighs straddle my hips, and she sits up. I hold my breath as she adjusts, shifting her hips over my erection. She's holding her arms over her chest. I reach, drawing my finger slowly along her crossed arms and watching her expression. I pull gently until she gives in. Strands of dark hair sway a thin curtain against the swells of white, unable to shield all of her. My gaze stops on the tight dark tip breaking through. My first glimpse of the fantasy I've had since I met her, coming to life. I trail a finger down the long strand, moving toward it. She's watching me with a tense expression, as if she's holding her breath. I hesitate and stop, dropping my hand. I can't read her exactly, but she's worried about something. I raise my torso and balance against my elbows on the mattress.

"Devi, you're beautiful, babe. There's not an inch of your body that I couldn't stare at all day." I lift a hand to her arm and pull her down for a kiss. She presses her palms flat on my chest and resists.

"Oh, no," she says, "that was ten."

I keep pulling. "I know, but I get a cool down kiss."

"There's no such thing as a cool down kiss," she laughs.

"Sure there is, you know, like when you're on the treadmill, you gotta cool down." She smirks, but her hands release the lock on my chest and she leans to me. God, I want her so bad my whole body aches, but I can't push too hard. The party is over, for now. I end the kiss feeling anything but cooled down. "Will you let me take you out to eat?" I ask.

"Sure," she says, rolling off me. I watch her bend and scoop our shirts from the floor. She holds hers to her chest and throws mine toward me. I catch it with one hand and pull it over my head as she retrieves her bra and slips into the bathroom. She flips the light and pauses a beat, watching me stare at her. Her arms drop, fully exposing the fantasy, and I watch the door close on the sweetest smile.

Chapter Six

Devin Grace

Gray clouds move against the night sky, emitting a low rumble of thunder. The first sprinkles of rain mist the air as Ben opens the door to the Sovereign Mixed Martial Arts Studio. I watch his powerful body move in front of me, radiating energy. My stomach is screwed into a knot thinking about him in a cage fight. I haven't given up hope that I can still talk him out of it.

The studio is an old industrial warehouse that's been converted into a training facility with a large arena in back. We move along with a crowd, following the arrow shaped signs marked "Cage." The distant sound of music and voices grows to a lively hum as we weave through a series of hallways. We turn the corner, and the narrow space opens into a bank of doors. Ben pulls four tickets from his pocket and hands them to the man seated on a barstool. I take a hesitant step into the arena and let my vision adjust. The bright lights beam through the dim space at a downward angle, spotlighting an octagon shaped platform, caged in by black chain link fencing.

The smell is familiar—rubber, like gym shoes with the faint scent of stale beer. It's loud, and I can feel the vibration of the music beating hard under my boots. Ben steps close against my back, places a hand on my hip, and moves to my side. "What do you think?" he asks, a glow of enthusiasm evident in his voice as he surveys the space.

"I think you're gonna get your ass kicked," I say.

"Thanks Dev," he lets out a low chuckle. "C'mon, you can help me get checked in, and then I want to look for my cousin." Ben has a cousin who lives in New York with her partner. He's been talking about inviting them out with us one night, and apparently he felt like this was the perfect opportunity—they can watch him get his ass kicked, too.

"We'll find the seats," Jett calls. Ben's fingers close on my elbow, and he starts to move down the aisle toward a table set up to the side of the cage. Ever since he told me he was going to compete in the amateur round tonight, my nerves have felt like they're wired to the outside of my skin.

"Ben Winslow," he says to the two women manning the table. "I'm signed up for the light heavyweight amateur round." A black fingernail scans the columned legal pad, stops and scratches out a note. She sets her pencil down and hands Ben a clipboard.

"Need your signature, here, here, and here," she says, licking her fingertips and flipping the pages.

I search the perimeter of the cage for anyone who looks like they might be his competition. A trio of men stands to the side of the registration table, cross-armed and laughing. They all have buzz cuts, square jaws, and tattoos, as if they're in some kind of a club. On the other side of the cage a large man is swinging his arms and tilting his neck side to side. Hmmm. He's not very tall, but he's as thick as a keg. My vision blurs over the black diamond fencing stretching around the octagon. *Shit.* None of these guys look a thing like my all-American Hollister model. I do not want Ben to do this.

I had two years of boxing training in high school and played around with a bit of kickboxing last summer. During the time I spent training I saw so many guys come into these amateur rounds having no idea what they were doing. Most of them could barely walk after the first round. I blink hard and take a deep breath.

"You all right?" He takes my elbow, and we walk a pace away from the table.

"Ben, you know, you don't have to do this for me. I mean, I already know you're a bad ass."

One side of his mouth edges up, and his voice hints at a tease. "You worried about me, Dev?"

"These guys are no joke, Ben—even the amateurs." I'm not bothering to hide my distress anymore, and his amused expression shifts to concern.

His voice lowers, and he steps closer. "Hey, I got this. You don't need to worry about me." He tilts his head down, and I see self-assurance in his soft green stare. I measure his words, his calm voice. I'd really like to think he knows what he's doing, but for some reason, I don't.

"And I'm not doing it for you, Devi."

"Then why are you doing it?"

He hesitates and shrugs. "Because I can," he says,

smiling. "C'mon, I'll get you a beer, you'll feel better. My weight class isn't up for a while, so I can sit with you before I hit the locker room."

We head up the inclining aisle. Jett is shouting Ben's name above noise of the crowd and waving us toward seats, halfway up and smack in the middle of the row.

Sitting beside Ryan is a spike-haired blonde and a tall, thin African-American woman.

"Awesome, my cousin and her partner are here," Ben says. "They're going to come out with us after the fight."

"If you can still walk," I mutter under my breath. My stomach sinks, and for a cowardly moment I consider making up some excuse to leave so I don't have to watch.

Ben kisses the cheeks of his cousin and her partner, who look to be a few years older than us, and makes the introductions. Mari-o. "It's short for Marisol," she says apologetically, twirling a finger around her ear. "My mom's a bit loopy—runs in the family. Call me Mario." I flash a sideways glance at Ryan and see her smiling. I know exactly what she's thinking—although a foot shorter and female, Mario could be Ben's mini-me. Her partner, Robyn, handles the introductions with the grace of a politician and the warmth of Mother Teresa. They are both instantly likeable.

Mario gabs on while Ben smiles warmly. "I loved going to Ben's for the holidays. I was an only child, and his house was so much fun. His sisters are such a riot—the shit they used to do. Nothing but trouble, that pack," she says, laughing.

"Hah, the shit they used to do is mild compared to current day," Ben says. "And now you've started talking about my sisters, the instant stress reminds me, I was going to get Devi a beer. Anyone else?" They all raise their hands, and

Jett volunteers to assist. Mario moves over a seat, and I sit between her and Ryan.

"How you doin'?" Ryan asks.

"Ben's all signed up to get his ass kicked."

She pats my leg. "He'll be all right. Here, have some popcorn."

I dismiss the white and red box, leaning back as Mario's hand extends, and she withdraws a clutched fist of popcorn.

Hoots and cheering erupt and I spot an older man in black trousers and a bright blue shirt moving into the cage. He introduces himself and the evening program. I'm half paying attention, distracted by the guy in front of me who looks like he's been drunk since Wednesday.

"Sporting events sure do bring out the best in people," Ryan says, pivoting her knees right to avoid the drunk's back as he sways. Laughter echoes into the air, and I look back to the cage. The door has opened and a red cape is spinning toward the center. A large costumed woman who looks like she belongs in some sort of Viking opera stops in the center. She's flexing her muscles, her mouth hanging open in an O as she roars at us.

"Yeah! Yeah!" Mario yells, clapping with gusto and laughing at her antics.

"Before we start the serious stuff," the announcer's voice echoes over the sound system. "We asked Helga here to help us warm up the crowd. Anybody out there wanna come up and play with Horrible Helga? We're looking for a volunteer. We need one female who thinks she can stay on her feet in the ring with Helga for 100 seconds."

Robyn throws her hand over Mario's lap. "No," she says. "Hell, no."

The announcer continues, "And the grand prize, if you're still standing for this round…" I narrow my vision and crane my neck, scoping out Helga. From this angle it's hard to see how big she is—there's really no point of reference.

"One thousand dollars," the announcer says, waving a rectangular piece of paper in the air. My mouth drops. Holy shit. That's a check. One thousand dollars for one hundred seconds?

"I'm goin'," I say to Ryan, bolting up.

"Devi! Are you kidding? Wait!" She stands with me and her fingers clamp around my forearm, but I'm already moving.

"Do we have any takers?" the announcer asks.

"Right here!" My hand shoots up, and I feel the people around me turn in their seats to stare.

"Devi, you can't be serious," Ryan says.

"Ryan, it's a thousand dollars!" I pause and look back at the cage. "If I win I can pay you back most of the money tonight."

"And if you get killed you can pay me back never."

"I won't get killed."

"You goin'?" Mario asks as I'm tapping her knee.

"Yep," I say, stepping past her. She throws a clutched fist toward the ground and yanks it back. "Hell yes, girl! Hell yes!" she shouts, patting me several times on the back.

I stretch a leg out into the aisle and pull the strap of my purse over my head. I take my lipstick and hand my purse to Ryan. "Can you hold this for me?"

"Shit, Devi," she says, taking the purse. We're walking down the aisle—two white girls from the suburbs, dressed more like we're ready for a shopping trip to Nordstrom than an MMA event. The crowd is laughing and cheering as I wave at them. They won't be laughing when I kick Helga's ass. I pull my lipstick case open, twist and apply.

"Do you really think lipstick is necessary right now?" Ryan asks.

"If she punches me in the mouth it will help keep my lips from splitting and I might as well look cute while I'm kicking her ass."

"Devi!" I flinch at the booming voice behind me. Shit! I forgot about Ben. I look back and see him coming down the other aisle, shouting. We're separated by a long row of people, and I pretend to ignore him and walk faster. He catches up so that he's even with us on the other side of the row.

"Devi!" My name pops from his mouth in a crisp demanding tone. "No fucking way! No *fucking* way!"

Wow. Ben's pissed. He's never raised his voice to me, and certainly I've never heard him swear at me, but I'm not stopping. I shake my head and press a tight-lipped smile back, waving him off with a hand. "Hey, you're signed up to get in that damn cage, and I can do it, too. Sit back down." The people in the row between us are ping-ponging their view, left and right as we argue.

"Fight! Fight! Fight!" The crowd starts to chant.

"Devi, I swear to God…" He bellows in a warning tone, pointing a finger over the crowd at me. I realize we're going to arrive at the cage at the same time and by the dead serious look on his face, he's going to try to intercept me. I pick up my pace and run the last steps.

The same lady that assisted Ben hands me a form just as a security guard steps in front of Ben. I scratch off my name by her X's and head toward the cage. A large man holds the cage door. "Gotta do a pat down first," he says. "Arms out. Show me your teeth. Good luck, fighter." I jump past him.

"Goddamn it, Devin!" Ben's voice erupts behind me as I slide through the gate. It rattles and clicks shut. Phew. I'm in! A cheer erupts from the crowd as I move to the middle of the cage. Two more security guards line up in front of Ben, trying to calm him down, and I feel a tinge of guilt at the tortured look on his face, but I have got to do this. I shouldn't have looked at him.

A stocky man with warm brown skin enters the cage holding a pair of gloves, heading toward me. He's one of the buzz cut guys I saw earlier, and his wide, flat face looks a little less threatening up close. "Come on over here, beauty."

A shadow looms over my shoulder, and I flinch at the vision of Helga breathing down my neck. The crowd laughs as Buzz shoves her away, grabs my arm, and guides me into the corner. He hands me a mouthpiece, and my heart starts to pound in my chest as I watch Helga. She's bigger than I thought.

"You ever done this before?"

"Once or twice," I respond, and he looks at me as if he's not sure whether to believe me.

"Give me a hand," he says.

I flip up my fingers and realize I'm still clutching my lipstick. "Shoot. Can you hold this for me?" I smile and he smirks, shoving it in his pocket. "Do not lose that. It's my last tube of Fearless Red."

The blue-shirted announcer dips his head between us. "What's your name, honey?" I stare a moment, trying to think of a bad-ass stage name.

"Fearless Red," Buzz answers, winking at me. "That

your boyfriend," he nods to Ben, whose argument with the big men around him is escalating.

"He's just my…friend." I press up on my toes for a better look. I see Jett behind Ben, pulling his shoulder, trying to get him to back off. There are three guys around him, and one has an arm against Ben's chest. *Shit.*

"You'd better tell him to settle down, or he's gonna get thrown out." I pull my hand away and walk to the edge of the cage.

"Ben," I scream over the crowd. "Hey!" I kick the cage and it rattles. Three out of four of them look up. "Ben! Stop fighting them." He stops struggling and they loosen their tight circle around him. Shrugging them off, he lets out a ragged breath and walks to the cage.

His entire face is flushed, and his jaw is set in a hard line as he crooks a finger at me. "Come down here," he says. I kneel on one knee, balancing myself with two fingers hooked on the fencing.

"I am so pissed at you right now." He shakes his head, and I'm glad there's a cage between us, but I can see he's at least trying to calm down.

"Well, go ahead, be pissed, but I'm doing this," I snap. He raises a hand, and his fingers curl around mine—gripping as if he doesn't want to let me go.

"Ben, you're out of line here. You don't have any right to tell me what to do and what not to do. You're not my… boyfriend."

His face falls, and he lets out a long breath of disappointment. I've got to stop doing that to him. I see the hurt on his face every time I say it that way. I squeeze his finger and lean closer.

"Ben," my voice is softer, pleading, "You don't know what it's like to not have a penny to your name. I have to borrow money from Ryan for a fucking hot dog." His forehead falls against the cage, and his shoulders slump. We are nose to nose, eye to eye. His head tilts and he sighs.

"I've got money, Devi. If you weren't so goddamn stubborn."

"I'm not being stubborn. I am not taking the free ride in my own life, Ben."

"Why the fuck not?"

"Because, free rides aren't real. I've been in that car. Eventually that ride stops, and you gotta get off, and then you're in a worse place than you were when you started."

He lets out a frustrated breath and shakes his head. "I just don't want to see you get hurt, babe." My heart melts. No one in my life has ever said that to me or looked at me the way Ben does.

"I got this, Ben," I whisper, trying to sound like as much of a badass as he did when he said it to me. He looks up, and I see the hint of a smile breaking. His eyes are piercing green, and I feel our deep connection. Despite my efforts to resist Ben, he occupies my mind constantly. I lean in and kiss his forehead, pressing my lips against his hot skin. I start to rise, but his fingers tighten—still covering mine through the fence, holding me in place.

"Listen." His chin lowers, and he pauses a beat. "You're going to have to move and move quick. You're faster than her, but stay out of her reach or she'll take you down in one swipe. Strike fast and get out of her zone."

He's on my team now. "Got it," I say looking back at Helga. She's shaped like a rock at Stonehenge, her thick form jutting into the air at an awkward angle, looking at me like I'm chum. She points two fingers at her own eyes and then at me.

"She's right-handed, so keep to her left," he says. I look back at him.

"Will you stay here?"

"Right here—in your corner," he says with a firm nod.

I move back to Buzz, and he finishes with my gloves, wrapping red tape around my wrists. Out of the corner of my eye I see Ben. He crosses his arms and plants himself by the cage. Okay. Time to kick some ass.

"Ladies and gentleman, I give you a real beauty willing to take on our BEEEAAASSSST. Armed with bravery, and brilliance, it's Feeaarrlleesss Rreedd." Helga is punching a gloved fist against her biceps. She spreads her arms open and turns as he announces her. Her thighs look like stumps, so heavy she has to lean to lift them. I'm jumping side to side, trying to release some of my nerves. I'm about to throw down with Horrible Helga—complete with ginger braids and a red cape. I've got to block out the "show" and concentrate on striking hard and fast.

"Hey, lookie here, beauty," Buzz says to me. "You gotta engage a little or they'll call you out, but don't try to take her down and she'll go easy on you. If you try to take her down she'll fight you full force—you don't want that."

"What kind of a match is it if I don't try to take her down?"

"Pure entertainment," he says.

"Well, I'm thinking it will be more entertaining if I kick her ass."

He tips his head. "Don't say I didn't warn you. You do

know how to tap out right? If you want to end the match you tap…" I swat his head.

"Like that?"

He smiles. "You got it. Hundred seconds and the money is yours. Good luck, beauty."

I hear Ryan's voice to my left, "Good luck Devi!" Then Jett, "Kick some ass, Devi." I say a quick prayer, take a deep breath, and turn. Helga hunches low and swings, growling like a snarling ape. The bell rings, and I fly at her with a running kick. It lands on her side, and she stumbles. The crowd raises a raucous roar. I throw my hands up and claim victory of the first strike. Out of the corner of my eye I see Helga lunge. I spin and she stumbles. The crowd erupts again.

"Stop fucking around, Devi," Ben yells. He's right. She wasn't expecting me to come at her seconds after the bell. That may be the only advantage I'll have for the remaining time. I'm pushing my luck, but I'm at least three times faster than ape woman, and having the crowd on my side will help throw her off.

I don't have to take her down, I just have to stay on my feet. Ten more seconds pass and no one has landed anything. We're circling each other with raised fists, but I manage to avoid each jab. If she lands one good shot to my head it will jar my senses long enough to give her the opening she needs. I can do this. *One thousand dollars. One thousand dollars.*

"Ouuuuuch." She lands a solid kick to my left side, and I feel an explosion of pain in my ribs—it flashes through my mind that I'll never breathe again. My knees dip, but I pull back up and gasp in a breath. Now that I've established her range, I know how close I can get. I move in and strike, twisting my body and landing my shin against one of the pressure points on the side of her leg. An audible "ummph" quivers over her flat lips.

It's more like fighting a side of beef than another woman.

She winds up. I jump back, far enough so that only her fingers graze my arm. While the momentum of her missed swing is still carrying her, I let loose a right hook to her face and then a side-kick across the front of her thighs. My shin connects with something hard as the crowd goes wild. She spins back to me and a murderous glare has hardened her features. I squint, concentrating on her square face. It strikes me—this is a guy. The red cape is fastened right at the spot on the neck that would reveal an Adam's apple. I'm fighting a guy, and that hard crack I felt against my shin was a cup. They put me in the ring with a guy three times my size.

I step in, forgetting myself for a moment. "You wearing a jock?"

The smile on Helga's face falls, and his close-set eyes move into a sinister slant. "Or are you small enough you don't need a jock?" I taunt.

"Come a little closer and you can feel for …"

"Umph," erupts from his chest as I land a solid kick. But this time I'm too close. He swings and connects. Stay up Devi. Just stay up.

"Move, Devi! Move!" I hear Ben's voice. I squint, trying to refocus and clear the white stars sparking around my head. "Twenty seconds, babe! Hang on!" I'm seeing double, blinking hard and dancing, trying to stay out of reach, buying myself a few more seconds. The stars are fading. I move in and throw two jabs, missing both, but I jump, duck, and slide back in time to miss his thrown fist. He's advancing faster now, and I'm moving as fast as I can but he's going to catch me. I hear the crowd counting down. "Ten, nine, eight…" I step in and throw a quick side kick, followed by a jab to his ribs. He swings and connects with my side. I stumble. "Four, three, two…" he winds up and throws a huge hook to my head just as the crowd roars out, "One."

The bell dings. I'm swaying on my feet—but I think I did it! I suck in a breath and I'm spinning, trying to find Ben. I see him pushing past the guy opening the gate, shoving Buzz out of the way. My joints feel strung together with rubber bands. I'm smiling, but Ben looks scared. He's lunging at me in slow motion. The lights are getting brighter, burning a white hole in my distorted vision. I'm sinking. Ben's arms close around my back as the black hole consumes me.

Chapter Seven

BEN

I drop onto the mat and lower Devi's limp body over my knee. *Jesus.* I thought setting myself up for a good amateur round would help me blow off the stress of my first week at a real job. *Wrong.* Instead I'm on my knees shaking Devi, trying to bring her back to consciousness while at the same time trying to pump blood back into my heart. I've had one other moment in my life as horrifying as watching Devi's neck snap back while the Beast pummeled her in the last ten seconds—when my sister Priscilla was nine, she jumped off the curb in front of me and got hit by a car. I watched her cartwheel through the air, and miraculously land on her feet. Devi's not on her feet, but at least I caught her, and she will be soon.

"Get your medic up here," I snap to the buzz cut guy that wrapped her gloves.

"We don't have a medic, but I know CPR," he says, dropping down beside us.

"What?" I reach a hand out and grab a fistful of his shirt. "You mean to tell me you don't have a fucking medic? You guys are going to lose your license."

"We don't need a license. This is New York," he says. "And I can't help your girl unless you let go of me." Devi moans, and I drop my hold. The back of her head rolls against my forearm. Her pale skin is marred with red indentations from the pounding. I start to shake her lightly, calling her name while the trainer smacks her cheek with the back of his hand. Her brows pinch, she gasps and immediately starts to resist us. She thinks she's still fighting. "Hey, hey!" I lower my chest against hers and tighten my hold. "Fight's over. Fight's over, Dev." She squints and blinks, trying to focus.

"Did I win?" Her voice is a frantic rasp. I smile and nod my head slowly.

"Thousand bucks, baby!"

Her body sags with relief and she grins. "Oh my God, I'm so awesome," she says but she sounds as if she's going to pass out again.

"Yes, you are," I laugh. "You gotta stand up though, babe."

"I'm so tired, Ben, I just want to lay here."

I start to rise, bringing her with me. "Later, I promise." The chant of the crowd picks up, hooting and hollering for the Beauty who conquered the Beast. "You all right, now?" I ask, holding her waist, waiting for her to stop swaying. Once I know she's got it, I step back and she moves into full Devi mode, waving her arms above her head and walking a slow circle around the ring.

"We might have a permanent spot for her in our pre-show," the trainer says, watching with a look of admiration.

I jerk my head and glare. "She's got a heart condition," I say, and I move to her side to end the show. "C'mon, killer," I say, putting my arm around her waist and ushering her out. Devi accepts congratulations from a dozen people gathered around the cage, including Ryan, Jett, Mario, and Robyn, as I move to the side table and withdraw myself from my own match—I've seen enough action for one night and I need to stay with Devi to make sure she's ok.

Trott Ventures has a resident doctor who works out of an office on the first floor of the building. Jillian said something about him being on call twenty-four hours as a concierge service to the Trott employees. I pull out my phone and text her—hoping she will grant me a favor and let me take Devi to see him. I want to make sure she doesn't have a concussion. I wait for Jillian to respond as I watch the announcer hand Devi an envelope that I'm assuming contains her prize money. Jillian texts back. Dr. Oscar can meet us at his office in half an hour.

"Let's get out of here," I say, breaking up the Fearless Red love fest.

"Where are we going to dinner?" Devi asks, taking her purse from Ryan and strapping it around her.

"You're not going anywhere until you've seen a doctor." Her mouth drops in protest but I keep talking. "I called in a favor, and the Trott physician can meet you for a quick check at his office in twenty minutes."

"Ben, I'm fine…"

"You should go, Devi," Ryan says.

"I have worked my ass off trying to find a job all week, and I just won more money than I've ever made in one paycheck. I want to go out!"

"I'll take you, and we can meet up with everybody after he sees you. It'll take twenty minutes, assuming you don't have a concussion or brain damage." She rolls her eyes but finally relents when our friends join in agreement with me.

We take the subway and walk three blocks to the Trott building. I'm watching her, trying to gauge how she's feeling. Other than walking a little slower than usual, she appears content. "I'm sorry I hijacked your fight," she says with a soft smile.

"No, you're not," I say, shaking my head at her. "You scare the hell out of me, you know that?" She laughs and reaches for my hand, holding it the rest of the way.

I open the door for her to Dr. Oscar's office, and we step in. He appears behind the front counter in jeans and a T-shirt and waves us in. We follow him to an exam room, and Devi sits on the table while I lean against the wall and explain what she's been doing for the last hour. I give him a detailed analysis of the hits she took, and Devi smirks.

"He's being dramatic," she says, "it really wasn't that bad."

Doctor Oscar asks her a series of questions, tests her reflexes, and looks in her eyes with a small light. "Well, I think you're fine. Don't do anything strenuous for the next twenty-four hours, and call me if you notice any other symptoms developing: slurred speech, problems focusing, nausea, anything like that."

"Can I go out to eat with my friends?" Devi asks.

"That should be fine," he says, and she flashes a smile my way. "Just stay away from alcohol and get to bed early." Her face falls with disappointment, and she gives me a dirty look, as if it's my fault she can't go out and party her ass off tonight. I raise an unapologetic brow, and we wrap it up with Dr. Oscar.

"I really think it'd be fine if we just go to the bar for one drink after dinner," she says, stepping close to me on the subway and looking up with an innocent expression.

"Not gonna work, Devi."

"Ben," she whines.

"No."

"I should be able to celebrate."

"We're celebrating the fact that you don't have a concussion. The verdict is still out on brain damage." She makes a face at me as I open the door for her.

We arrive at the restaurant and find our gang halfway through two large pizzas and three pitchers of beer. I pull out a seat for Devi and move the pitcher of beer away from her empty plate to the end of the table.

"You are an absolute buzz kill," she whispers.

"Yep," I take the open seat across from her and next to my cousin.

"Everything check out okay?" Ryan asks.

"For the most part, but she's got to take it easy for the next twenty-four hours."

"I'm fine," Devi says.

"Here's to Fearless Red." Mario raises her beer, and we toast with the rest of the table, including Devi who raises her red plastic water glass.

"So how you doing, cousin?" I ask Mario.

"Life is good," she says, "I got no complaints, just living the dream here in the Big Apple."

"How's your mom?" I ask. Mario and her mom are my only living relatives from my dad's side of the family, and since I haven't seen my dad in more than ten years, she feels like a connection.

"She's good. I talked to her this morning, and she said to say hello. She was happy you'd moved to New York. She'll probably come for a visit over the holidays and said she wants to see you."

"That'd be great," I say, feeling a little guilty that I don't really mean it. It's hard to see my aunt without thinking about my dad, and anytime I have seen her, she always brings him up. I define my dad as the guy who deserted his wife and four young kids to move himself and his business to Switzerland. He left each of us with a huge trust fund and checked his family off his list of responsibilities. Other than the occasional birthday call, he's non-existent. I can handle what it did to me, but the thought of what it did to my sisters—watching them on their birthdays take his call a day early, or a few days late, or not at all. It turns my stomach to think about it. No kid should have to deal with that shit.

I turn my gaze back to Devi, catching part of her conversation. "I oughta get some credit for gettin' a couple good shots in on that guy," she's saying, reaching for the hot pepper shaker. That's the third time she's called Helga a guy.

"Are you joking about the whole guy thing?" I ask her.

She pounds the bottom of the shaker, turns it over, and inspects it for a jam. My fingers close over hers, and she looks up as I take the shaker out of her hands.

"No joke. Helga's a guy in drag."

I press my lips together and shake my head. That fucking promoter is going to hear it from me. I unscrew the top of the shaker, stir it with a butter knife, close it up and hand it back to her. "You sure?"

She sprinkles red pepper flakes over her pizza. "He had a cup on and when I called him out, he told me to come feel for myself."

I look at Jett to see if he's hearing this. "Can you believe that shit?"

"No. That's fucked up," he says.

"I don't really see what the difference is," Devi interrupts. "I saw the guy before I got in the cage. I volunteered."

"There's a big difference." I recall the words of the buzz cut guy who was assisting Devi. "That guy in the cage said something about amateur rounds not needing licenses in New York."

"That's true," Robyn says. "Professional cage fights are banned in New York but there's no prohibition on the amateur rounds—kind of a loophole. The legislature has been trying to pass a bill that would require licensing for several years now, and it keeps getting jammed up."

"Well, that explains a lot," I say.

Robyn returns to her conversation with Ryan, talking to her about law school. Robyn graduated from law school in Chicago, and that's where she met Mario. She worked for the prosecutor's office for a few years in the juvenile justice division before deciding she wanted to spend more time helping kids rather than locking them up. They moved to Manhattan six years ago when Robyn was hired by The Children's Center, and they've been here ever since.

"What do you do, Devi?" Mario asks, pulling another triangle of pizza off the silver pedestal. "I mean when you're not kickin' some dude's ass."

Devi smiles. "I have a full-time job delivering resumes," she says, her voice sounding tired. "Shitty pay and no benefits.

I'm thinking about quitting."

"What are you looking for?" Mario asks.

"A paycheck, preferably from somewhere that doesn't have a neon 'half-off shooters' sign," Devi says.

"Well, we're hiring where I work at The Children's Center. We're a temporary house for kids before they're placed in foster homes."

Devi's expression lights up. "Seriously?"

"Yeah. I can get you an interview if you want."

"I want one. But are you sure?"

"I'm sleeping with the director," Mario says, tilting her head toward Robyn.

Robyn smiles and addresses Devi. "Can you be at my office tomorrow morning at nine a.m.?"

"Of course," Devi says.

"Bring your resume. I'll tell you what we have open and we'll see if it's a good fit. I have to warn you, some of our kids come to us a bit rough around the edges, but I imagine Fearless Red can handle anything."

"Thank you so much," Devi says, her voice a mix of excitement and exhaustion.

Ryan and Jett are talking about heading to a bar to meet some friends Ryan met at NYU. I lean over and tell Jett I'm going to take Devi back to the apartment. We say our good-byes, hug Mario and Robyn, and head for the subway.

"How you feelin', killer?" I ask her as we're waiting on the platform.

"Tired," she says, crossing her arms and leaning to look for the oncoming train. "You don't have to take me home, Ben, I know the way. No sense in spoiling the night for both of us. If you want to go out with your cousin or Jett…"

"No. I'll take you home."

The train swooshes to a stop in front of us, carrying a gust of warm air. We step in and Devi leans the side of her face against a silver pole, closing her eyes. The doors seal and she stumbles to catch her balance as the train starts. I move behind her and drop an arm around her shoulders, pulling her against me. Her body relaxes into mine, and I grip the pole above her head. The rails echo a tin-can sound as the train flies over the tracks. There's a thin crowd in the car that clears to a few lone riders at the first stop, leaving us alone in the back of the train. The doors seal over the smell of exhaust, and the wheels squeal as the train leaves the platform and glides into a tunnel.

Devi leans her head back on my chest. "Thank you for taking care of me, Ben." I smile and kiss her temple.

"Always."

The train sways under our feet and her body rocks softly against mine. I flex my fingers against the pole, suppressing the urge I have to lock my hands on her hips and let her feel what she does to me anytime we're close. I grit my teeth as her ass continues to brush my groin—I'm wondering if she's doing that on purpose or if it's my imagination.

She turns in my arms, and I watch her gaze move slowly to my mouth—definitely not my imagination. I know where this is going. I know exactly what she wants, but this time I'm going to make her admit it.

I speak in a low voice. "I want something from you, Devi."

"I want something from you too, Ben." She presses up on her toes.

I pull away and turn her in my arms so that she's facing the pole. If I'm going to hold out I can't be looking at her mouth, or watching her look at mine. I gather her in my arms and speak low in her ear. "I've got what you want, babe." I know she can feel me pressing against her ass. A deep, soft sound echoes from her throat, and she reaches back to grip the sides of my thighs. I find her hands and pull them above her head. Her fingers curl around the pole, and I lock one hand over both of hers to keep them still.

"I want you more than I've ever wanted anyone, but I'm not willing to do this with you anymore. You are driving me crazy with this whole 'just friends' thing. Enough." My fingers graze the skin on the back of her neck as I move her hair to the side. I trail my mouth over the delicate bones curving up. She lets out a slow, deep moan and rocks her hips. "Every time you say those words 'just friends', it's like a sucker punch to my heart. I am not just your friend, and you know it."

I take a breath and keep going. "I'm the man that wants to kiss you, tease you, bite you. I'm the man that wants to fuck you hard all night and make love to you in the morning." I feel her shudder in my arms. I know I'm pushing her. But I can't take it anymore. Something about watching her in that ring has blasted a hole through my restraint.

"Ben," she says my name in a pleading tone, but I'm not done. I strengthen my hold around her.

"I am not willing to stand outside of the cage anymore." I rest my mouth over her ear. "You gotta let me in, Dev." I hold her, and we are both still for a moment. A breath deflates in my chest, and I think I've said too much. But I feel her head nodding, slowly at first and then with conviction.

"Yes," she whispers and then again, "Yes." I turn her in my arms and her gaze locks on mine. She's smiling and I'm elated, if I understood her right.

"Yeah?"

"Yeah," she grins. "No more just friends." My knees bend, and I wrap my arms around her and pick her up. She laughs and kisses me, then shifts and winces.

"Ah, Ben, it hurts my ribs," she says in a raspy voice.

"Sorry," I say. I lower her slowly and drop my forehead on hers. This night just went from being one of the worst in my life to one of the best. Her hazel eyes are filled with light and happiness. I slide my hand to the side of her face and kiss her again, as deeply and as gently as I can manage under the circumstances. She starts to pull away but I hold her to me, wanting more. The sound of the doors opening and the realization that the train's movement has stopped hits me. I grab her hand and we jump onto the platform as the doors slide together.

I take her keys from her, unlock the door of her apartment and flip the switch.

"Do you have any Advil?" I ask her.

"No."

"I've got some at my place. I'll bring the bottle. You should keep ahead of the swelling."

When I come back to her apartment, she's in the kitchen with a glass of ice water.

"Thanks," she says, popping the pills into her mouth. Her throat ripples as she drinks. I move closer, put my hand on the side of her face and tilt her head to mine. She kisses me full on, no resistance, and I feel like we've just made it through the desert to the oasis. I take the glass from her hand and lift her onto the granite countertop. She hooks her arms around my neck, pulling me close. Her legs spread and lock around my waist, and we kiss in slow sensual strokes. She draws my tongue deeper, sucking. I tighten my grip on her thighs feeling the heat building fast. I need to step back.

I drop my forehead against hers and shake it back and forth slowly. She raises a questioning brow. "I can't believe I'm going to say this, but I can't have sex with you tonight."

"Why not?" she says with the most disappointed look on her face. I spread my hands out in front of my body.

"Devi, look at me. I'll absolutely crush your ribs. You're already bruised and tomorrow you'll be swollen and sore. I don't think I should add to that."

Her fingertips trail slowly down my chest and slide into the waistband of my jeans, tugging. Her eyes cast a seductive spark and she whispers, "It'd be the right kind of sore though."

I shake my head at her smiling. "You stiff arm me for six months and now you can't wait."

"Exactly, I've been wanting you for six months," she says.

I lean my chin against her head, kissing her hair and let out a deep moan.

"I wouldn't trust myself, Devi. I'll apologize now because when it does happen, I don't expect I'll be able to go slow or easy, at least the first time."

"Well, now you're just teasing me," she says.

Me teasing her? Ha. That makes me laugh. "We've waited this long, another few days isn't going to kill us." She drops her forehead into my chest and lets out a soft sigh as I run those words back through my head—at least I hope another day isn't going to kill us. I can't believe I just said that, but it's the right thing for her.

"Will you stay with me, Ben? Just to sleep."

"Mmhmm."

"I'm going to go change and then I'm ready for bed."

I head back to my apartment, brush my teeth, and grab my overnight case from the bathroom. I hesitate. I know there are condoms in there, and if I were smart I'd just leave the whole thing so I have to get up in case things go too far, but I think about what happened with Jillian in the summer and decide I'm never going to take another chance like that.

When I come back to the apartment Devi's in her bathroom. Light spills through the cracked door. She's changed into pajama pants and is in the process of pulling a white T-shirt over her bare breasts. I press the door open with my fingertips and lean against the wood frame rubbing a hand over my jaw and watching her. Her smile is sensual and her movements slow. Her back arches and her chest strains against the thin fabric of the white T-shirt as her hands work, threading her hair through a ponytail holder. "I would have worn something sexy but since we're not going to…"

I clear my throat, staring down at her dark nipples. She's definitely teasing me. I dip my hand into the V of her shirt and skim a slow pattern with the back of my fingertips. "You're going to pay for this," I whisper, pulling her close. "It won't be tonight and it may not be tomorrow, but it's gonna happen."

Chapter Eight

Devin Grace

"Excuse us, miss," a deep voice says. I flatten my back against the wall as a mattress passes, gripped on both ends by tan work hands. I'm in The Children's Center holding a file folder with my resume. Mario's voice is giving directions in the background. The mattress glides past and she appears in front of me.

"Hey! You found us!" she says, throwing her hands up.

"Yes. I was beginning to think I was in the wrong place."

"Oh, you mean the moving. We're expanding the Center," she says. "We just finished renovating a portion of the second floor, and we've got twelve new rooms. It's a good thing too because we need the space. C'mon, I'll walk you to Robyn's office."

My heels clip over the terrazzo floor as I follow her down the wide hallway. Scenes of aquatic life bubble past us on the cinder block walls that are painted light blue; a string of small turtles, a school of primary-colored fish, and a large stingray that melts around the corner, dopey-eyed and smiling. I float alongside Mario, glancing left and right as she points into the rooms we pass and explains what they're used for.

She stops beside a low drinking fountain.

"So how long have you and Ben been seeing each other?" she asks on her way down for a sip.

Since last night, I think to myself but I pause before I speak. "We met at an entrepreneur competition last spring and we were…" I stammer, catching myself about to say "just friends." I recall what Ben said last night about every time I say "just friends" it's a sucker punch to the heart. Now that I know how he felt hearing me say it, every time I think it, it's a punch to *my* heart. I promised myself I'd never refer to us as "just friends" again.

"I just can't believe it's only been six months since we met. It seems like we've known each other forever," I say.

The sound of running feet ehoes into the hallway and we turn to see two elementary aged girls coming at us. "Miss Mario, we're supposed to come find you so you can help the movers with Hoss and Honeybear. They said it's not in their contract to move tarantulas."

"Yeah, I told them I'd help with that," Mario says. She turns back to me, "Robyn's office is the second one on the right. She's expecting you." She waves over her shoulder. "I'll catch up with you later."

I hear Robyn's voice as I draw closer to the office. I step in and see her behind a glass window in a smaller office. She looks up, shifts the phone she's holding to her ear and holds up her index finger, indicating for me to give her a minute. I turn to the molded plastic seats just outside her office and my vision fills with the image of a stocky little African-American boy. His hair is cropped and squared off at the top, and he looks to be around seven or eight years old. "Hi there," I say.

"Hi," he says in a timid voice. I take the seat two down from his.

"Are you waiting to see Miss Robyn too?" He shrugs and looks away. He's wearing a dingy gray sweatshirt that looks like it might have been white at one time. His jeans are worn to white threads at the knees and look like they came from a picked-over lost and found bin. My heart starts to swell.

"My name's Devi." He doesn't say anything, just stares. I clear my throat, lean over and whisper, "I'll tell you a secret, my real name is Devin Grace Dalton. Devi is my nickname." I wink at him.

"My name's not a nickname, but everybody think that. My daddy named me Gator 'cause he said I had a big mouth."

That immediately strikes me as mean, but I hold my smile. I notice the slight sag of his left eyelid. My stomach dips, but I keep my voice level and matter-of-fact. "I bet your daddy and my daddy were a lot alike."

A spark of interest lights his face as I continue. "My daddy used to call me motor-mouth because I liked to talk."

He grins and we both start to giggle.

"When I was little I didn't think it was a good thing to have a mouth that worked a lot, but when I grew up I realized it's a really good thing—you know, if you have a big mouth that's not afraid to talk, you can use it to tell people when they're hurting your feelings. It takes a little practice, but you and me—we're so much luckier than all those other people who have itty-bitty mouths that barely work."

I see the reflection of movement out of the corner of my eye. Robyn has come out of her office and is leaning against the doorjamb listening. "Well, I see you've met our newest resident," she says, nodding at Gator. His head lowers to his untied shoes. He reaches between his legs, pulls a plastic shopping bag on top of his lap, and circles it with his arms. "Would you mind waiting a few more minutes Devin? I need to chat with Gator a bit more."

"Of course. No problem." Gator stands and shuffles toward Robyn. She puts an arm around his shoulder and ushers him in as the untied laces of his shoes click around his ankles. Through the glass window I see him sink into the chair in front of Robyn's desk, his profile visible from the neck up. I pick up a copy of The Children's Center Newsletter that's lying on the table beside my chair and try to look occupied.

"Well now, Gator," Robyn begins, and I realize she's left the door ajar. "Do you know why you're here, honey?"

"I know my momma took a lot of drugs and now she's really sick. She can't take care of me anymore."

"That's right. This is a safe place, and there are a lot of kids here like you whose mommies or daddies are sick. Your mommy's doing what she can to get better, and until then you're going to be here with us. One of the best things about being here with us is there are a lot of people here who care about you. We always have enough love and enough food for everyone. Okay?"

"Okay."

"Is there anything you're scared of or anything you want to talk to me about?" There's a pause in the conversation, and I see Gator shifting in his seat. His voice is raspy when he responds.

"I'm scared my daddy, he won't be able to find me 'cause I don't live at home anymore." A tear falls, and he swipes it with the dirty cuff of his hoodie.

I want to bawl. I draw a deep breath. I can't go there. If I'm going to work here, I'm going to see this and feel this. I have to be able to handle it. My crying won't help anyone, especially not Gator.

"Well, I am going to do my best to find your daddy," Robyn says.

Gator's eyes and mouth tighten to thin seams in his round face. He's trying to control his tears. I squint and press my lips flat, mimicking his expression, wondering if that works. He nods but doesn't say anything, and I brush a tear from my cheek.

"Your job while you're here is to follow the rules, be happy, and have fun. Okay?" He nods, and Robyn pulls a piece of paper from her printer. "I'm going to give you this, and you can write down as many things about your daddy as you can remember. On the back you draw me a picture. I'm going to talk to Ms. Devi now."

I turn the page of the yellow newsletter and tilt my head, pretending to be interested in the stick figure illustrations dancing across the top. Robyn points Gator to the small table beside the row of chairs. "Okay, I'm all set for you, Devi."

We exchange sympathetic smiles as I walk in and hand her my resume and she closes the door. "First and last days are always the hardest—for all of us," she says, dropping into her swivel chair and lowering her glasses. Her index finger smoothes an arched brow as she scans my resume. I feel my nerves rising. My only experience with kids is the nanny position I held two years ago. I glance out the window and see Gator's head bowed over his assignment. A wave of determined emotion washes over me. I want this job.

"I don't have a lot of educational experience with children, but I have a lot of practical experience. I've tutored kids in math and in the languages I speak." Robyn nods but she's still reading my resume. "I know I don't have the social science degree you're probably looking for."

"Actually, we have enough people with social science degrees. I think someone with a business degree would be a good move for us," she says tapping the eraser of her pencil on her desk. "I have to forecast and maintain our budget every month. And we don't have nearly enough math tutors here." She smiles and sets my resume down.

"Are you sure you want this?"

"Positive," I say. I look over at Gator. "I won't claim to know exactly what it feels like to be that kid, but I know enough."

"Are you good with money and budgeting?"

The vision of three Sacageweas in a baggie at the bottom of my purse flashes through my mind. "Absolutely," I say, trying not to blink.

"I'd like to offer you an administrative position. You'd be in charge of balancing our budget, and working within that budget to order all the supplies the household needs and things the kids need. We have special events that require more budgeting, for example, our Halloween and holiday

parties. I'd also have you come with me to help solicit dona-
tions from corporate donors."

"I can do that—all of that. I'd like to be able to interact
with the kids, too."

She laughs. "Oh, don't worry about that—there's plenty
of work in that area. You won't be able to help but be drawn
in."

"It's eight thirty to four thirty, full benefits, three weeks'
vacation, salary starts at fifty-five thousand." She raises an
eyebrow and looks at me.

"I'll take it."

"When can you start?"

"I just did."

I spend most of the morning touring the center, meeting
the staff and acquainting myself with the inventory the
Center keeps. We have forty-four kids and sixteen full-time
adults who rotate on seventy-two hour shifts.

After my tour, Robyn leads me up a short series of
stairs and flips a switch, introducing me to my new office.
It's an old janitor's closet on the second floor—a little ways
from the main offices but I have my own desk, a file cabinet,
enough room for two chairs, and the best part, a window.
She leaves me to get set up, and I start to clean and organize.

At three forty-five I hear the screech of brakes and look
out my window to see a stream of kids clutching backpacks
and filtering off the bus. I make my way to the dining room
where the kids have after-school snacks, and Mario introduces Gator and me to the rest of the kids. I sit with Gator eating carrot sticks and goldfish from Dixie cups, silently praying that some of the children will come to sit next to him. By
the end of snack a thin boy named Diego and a precocious

blonde named Louisa are standing beside us, swinging their arms, and asking questions. Although he responds with one-word answers, Gator's face looks a little more relaxed, and he even manages a small laugh when Louisa flips a goldfish into the air, tries to catch it in her mouth, and misses.

"Hey, Devi," I turn to see Mario standing behind me. She scratches her head. "I have a small favor to ask. Would you be willing to disassemble, move and reassemble the twenty-gallon fish tank for us?"

"Sure," I shrug.

"Ooh, ooh, can I help you, Miss Devi?" Louisa asks, jumping at my side.

"I can help, too," Diego offers.

"Gator, would you like to help as well?" I ask. He nods and stands, and we follow Mario for a briefing on the task.

An hour later I'm staring at Gator's brown arm as it swishes back and forth like a windshield wiper over the in-side of the empty fish tank. Diego and Louisa are squealing with fits of laughter over the bucket that we transferred the fish into, poking their fingers into the water and thrusting back as the fish swim to the surface to nip at them.

"You guys be careful over there. You don't want to tip that bucket over," I say, scooping a paper cup full of turquoise pebbles from the bottom of the tank. "You're doing a good job, Gator. You ever had fish before?"

"Nope. I ain't never had a live pet." I hear my phone chirp and take a break to dig it out of my purse, hoping it's from Ben.

Bingo. *"How's your day going? How are you feeling?"* he asks. I smile and text back. I've been thinking about him all morning. *"I got the job! Feeling great!"* I text.

"*You're awesome! Want to meet me at Monkey Kick after work and celebrate?*"

"*Yes! How's your day been?*"

"*It just improved. See you six-ish.*"

Behind me, Louisa lets out a blood-curdling scream. I flinch, turn, and lunge instinctively toward her. She's spinning in a wide circle, her blond curls flying up at the ends. Her mouth gapes and her face is pinched as if she's in pain. She's holding up her index finger, and in the blur of movement, I realize there's a fish attached to it.

"Louisa, Louisa, hold still," I shout as I move toward her. She stops twirling and starts to flick her finger violently. I widen my eyes and match her horrified look at the realization of what will come next. The fish flies into the air in a white streak leaving both of us staring at her red-tipped finger.

I lunge to catch the fish, knocking Diego into the bucket. The force of his small body tips the entire contents. Water spreads a wide dark spot over the carpet, leaving three silvery twitching fish. I grab the bucket and look for a water source. Nothing. Diego starts crying. I stoop, pinch the tails of the fish, put them in the bucket and scramble out of the room. "We need a faucet," I yell. The kids are running behind me. Diego is crying, Louisa is screaming, and Gator is huffing with every heavy step. At the end of the hallway, Mario appears. Her eyes pop at the vision of us charging down the hall with panicked faces. "We have an emergency here," I shout to her over Louisa's screams, "We need water! Now! Water for the fi…"

"Holy mother!" she says stumbling back. She looks left, then right and focuses on the small red box attached to the wall. Her hand reaches out.

"No!" I shout, but it's too late. She pulls the fire alarm and sirens shriek with mind-numbing volume around us. Louisa raises her scream into a pitch that matches the decibel of the alarm. Diego wails.

We reach Mario, and I yell over the alarm. "We don't need water for a fire. We need water because we spilled the fish bucket." I hold it out and she peers into the aluminum at the half-dead fish. I spot a drinking fountain and move toward it. Shit! I want to cry and laugh at the same time. I stand filling the bucket with the small thin stream. "There's no fire," I yell to Mario. "No fire." Her expression falls, she turns and starts to jog toward the dining hall.

Once I have enough water to float the fish, I swirl gently, trying to revive them.

We descend the steps into the front yard, where the kids are gathered, holding hands in a long line. I direct Gator, Diego and Louisa into the line and move to find Mario. She's in front of Robyn, staring at the ground and running a hand back and forth over the top of her spiked hair.

I walk to them, carrying my bucket and the sirens finally stop. I move my gaze between them, trying to think of something to say. Suppressed laughter pinches Mario's expression. A loud snort erupts through her nose, and she lets loose. Robyn and I join her, and we laugh until we start to draw attention.

"All right kids, great job, great job," Mario says, directing the line back into the school. "That was record time," she says, raising a triumphant fist into the air. I start clapping and Robyn adds a hoot of encouragement. Gator is smiling over his shoulder at me as the line tugs him forward. I wink at him and he winks back.

I move through a sea of guys searching for Ben. It's six fifteen, and the Monkey Kick is already crowded. This was our old haunt when we were all competing in the entrepreneur competition back in the spring. I texted Ryan earlier and she said she and Jett and Vaughn would meet us, too.

Small nerves are tightening in my stomach in anticipation of seeing him, which seems ridiculous considering how long I've known him. But it's different now. I'm completely high on him, on us.

I was only half-conscious when he woke up this morning and left for work. I told him I'd make him coffee, but he kissed my hair and whispered in my ear not to get up. I should have just gotten up, because after he left I couldn't get back to sleep. I rolled over into the warm indent left from his body and basked in the smell of Ben all around me. I've missed him ever since the door clicked shut.

A flash of dark blond hair moves at the end of the bar. His back is turned, and he's talking with a man I don't recognize. The man stares at me as I approach causing Ben to turn. God, he looks great. I'm so used to seeing him in jeans and T-shirts, I'd forgotten how good he looks in his work clothes. He's taken his tie off, the top button of his white shirt is undone and his cuffs are rolled. He smiles at me, and I feel my heart expand. I can't wait to tell him about my day. I'm so relieved to have a job and to have let go of my fears and given in to Ben. I dive at him and he catches me.

"Hey, babe," he says, circling my back with his strong

arms.

"Hey," I say as he lifts me into a tight hug. I kiss his cheek, and he lets out a low seductive growl. I press my eyes closed and smile, hanging on his shoulders.

"You look great," he says, and that makes me laugh. I knew from the minute I walked through the door of The Children's Center this morning that I was overdressed. After the day I've had—converting a janitor's closet into an office and cleaning a fish tank—I'm sure I don't look great, but I'm happy.

"I had the best day," I say, kissing his cheek again. I slide down his body feeling the starchy fabric of his shirt against the inside of my arms. His eyes are smiling, and I swear I want to jump him. It's only been one day since we declared our "not just friends" status, and now that I have allowed myself to go there, I really want to go there.

"Let me get you a drink and you can tell me about it."

He signals the bartender and listens with a warm smile as I talk about the Center—what I'll be doing, what I'm in charge of, all of the kids, and especially Gator. He pulls bar stools out for us and sits, but I'm too wound up to do the same. I stand between his long legs and move my hands in grand gestures as I describe the fish tank fail, and we laugh. "And the best part of the job is I get to wear jeans and flats, every day. No more walking on pegs."

He tips his bottle against mine. "That's awesome, babe."

"Funny, I never thought it's what I'd be doing with a business degree, but I am so excited, Ben." His gaze raises over my shoulder and I turn to see Jett, Vaughn, and Ryan coming toward us. Jett kisses my cheek, and I give Vaughn a big hug and then Ryan. Ben tells them I got the job, and I repeat the abbreviated version, giving them the best details.

We take our drinks and head to the back room where it will be quieter. I sit beside Ryan and fill her in on things with Ben and me. We lean together holding a private conference, whispering and laughing as the guys talk.

"Oh, Devi, I'm so happy for you," she says, patting my knee. I glance up to make sure the guys aren't listening and pause at their solemn expressions.

"What's going on?" Ryan asks. "Those aren't happy hour faces."

Jett and Vaughn stare at Ben. "No," he says. "We're just talking about life at Trott Ventures." I sense the reserve in his voice, and it hits me that as I've been going on about my day but haven't asked him how things have been at Trott.

"Rough day?" I ask, feeling a little concerned that they seem so sober talking about work. "What do they have you guys working on?" I ask, looking around the table.

"They've separated us. I'm working with Robert on new business development, Ben's working on Jillian's team, which is mostly operations management, and Vaughn's working with Mr. Trott directly."

"Well, you're the biggest winner in that toss," I say to Vaughn not bothering to hide the sarcasm in my voice. He returns my smile, and his dark eyes angle softly.

"Yeah, and judging from this week, Ben's the biggest loser. Every time I've seen Jillian's team, she's either glaring or sniping at Ben. You must have done something to piss her off. I used to think you were her favorite," Jett says.

"I just can't believe they split up the dream team," Ryan interjects with mock indignation. "What were they thinking? I mean, don't they know who you guys are?" The dramatic tone in her voice increases. "Did you explain to them that you went to Michigan?" She smiles at the appraising look Jett is giving her and sips her gin and tonic.

"Brilliance needs no explanation, Ryan." He flashes a challenging smile, waiting for the volley return.

"Exactly, that's why you need to explain yourselves."

I lean into Ben's arm and look up at him. "I think Jillian acts that way toward you because she wants you. And she's probably pissed that Ryan and I have moved to town." He takes a swig of his beer, and his brow tightens, as if something is disturbing him.

"She has a boyfriend now, and apparently they're pretty serious. Robert told me they're engaged," Jett says. "He's working at Trott. His name's Henri—and he's on Ben's team, too."

"She wasn't dating anyone when we were here in the spring. Seems kind of quick that they'd be engaged already." Ryan says, swirling her ice cubes with her straw.

Ben is rubbing a hand over his jaw, and he looks tired. I'm feeling for him right now. There's no way I could work with Jillian. As badly as we wanted to win that competition, I'm glad we didn't now. Ben sees me watching him and raises his longneck out over the table.

"Enough about work. Here's to the weekend."

Vaughn clicks his bottle against Ben's, and we all join in. "Hear, hear."

"Let's send Jade a picture," Ryan says, pulling her phone out. Vaughn holds his arms open for us, and we move to his side while Ryan hands Ben her phone. He snaps a series of poses: Ryan and I kissing Vaughn's cheeks, me with my hand on my hip, lips puckered. "Ok, a little more skin now, girls,"

Ben says from behind the camera.

"How's this?" I say flipping up my middle finger.

"Oh, yeah baby, talk dirty," he says smiling.

"Let's get one with all of us," Ryan says, and we all move around the table and pile on Ben, laughing.

He grabs my hip, and I wrap my arms around his waist. The iPhone flashes and we start to untangle, but Ben holds me close and I don't bother to resist. He tucks a hand to my cheek and pulls my ear close to his mouth. The soft bristle on his jaw scratches my cheek as he whispers, "I've been waiting all day to have you back in my arms." I smile up at him, and his expression intensifies. He tilts his head lower. "How are your ribs today?"

"Completely fine," I say, lying through my teeth. I am not used to being treated like a delicate flower by anyone— nor do I want to be, and ever since his teasing last night, all I can think about is sleeping with him. I don't care if I can't breathe, it'd be worth it to feel him on top of me. I'm not going to give him any excuse tonight.

"You wanna dance—like not just friends?" he asks.

"Mmhmm." I follow behind him with my fingers entwined in his, staring at the slope of his broad shoulders and excited about the prospect of hitting the floor with Ben again. He is simply the best man I've ever danced with. You'd think being so big he'd be only mildly tolerable, but it's the complete opposite—like one of those football players you see on *Dancing with the Stars*. Full of rhythm, grace, and smooth moves, he never lets me go. He swings me, spins me, dips me, and rocks me against his whole body.

I follow him to the floor. "Just a Dream" by Nelly starts, and he pulls me into him and we rock together. The hardness of his thigh brushes between my legs. His hand moves behind my neck, and I tilt my head into his palm. He kisses me as I breathe him in, licking his bottom lip. He stops dancing, brings his other hand to the side of my face, and deepens the kiss until I feel dizzy. He pulls back an inch, and all I see are his green eyes staring intensely, a slow smile creeping into the corners. He runs his fingers through my hair and mouths out the words, "My lover, my life…" I'm laughing at him and he's laughing, too, but not the least bit discouraged. He just keeps right on throwing down to the music with the wild abandon that's Ben.

His head starts to nod to the beat. I hold his hand and grip his shoulder; he spins us with his hand on my lower back. Several songs have played and I'm lifting my hair off my sweaty neck and arching into the feel of his strong hands. I roll my head side to side, taking advantage of the quick breeze our movement is creating. It's getting harder to ignore the pinching feeling in my ribs and I'm going to need to stop soon. Thankfully, the beat slows and the crowd thins. Ben's arms tighten around me, and we rock pressed together.

"The Trotts are hosting a reception to celebrate the grand opening of their new building in midtown," he says over my ear. I pull back and look up at him. "They invited Jett and Vaughn and me to attend. I was hoping you'd go with me."

"Sure," I say, but I immediately begin to think about how unappealing interacting with Jillian and her crowd of hobnobbing elites sounds. What am I going to wear? Is Ryan going, at least?

Ben is watching my face, smiling. "We can cut out after dinner if it's dull. Jett and Ryan are planning on it."

"I'm sure it will be a blast," I say, but my voice doesn't quite reflect enthusiasm.

I thread my fingers behind his neck, feeling the warmth of his shoulders against my arms and all I can think about in this moment is how I want to be alone with him. "Do you want to go?" I ask.

He looks at me as if he hasn't heard me right and then his mouth turns up and he nods to the music. He glances to where Jett and Ryan are dancing. I tug his arm. "Let's just go, I'll text them." He raises a brow and starts to lead me off the floor, toward the back door of Monkey Kick, which is much easier than fighting our way through the crowded bar to the front exit. He presses down the heavy handle and holds the door open. A sour smell fills the air as we step into the alley, pass the row of dumpsters and turn onto the street.

"You feel okay?" he asks.

"Yes, do you mind we're leaving?" He lets out a low laugh.

"Not a bit." I pull out my phone and text a group message to Ryan, Jett, and Vaughn. "I knew they would totally know what we were up to if we told them we were leaving so soon."

"What are we up to?" he says with a sly look. I pause and measure his expression. He knows as well as I do.

"I'm going to take you home and fuck your brains out," I say.

His laughter echoes up. "Game on," he says.

"Your place or mine?" he asks as we're approaching our apartment building.

"Mine, but I want to take a quick shower."

"Perfect, me, too," he says.

"Well, I didn't mean together." I laugh, a little startled. I'm ready for this but I don't think I want to stand under the bright lights in the bathroom completely naked, without any blankets—umm, no. When it comes to my body I am not a brave girl. To add to it all, I have three huge blue bruises on my side, and I don't really want him to see those either.

We step into the elevator, and he pulls me against him. "We could put some candles on, turn off the lights," he whispers, as if he's read my mind.

"Hmmm. That might work."

Ben stops at his apartment, and I take the opportunity to change into a short black robe. I'm in the kitchen looking for matches when I hear the door open and he steps into the living room. He's holding a T-shirt and a University of Michigan hoodie in one hand and two longneck beers in the other. He's changed into jeans and I stop what I'm doing to stare at his bare chest. He gives me an appreciative smile, sets the beers on the island and twists the caps. There's not an inch of his chest that's not rising or falling into a line of hard muscle. His skin glows golden, and I know from past experience when I lay my hands on him he'll be warm and smooth. His jeans hang on his waist, the edge of his boxers are just barely visible above the waistline. I feel a flush of heat slowly overtaking my body.

I am *not* the female equivalent of Ben in the physique department—his body is worthy of a shrine. I raise my gaze to his and watch him slowly pan my body. I swallow hard and bite my lip, moving toward the beer on the counter. I don't want to be drunk for this but a slight buzz to take the edge off my inhibitions would be nice. I tip the bottle back and open my throat. The corner of his mouth raises, and he steps close, circling my waist with his arms.

"Are you nervous, Dev?" I look up and consider lying

but I know he sees it.

"Are you?" I ask.

He kisses my cheek and whispers above my ear in a definitive tone. "No."

I smile, pushing his chest with my fingertips. I hand him my beer and pick up the long pillars from our kitchen, glancing over my shoulder as we walk to the bathroom. He's following me, drinking his beer and staring at my ass.

I start the shower and reach for my bobby pins, holding a few between my lips while I work, piling my hair and pinning it up. Ben finishes his beer, watching me with a devouring look. I pull a book of matches from the vanity drawer, cup the tip of the taper, and light the candles. He moves close behind me—his body strong and tall against my back. His fingertips skim my shoulders, moving down my arms and spreading a tingling sensation. I turn and touch the warm skin of his chest, moving my hands upward.

His fingers slide into the deep V of my robe, the back of his knuckles brushing cleavage in a slow caress. The silk drags over my breasts as his fingers move underneath, tightening my nipples. I feel the thin black ribbon tied at my waist loosening.

"Ben, the lights."

He smiles, reaches an arm out and drops the switch. Darkness surrounds us for a moment as my vision adjusts to the flickering glow.

"I can't wait anymore," he says, wrapping a big hand in the fabric of my robe and pulling it off in one fluid motion. My fingers fumble over the button of his jeans, sliding the zipper, and I'm thankful to have something to focus on other than the fact I'm standing naked in front of him—it's unnerving even in the darkness.

He kisses my neck, and I tilt my head up. The steam of the shower swirls a smoke-like pattern against the ceiling, and the sound of the rushing water soothes my nerves. He holds my chin gently and his mouth moves against mine, kissing and whispering. "I have wanted you so badly, for so long. You are the definition of my fantasy, living and breathing." I let out a small laugh. "I swear to God, Devi," he says, but it's hard for me to believe.

Right now though, I'm determined to push my own body image issues aside and concentrate on being the woman he thinks he sees. I want to be good for him. He's been so patient with me. He deserves this. I drop both hands back to his jeans and tug the sides down, taking the boxers over his warm skin. His erection springs free. I clasp one hand around it and then another. I drop to my knees in front of him and take him in my mouth. His sucks in a breath, and his hands catch and brace against the edge of the vanity as I move.

"Devi," he says my name with breathless urgency. I ignore his call and take him deeper. "God, Devi," he says, more firmly this time, reaching for my shoulders. He pulls me up. "Shower," he says.

I hold his hand and step under the hot stream, crossing my arms against my chest. The water beads at the tops of my breasts, sliding down my stomach and over my thighs. Ben steps behind me and hugs me close. His powerful body, warm and smooth, surrounds my senses. His cock is rock hard, sliding slowly over my lower back. I arch against him and moan. The side of his face drops to mine. "Mmm," he says over my ear.

He reaches above me for the soap. His hands grip and massage the white cake until the lather drips between his fingers. "Put your arms down, babe…to your side." He dishes the soap and brings his hands to my waist. They run slow circles over my hip bones to my stomach, then lower to the sensitive area just above the thin strip of curls. I close my eyes and reach my hands back to grip his thighs. His fingertips massage, moving deeper. Sensations are erupting, spreading a thousand tiny pins over my body. I bite my lip and groan his name, trying to focus on the feel of his hard thighs under my fingertips. His hands stop the exquisite torture and move up to cup my breasts. "I love the way your curves fill my hands." He lifts the heaviness and lets them slide over his hands, grazing my nipples with his fingertips. "Like you were made for me." His mouth comes down to nip my ear, starting a shiver that spreads down my spine.

"Do you know how long I've wanted to touch you like this?" I swallow over the dryness in my throat as his thumbs circle my nipples. His cheek lowers and rests against the crook of my neck, and I arch in his hands. Our bodies move closer into the stream of water and the tiny bubbles slide between the cleft of my breasts, teasing my hot skin. He turns me to face the wall so that one shoulder rests against his chest and the other is under the stream of water. He reaches for the soap again and lathers. I watch his bicep twitch in front of me as he works and then I feel his hand, slick with soap, massaging and sliding slowly down my backbone. He presses a finger into the crack of my ass and I squirm but he tightens his hold with a firm grip.

I can't take it anymore. I sneak my hands over my soapy hips as he's massaging me with strong steady strokes. I reach to the side and capture his cock. He sucks in a sharp breath, releases it and smacks my ass. I flinch at the quick sharp sting and grip him harder. A low rumble builds in his throat and his hands turn me so that I'm leaning against the cool white tile of the back wall. He presses his body full against mine, hot skin on hot skin, and we kiss until we're breathless. I can feel him pressing hard against the slippery skin of my stomach, and it's impossible to hold my hips still.

"We have got to get out of this shower," he whispers against my mouth, and I nod my head. I rinse as Ben lathers the rest of his body. I move behind him and hug his back while he dips his head and face in the stream.

"Go get in bed," he says, reaching back and smacking my ass again, "and don't put any clothes on." I step out of the shower and dry off as he's finishing. I hand him a towel and head for the bedroom with one of the long pillar candles. I pull the covers over the end of the bed, and I'm climbing in when I feel his hand cup my ankle. I gasp and laugh as he starts to pull me toward the edge of the bed.

"That is the best view ever," he says, staring at my uplifted ass.

"Ben," I whisper.

"I want you like this, babe." His hands catch my hips and he pulls me up on my knees. I feel the rough brush of towel across my backside as he yanks it off his hips. It lands with a soft thud on the floor, and I feel his erection pressing against me. He moves to his knees on the bed in back of me and slowly spreads my legs with his thighs. He slides the shaft of his cock up and down and through the haze in my mind I'm grateful he's already put a condom on. He's murmuring encouraging words to me, and I'm squirming against him, wanting more.

"Ben," my voice is a tortured whisper.

"I'm right here, baby," he says, continuing to stroke and tease.

"Ben."

"Right here," he says again, and I hear the tortured rasp in his own voice.

"I need you," I feel him slowly easing. I suck in a ragged breath and then another. His thighs press against the back of my legs, spreading me further, and I grip the sheet as he's easing deeper. I'm holding a breath, waiting for the threshold between pain and pleasure to open, and my head is spinning. He's buried inside of me, holding my hips still and tight. His fingers spread and move in a caress up my back, until he's leaning over me. He's waiting for me to move. I pull my hips slowly off of the hard length of him and drop back hard against him.

His breath catches in his throat. I try to move again but he catches my hips and reaches his fingers around between my legs. He's telling me to spread my legs farther and when I do, he starts a slow methodical stroking with his cock and fingers, rocking in and out. My breath is coming harder, I'm struggling to concentrate on anything other than the feel of him between my legs and the rhythmic stroking of his fingers. Heat is building and moving up my body, into my chest and over my neck, rushing in my head. I call his name in a voice I hardly recognize as sensations pulse through me. I'm gasping for breath, and my limbs feel heavy. I collapse my face on the bed and reach back to grip his wrist. Stop.

He moves his body, rolls me gently onto my back and lays half of his weight on top of me. I'm cocooned between his forearms as he holds himself above me. His hand rests on the side of my face, thumb moving slowly under the line of my cheekbone. He wasn't ready to stop, I can feel the evidence of that still hot and hard against my inner thigh. But his expression is serene, and the corners of his eyes hold the crease of a soft smile. He's waiting for my mind and body to come down from the cloud. I'm still trying to catch my breath. He kisses my forehead and his mouth moves against my skin. He's humming a soothing tone—basking in the aftermath of bliss with me.

I push my hands lightly against his chest, and he rolls onto his back pulling me on top of him until I'm straddling his hips, positioning myself over him and easing down. He's watching me move a slow rhythm with my hips, and I'm emboldened by the expression on his face. I raise my arms, gathering the hair that's fallen loose and raising it off my body so that I'm completely exposed. I arch my back as he grips my thighs, and I feel his stomach muscles contract as he moves inside of me. Five deep strokes, and his entire body tightens. His torso arches, and the tiny muscles around his eyes strain. I feel him hard and pulsing between my legs as he growls out a low breath. I smile and watch as his breathing slows.

I lean down to kiss his lips. He returns my smile and laughs through a breath. We stare at each other for a moment as I run my fingertips up his chest, massaging behind his neck. His gaze moves slowly over my face, and he raises a hand to move my hair back. "I'm madly in love with everything about you." I raise a finger to his lips and trace the outline.

"I love you too, Ben." He captures my hand in his and kisses the inside of my wrist.

"I should have known." I say, resting my hand on the side of his face. My voice echoes with a hint of regret and my words trail off as I realize I've said it out loud.

His gaze narrows with tenderness. "Should have known what?"

"That it would be this good between us."

"I've always known, Dev. From the moment I met you."

A white-hot pulse shoots through me, and I feel the sting of tears from his words. Since the day I met Ben, I have felt connected to him. The best kind of connection, mixed with laughter, acceptance, and a feeling of being wanted. All I've given him is glimpses of how good it could be — and a hard time. I pause a beat, stepping up to the apology in my mind. "I'm sorry I pushed you away this summer, Ben. I was scared." My excuse sounds so lame. I'm embarrassed.

He's silent for a minute watching my face. He rises slowly off the mattress, resting on the back of his forearms. "Kiss me, Devi." I lean into him and press my lips against his.

"Forgiven," he says.

He pulls me down, and I lay flat against his chest. Moments pass in silence, and were it not for his hand moving slowly, rubbing my back, I would think he'd fallen asleep.

He breaks the silence. "You feel okay? Your ribs doing ok?"

"My ribs are fine, but my stomach is growling. I'm starving."

"Not very gentleman-like to have taken you to bed without even taking you out to dinner first," he says laughing.

"Well, I think it was my idea to come straight home." I run my hands over his shoulders, curving my fingers along the slope of muscle. "I have some pizza left over from yesterday. Want me to heat it up for us?"

"Works for me," he says.

I pull on my jeans and a T-shirt, and I'm in the kitchen watching the seconds on the microwave count down when Ben comes out of the bedroom. The microwave beeps, and I pull the plate of pizza out and set it back in the box.

He moves behind me and circles my waist. "I want to take you somewhere," he whispers in my ear, reaching for the box. "We can bring the pizza with us. Grab my sweatshirt, will you?"

"I'll follow you," I say. I grab his sweatshirt and two more beers from the fridge and follow him out the door. We pass his apartment and my curiosity grows. A few more steps, another door, and we're in the stairwell.

"You all right back there?" his voice casts a lingering echo through the cavernous space, and I feel as if he's just busted me staring at his ass as he climbs.

"Yep," I say, smiling. We arrive at a landing with nowhere to go except through the door in front of us. Ben pushes it open, and a cool breeze ruffles over us. I step out onto the roof of our building, terraced on all sides with waist high walls of glass. Sparks of light from the cityscape dot the dark blue sky. It's like we've stepped into another world, isolated and peaceful, yet open to the beauty all around.

I follow Ben as he walks onto the long terrace. There's a bar, and high-top tables are scattered over half of the rectangular space. At the other end there's a massive outdoor fireplace surrounded by low sectional furniture and the best part of all—the space is completely empty.

"What is this place?" I ask in amazement.

"Jillian told me it was here. The Trotts use it for enter-taining. Most of the residents of the building don't know about it, but she said the door is usually left open. It may not be five-star dining, but we'll be under the stars at least."

"I love it," I say.

"I think I can get the fireplace going," he says, setting the pizza box down on the low table in the middle of the sectional. "That sweatshirt's for you, if you get cold."

I look down at the blue Michigan sweatshirt I'm carrying. "I'm a Spartan girl, I can't wear this. It's bad enough I have the tattoo. At least I can cover that up."

"Yeah, and I know how you covered that up by the way. Don't think I didn't notice how you weaseled," he says, as the fireplace poofs into a low flame.

"That's not weaseling. That's outsmarting your competition."

He turns to me and rests his hands on his hips. "Well, Dev, if you'd outsmarted us, you wouldn't have a tattoo of the Michigan M on your ass now, would you?"

It's hard to argue with that, and I laugh. "I didn't think you noticed that Spartan fist crushing the M. You didn't say anything about the tattoo."

"I noticed. I was just too busy noticing other things."

We sit by the fire eating pizza, drinking beer, and recalling some of the more comical moments of the entrepreneur competition last spring.

Despite the soft glow of the fire, I feel the chill of a late summer evening and relent, turning his sweatshirt inside out. I pull it over my head and roll the cuffs. Ben's sitting against an end of the sectional with one leg bent while his arm rests against the top of the cushion. He takes a sip of his beer, and I crawl up to sit beside him. He curves his big arm around my shoulders. I lay the side of my cheek against his chest and crook my leg over his knees.

"This is amazing," I say, gazing up at the tiny white sparks of light in the sky. "Thank you for not giving up on me, Ben."

"Never," he says, kissing my forehead. "You said earlier you were scared. Will you tell me, what you've been scared of?"

I pull his big hand and hold it above me, studying the lines of his palm that glow pink in the tint of fire and moonlight. An uneasy feeling sways through me at the thought of trying to identify my worries with enough precision to describe them.

"I've just always believed when two people come from such different backgrounds, it's hard for their lives to fit together and maybe it leaves one person feeling like an outsider. Well, you saw a little of that when you picked me up at my house. It's scary to think we would start this great relationship and then I'd find out I didn't fit in your world, and I don't know why you'd want to fit in mine." I laugh thinking about my run-down little house, my brother's problems, and my mom's financial struggles. "I just don't want to go back to where I've been."

"Where have you been?" he asks.

I push myself up, off of his chest and sit. I've never talked about this. Not even with Ryan. I've thought about it, but the words are just physically hard for me to say. Probably because I feel like it's calling my mom out for mistakes she made and like it's a confession of my own inability to deal with it. I let out a long breath and hug my knees to my chest.

"My real dad was a joke, and dad number two, my stepdad, wasn't much better. He was really well-off, and we were always flat broke. My mom tried to fit into his world and to live up to his expectations, and she tried to fit Josh and me into that world. Josh was six and I was ten—and my brother was never an easy kid. My stepdad was interested in having my mom in his life, but not us. He never came to any of my extracurricular activities or school stuff. He never picked us up or dropped us off. Dinners out were always reserved for just him and Mom. After a while you catch on."

I let out a long breath and smile at the tenderness I see in his eyes. "It's a horrible feeling, knowing someone in your immediate family doesn't want you around—you start to feel like you're an outsider in your own family, and Josh and I both felt it. It's hard not to think some of what happened in those years contributed to his problems today. I also think my mom feels guilty, and that's why she gives him a pass on so many things."

Ben's arm raises and he rubs a hand over the back of his neck. "My dad walked out on us—left my mom with four kids," he says. "I was thirteen. I remember being so shocked. I just couldn't believe that he had packed up and left one day. Gone."

My heart twists. I did have the feeling his dad wasn't in the picture anymore because I've never heard him talk about him. I try to picture Ben as a kid, blond hair, big green eyes. His tender heart is such a contrast to his powerful frame but I know how deep he runs. "That must have been awful," I say.

The corner of his mouth lifts slightly. "I didn't have much time to think about it really. I spent most of my time trying to prop everyone up. The worst thing for me wasn't that he left. It was seeing my sisters cry every day. That was a bad, bad year for the Winslows."

"Did your mom every remarry?" I ask.

He lets out a little laugh and shakes his head. "My mom's not that easy to get along with—she's a constant drivel of unsolicited advice. It doesn't matter if you're the greeter at Walmart or a Congressman, and it sure as hell doesn't matter if you're her kid. She'll tell you if you use the wrong tone to say 'hello,' she'll tell you if your constituents think you're a buffoon, and if you're her kid, she'll tell you a dozen things you don't want to hear in one conversation. She's a self-declared expert on everything, yet professionally qualified for nothing."

"Sounds charming," I say, and we laugh together.

"Well, she's my mom, and I do love her. But the best part of being where we are in life right now is definitely the opportunity to create the world we want."

I have no doubt in my mind that Ben believes this to be true—and I am going to try like hell to prove him right. But I swear to God, sitting here on top of Manhattan, under the stars—in our marble floored apartment building with a doorman—it all seems too good to be true.

Chapter Nine

BEN

I'm in the boardroom on the ninth floor of Trott Ventures listening to Jillian ramble on. I'm making a mental list of all of the things I've done that could possibly have resulted in someone up above punishing me with the torture of being placed on her team. She is primarily responsible for overseeing the human resources department at Trott Ventures, and our team has been tasked with rewriting the Trott employee manual.

Why in the world Mr. and Mrs. Trott would put her in charge of their human resources department when she has the social skills of a snail is beyond me. I have seen another side of Jillian. Beyond the tight bun, quick shifting eyes, and flat expression, there is a fairly attractive human being in there. Unfortunately she never presents it in the boardroom. As their only daughter, the Trotts probably see Jillian as generous and kind-hearted. A burst of laughter slips out, and I attempt to mask it with a cough. Jillian's close-set eyes dive my way. I adjust my seat. "Excuse me."

She starts every morning with a lecture on the importance of the employee manual and how anything we put in the manual can be considered a contract between Trott and their employees. What she's actually trying to tell us is that we shouldn't put anything in the manual that actually benefits the employees.

"Let's turn to the dress code rules," Jillian says. I look around the room for something sharp to poke my eyes out with.

"Page three hundred twelve, I have a revision under section three, letter D. Earrings," she says, as if it's a bad word. I flip the page of the binder in front of me and sit up trying to revive myself. There are six of us on this team including Jillian and her new boyfriend, Henri. I'm not sure what Henri's background is. Physically he fronts a good show, appearing every morning in a custom-made suit, initials embroidered on the cuffs of every shirt he wears. He has a swarthy look about him, maybe French descent, a few inches thinner and taller than Jillian.

"I want to talk about chandelier earrings," Jillian says. *What the hell are chandelier earrings?* My mind drifts to a picture of Devi and I tune Jillian out. We were at the Monkey Kick playing pool last night, and her earrings were dangling every time she leaned for a shot, threw her head back to laugh, or moved her hair.

Despite the mundane agony of the day job, at least I have Devi and the fresh memories of our hot nights to occupy my mind. *Thank God.* She wants me to make the same agreement that Jett and Ryan have—that we only spend the night together on the weekends, so we don't end up living together. At least I talked her into starting that next week and giving us time to have a dating honeymoon.

Jillian's voice breaks through my fantasy. "I want to make a rule prohibiting the wearing of any earrings that drop below the lobe." Is she totally serious right now? Jillian and Henri want to take the rules section of the manual from fifteen "strongly encouraged guidelines" to "sixty mandates, which if violated could result in immediate termination."

"Why don't we just call it 'Rules for Stupid Shit?'"

"What?" I stare at her offended expression, and it occurs to me that I said that out loud, but I'm too annoyed to even care.

"Come on, Jillian. Do you really think it's necessary to dictate to people what kind of earrings…"

"Well, let's take a vote," she interrupts me and looks around the table. "All those in favor." Four hands raise—four hands that belong to people who need their six-figure jobs. "Opposed?" she asks smirking at me.

I lean forward and say, "Nay," in a challenging tone.

"Motion passes. Note the revision, Claire."

"This sounds like a good time to break for lunch," Henri says pushing back from the table. He saunters out, without waiting for Jillian's agreement.

"We'll meet back here at one thirty," she says, following him.

The rest of the team gather their materials and head out. With the exception of Claire, they avoid looking at me. "You'll make things a lot easier on yourself if you just agree, Ben," she says. "You're on her bad side, and she's going to get her way anyhow."

"Mmm." I acknowledge her comment without agreeing, and she walks out. Part of my frustration comes from the fact that every suggestion I have made this week has been immediately shot down by either Jillian or Henri. The only thing different about today's discussions is I've decided I'm not going to sugarcoat my comments anymore. But this strategy isn't working either.

I take the elevator down, exit the building, and head across the street to meet Jett and Vaughn for lunch. They're seated at a high-top table eating burgers.

"Hey, we didn't think you were going to make it," Jett says.

"I didn't think I was going to make it either." I let out a long breath and massage the tight muscles behind my neck.

A young waiter approaches our table. "What can I get you?" he asks, setting a napkin square in front of me.

"I'm fine," I say nodding him off. Jett and Vaughn stare at me with a concerned look. I never miss a meal, but I'm so preoccupied with this, nothing sounds good.

"I've got a problem," I say. I haven't told them about the night I spent with Jillian. I rub my hand over my mouth and fess up.

"When we were here for employee training in July…" I pause a beat and Jett raises a brow. "I slept with Jillian."

Jett drops his chin and stares.

Vaughn picks up his burger.

"That was a mistake," Jett says.

"No shit." I say, "The night that I didn't get back to the hotel until after two a.m., she asked me if I would walk her home. Big mistake. Now she despises me and her new boyfriend does, too, and I've got to be in the same room with them every fucking day for the next year. I can't take it."

"Does Devi know?" Vaughn asks, and the tone of his voice heightens my guilt over the whole incident.

"No." He takes another bite of his burger. "We weren't dating at the time, and I was hoping to just forget the whole thing. But obviously Jillian's holding on to some bitterness."

"Have you said anything to Jillian about it since you started work?" Jett asks.

"No, I don't really have anything to say. I mean, am I supposed to step up and say it was a mistake? 'My judgment was clouded with alcohol and I really don't like you that much?'"

"Just be mature about it and tell them, you don't want them to feel awkward and you respect their relationship," Vaughn says.

Jett nods. "And downplay the whole thing. Don't blame Jillian. That way Henri can save face. Right now it's just an elephant in the room that's getting in everyone's way."

"You think that will turn things around?" I ask.

Jett shrugs. "I doubt things could get worse."

"I didn't say anything to you when it happened because I didn't want to put you in a bad spot with Ryan. I gotta figure out some way to tell Devi now that it looks like it's lingering."

"Yeah, well, let us know when you're going to do that so we can make sure we vacate the building. And give me time to get Ryan out, too."

"So glad to know you guys have my back."

"You should probably remove all the sharp objects from the apartment."

"Wear your cup," Vaughn says.

"You going to finish that?" I nod to Vaughn's basket of fries, and he pushes them my way.

By the time I return to the conference room, the team has assembled. I nod to them and take my seat. We usually take a break at 3:30 and I'm going to talk to them then. "It's one thirty-three, Ben. We start at one thirty," Jillian snipes as I take my seat.

"Sorry. My fault," I say, practicing my humble voice. She looks back to the open binder in front of her and clears her throat. For another two hours we listen to her strike, delete, and add the word "shall" in front of a dozen more sections.

"Next section, employee relations with one another," she announces.

This ought to be interesting and incredibly awkward. On the other hand, it may lead to just the opening I need.

"Another revision. No relations between employees," she says. I look up and we exchange a quick glance.

"And so your parents? And the two of you?" I glance between Henri and Jillian.

"Well, obviously, it doesn't apply there," she sneers.

"Well, we should probably have a provision saying that, then," I respond.

"I think it's time for a break," she says. The team scurries out of the room leaving Jillian and me staring at each other. Henri leans back in his chair and swivels with the casualness of someone who enjoys the tension of disagreements.

"What seems to be the problem, Ben?" he says to me, as if he has some higher position of authority on this team than the rest of us.

"My problem is that I don't agree with half the revisions

this 'team' is making. And I don't really believe we're acting like a 'team'. I believe everyone is kowtowing to what Jillian wants, no matter how warped it is, including you." He sits up and lowers his arms onto the table as if he's going to object, but before he can, I'm going to complete my thought.

"I want to clear the air with the two of you. Jillian, I'm sorry about what happened between us this summer. It was a mistake. In hindsight I think we can both agree on that now, and I don't want…" Her eyes widen as if I've just dumped a bucket of cold water over her. I pause. I think I've offended her, and I put up my hands and try another approach.

"I know we both had too much to drink. I'd like to just put it behind us, and I want the two of you to know I totally respect your relationship." The color has risen in Jillian's cheeks, and she still seems shocked. Something's not right here. I follow her gaze at it moves slowly down the table to Henri. He is staring at her with the intensity of an axe murderer mid-stroke.

Jett was wrong. This just got so much worse.

Jillian never told him. *What the fuck! Then why are they acting so pissed at me?*

With an abrupt jolt Henri stands. His chair swivels and makes a loud thwacking noise as it hits the wall. "Henri, wait." Jillian starts to plead, and for a moment I'm worried he's going after her. I stand up as he marches toward her.

"You lying bitch," he bites out, hitting the table in front of her and leaning too close.

"I never lied. I never lied," she says, but her voice sounds panicked. Was she seeing him when we slept together? Did she fucking tell him she was a virgin or something? He pushes past her and walks out. She turns to me, and for the first time since I met Jillian I see the concrete mask of composure she always wears crumbling. Her jaw is trembling, and the tremble is moving up her entire face. Her small green eyes are pooling up.

I spread my hands out. "Jillian, I'm so sorry," I stammer.

She closes her eyes and her brow furrows as if she's trying regain the composure she's lost. Two of our team members are laughing and approaching the conference room door.

Jillian slams the cover of her manual shut. "We're done for the day," she says, pushing past them as they enter.

"What just happened?" Claire asks, staring at Jillian's back.

"I don't even know," I say.

Leaving work early gives me a chance to run over to Julliard's campus for my sister, Cate. She's thinking about auditioning for their drama and voice program and possibly transferring. Before she decides, she wants to know how big their dorm rooms are. She's been texting me for the last week asking me to do a site visit for her. I walk toward Lincoln Center, rolling the events of the day through my mind.

If Henri didn't know about Jillian and me, why has he been acting so goddamn cocky toward me? Is he that much of an asshole? I can't figure those two out. Everything bad that happened this afternoon doesn't scare me half as much as telling Devi. After seeing Henri's reaction, is that what I can expect? There's got to be something Jillian wasn't straight about that he's pissed off at, right? Devi will understand—I think. She's not crazy. And she's not a bitch. But one thing is for sure—I have got to tell her. Tonight.

Chapter Ten

DEVIN GRACE

The thin bones of Diego's fingers press into my palm. In my other hand I'm holding a small flashlight, and I have a balloon tied to my wrist. I had thought Mario was kidding when she told me she was planning a candlelight vigil for the fish. Nope.

We're in the backyard of the center with our flashlights pointed to the sky listening to Mario deliver a heartfelt fish eulogy. Thunder rumbles in the distance as if on cue—leftover from the rain that just moved through. Mario raises her palms to the air, incorporating the sound effect into her act, and Robyn casts me an "is-she-serious" look.

"Ms. Devi," Louisa whispers in an urgent tone. "Since we already flushed 'em, can we go to the pet store after we're done?"

I cast a firm expression her way and pout my lips into

a low "shhh." I'd told Louisa, Gator, and Diego we'd go the pet shop and pick out new fish once we had the service. I didn't actually mean *right* after. She gives me an annoyed look and drops her head to her rainbow-colored sneakers.

"Time to set the souls free," Mario says, raising her hands to the sky as if she's signaling the fish heavens to reel the gates open. Rustling erupts and the children fumble to free the balloons from their wrists. Mario counts to three and blast off.

The yard erupts in dark balls of red, blue, and orange. The children begin to scramble, crossing back and forth, giggling and shrieking as they follow their own launch with thin beams from their flashlights.

I join Robyn and Mario in the center of the yard. "I have always thought that fish exist to teach kids about death," Robyn says, looking skyward.

"Amen," Mario affirms.

I feel a soft tug on the back of my jacket and turn to see Diego staring up at me with a concerned look. "What's up, D?" I ask, bending down.

He leans in and whispers in my ear, "Gator's crying." A pang ripples in my stomach.

"Is he hurt?" Diego shakes his brown curls. "Can you show me where he is?"

He turns and I follow him across the yard, weaving through the maze of kids. I see the dark shadow of Gator crouched against the fence. He's on his knees in the grass with his hands pressed to his face. Louisa and her friend Georgia are standing over him. I drop down beside him. Wetness seeps through my jeans from the damp ground as I put my arm on his back. "What happened?" I ask them.

Louisa shrugs her shoulders and raises empty hands, "Hell if I know." I blanch at her word choice and snap my fingers at her. "Language please, Louisa."

"He can't find his bag, with his stuff," Diego says. I rub Gator's back and lean down to his ear.

"Gator, are you okay? Are you hurt?" he shakes his head against his hands. "Are you upset because you don't know where your bag is?" He nods forcefully against his palms. Gator carries that bag with him everywhere he goes, determined to be ready when his dad comes to pick him up. It's heartbreaking. I know he had it when we were walking out to the yard—he was telling me his name was drawn as "Person of the Week" at school, and he asked me if I'd help him make his "All About Me" poster after the ceremony. I glanced at that crinkled plastic bag dangling from his wrist, thinking how challenging it was going to be to create a "happy" poster for a child whose eight-year-old history can be summed up by the contents of a wrinkled grocery bag.

"Gator, I know you had it with you before we let go of the balloons. It's gotta be here. Let's start a search, okay?" He raises his face, which is streaked with wet lines, and the slight droop of his left eye is now a tear-shaped welt. He wipes an arm across his nose, sniffling and nodding. "Louisa, you and Georgia take your flashlights and search over by the play structure. See if you can get some other friends to help, too." I stand up and reach a hand down to Gator.

"What's going on?" Mario asks, appearing behind me.

"Gator can't find his bag. He had it when he came out."

Her face falls, and she puts her hand on his head as he stands up. "We'll find it, bud."

After thirty minutes and a thirty-person search party, all

we've managed to find is a spoon, two hair clips, and a golf ball. I can feel Gator's growing unease in the tightening grip of his hand. My stomach swirls with the dread of bad news. I see Robyn coming our way, and I know what she's going to say. She puts her hand on Gator's shoulder. "I'm afraid we have to give up for tonight, Gator. We can look some more tomorrow." He nods his head, and I look down at the dark shadow of his flat-top haircut angled to the ground.

Is it not bad enough he has to carry the tattered shreds of every memory he has in a plastic bag? Now that's lost too—all because his parents couldn't fuckin' figure out life? On top of feeling like my heart is being squeezed, I really wish there was someone left in his life—one face that I could point my finger at and growl, "Now you listen to me, asshole. Get your shit together!" But there's not a trace of a DNA connection left in this kid's life. Every lead Robyn had for finding a family member has died, literally. Yet Gator still insists his dad is coming for him. I shove all of that out of my mind, bend down and hold his shoulders.

"Maybe someone carried it in with their stuff." It occurs to me that I have the excuse I've been waiting for to ask him what's in that bag he always carries. "If I'm going to keep looking you should probably tell me what's in the bag, Gator—so if I do find it, I'll know for sure."

He rubs his nose on the back of his hand. "There's a book that my Mama gave me before she got sick, and a necklace, some notes, fourteen dollars, some army guys, oh, and a rabbit's foot lucky charm."

"Okay. I'll keep looking," I say as we walk back to the porch, but now I'm more determined than ever. I have to find that damn bag.

"And a Snickers bar," Gator says, raising a sheepish grin. "Promise you'll keep looking?"

"A Snickers bar? Heck yeah, I'm gonna keep looking." I open the door for him. "I'll help you work on your poster for a bit, okay?"

Three hours later I'm walking into our apartment building. Although we didn't find Gator's bag, I was able to help him come up with some ideas for his poster. We drew pictures of his Mom in a hospital bed and two pictures of his dad, one with an angel's wings and one without. Then he drew pictures of Robyn, Mario, Diego and one of me holding his hand — his insta-family. But the thing that made staying late worth it was what he wrote across the bottom of his poster under the pictures: "People I love."

My mom used to tell us when we went through bad times, "Things could always be worse." I must have repeated that to myself twenty times tonight on Gator's behalf. It never would have occurred to me how difficult a class project could be for a kid like Gator. I'm sure "Person of the Week" is intended to give a child a chance to be in the spotlight, but when the spotlight beams and all that's left is empty space created by a parent's bad choices — it's just hard. Mentally, I'm exhausted, but it could always be worse.

I had texted Ben and Ryan earlier today and told them I was going to work late so that I could attend the flashlight-fish vigil. Ben told me he would wait up, but helping Gator on his poster took me longer than I expected. I ride the elevator to the eleventh floor and nervous anticipation grows at the thought of seeing Ben. I want nothing more than to fall into his chest and feel his arms around my back. I turn into our hallway and smile. His door is wide open.

He's stretched across the couch, ankles resting over the end. One hand is tucked behind his head and the other is on his stomach. The big screen casts soft shadows of flickering light over his handsome face. There's a pizza box on the table in front of the couch, along with several empty beer bottles.

He's not awake, but I know he's waiting for me. I've never had anyone in my life who waited for me to come home. My mom has worked the night shift for the extra money as long as I can remember.

I sit next to him, lean over, and kiss my giant sleeping beauty. He stirs but doesn't wake. I kiss him again, more slowly this time. I start to pull back but he catches me with a hand on the back of my head. He kisses me gently and soft green eyes fill my vision.

"I was having the best dream," he says.

"Mmmm." I kiss him again.

"Sleeping on the couch after beer and football, and this beautiful brunette walks in. She starts kissing me." I smile against his lips. "Lower." I move my mouth down his neck and nip his skin. His hands grip my shoulders. "And she's got the greatest tits–pressing against my chest—and I mean the greatest—like first place wet T-shirt tits."

I laugh. "More like first place at the local bowling alley cleavage contest," I say.

"Hey," he says, "this is my fantasy. Stop dissing yourself. You've got an amazing body, babe."

"There's just a little too much of it," I say.

He stares with narrowed eyes. "Look at these hands, Devi." His palms raise and flip between our faces. I study the long, smooth-boned fingers and the thick palm stroked with lines. "I've never wanted to date anyone who's a size two. I want to be able to feel you when I touch you."

I reach and cup the top of his fingers. "Well, that shouldn't be a problem," I say.

"Now, stop interrupting my fantasy. Where was I?"

"You were here," I say, pulling him toward me and leaning my first place tits into his open palms. He closes his eyes and lets out a low sound.

"Yeah, I was definitely here," he says. "She unbuttons her shirt and takes off her jeans."

I lean down and kiss his lips. "Mmm, you are dreaming," I say, smiling against his mouth. His eyes crease at the corners as I sit up. He raises a hand into my hair, twirling a thick strand slowly around a big hand, drawing me gently back for another long kiss. "Me and my first place tits are exhausted," I say. "And I need to be back at the center early." I stand and hold a hand out, pulling him up.

"Want me to heat up some pizza for you?" He asks, smoothing his hands over jean-clad thighs.

"No, I'm fine." He closes the lid of the box and his face stills, as if he's contemplating something. "I just want to sleep," I say. He blinks, dismissing whatever it was he was thinking about.

"Can you have dinner with me tomorrow?" he asks.

"Sure," I say, reaching for the beer bottles on the table.

"I want to talk to you about a few things," he says.

"More work stuff?"

"Sort of," he says.

"I miss college," I say.

He lets out a low chuckle, sounding more sad than happy. "Me, too."

We put the beer bottles in the sink, and he walks me

to my apartment door with his fingers resting in the front pockets of his jeans.

"I guess this is what it's like to live in the real world," I say.

"Real world, real problems." The sadness I hear in his voice concerns me. He tugs my hand and pulls me into his chest, wrapping heavy arms around my back. I'm about to ask him more about his day but he kisses my cheek and starts to walk back to his apartment. "We'll talk more tomorrow," he says, rubbing the back of his neck and looking at his bare feet. As bad as my day was, I think Ben's must have been worse. I've never seen him seem down. I'm sure we'll feel better tomorrow. It could always be worse, right?

Chapter Eleven

BEN

Devi stands in front of me straightening my tie. I'm waiting for her to look up. She's stunning; black dress that's tight in all the right places, heels, and a long silver necklace sparkling over her cleavage. I reach and hook a finger behind her earring. It's silver and cut into long layers of teardrops, as iridescent as a sunfish.

"I like these," I say, as I recall the ridiculous discussion my team had on the length of earrings appropriate for employees. Her glossy brown hair flows over her shoulders in waves, framing bright eyes and red lips. She's still fidgeting with my tie and twisting her lips and her expression is distant, lost in apprehensive thought.

Devi ended up staying the night at the center last night. They asked her to fill in for another staffer who had an emergency. As a result, I was not able to talk to her about my history with Jillian. I am really hoping we make it through the night without incident. Things have settled down a bit at work. Henri has called in sick for the past two days—or at least that's the excuse Jillian is going with. And Jillian has ignored me for the most part. I tried to apologize again and she dismissed it, saying something about it being more complicated than that with Henri. Whatever. All I care about is handling this with Devi the right way.

"Thanks for coming with me, babe."

She nods her head and steps back, but she's still not looking at me. Earlier this week she admitted that five-star events with "too many silverware choices" make her nervous, and I'm sure her anxiety has a lot to do with her experience with her stepdad and being raised poor—as if people with an income tax return in the top three percent are naturally more skilled at socializing with the elite. If she had the experience that I do with that top three percent, she'd know what I know: Economic status has nothing to do with class, ethics, or what kind of a person someone is.

She raises her hand back to my tie for more fidgeting. I catch the faint smell of lavender and lift one of her hands, turning it in to kiss the soft skin of her wrist. She raises her head to meet my gaze and forces a smile.

On top of her fancy silverware insecurities, she doesn't like Jillian, and she knows Jillian doesn't like her. I'm sure it will be a cool reception—but I'm praying that's all it will be. I'm also praying that I haven't crossed too far beyond the line—when not telling someone you love about something goes from being not really necessary to a blatant attempt to hide something.

If only Jillian could have been mature about the whole

thing and admit that we both made a mistake and treat it with the same respect you'd treat a fart in a boardroom—pretend like it never happened, ignore the lingering regret until you can't smell it anymore, and laugh about it later. I would have told Devi eventually, once our relationship had more foundation underneath it.

Still, I know it's not going to make her happy. She and Jillian share a special abhorrence for each other, the kind borne from one lacking something the other has an abundance of. Devi's abundance is her beauty, both inner and outer—she lights up a room. Jillian's only abundance seems to be money—and her ability to darken a room with snide comments. When we were competing last spring, Jillian's brother, Robert, warned me about her. I didn't pay too much attention because I had made it obvious to everyone I was interested in Devi. I guess if Robert's words were true, and Jillian was interested back in the spring, that would explain why neither Jillian or Devi have ever had a kind word to say about each other. My goal is to keep Devi by my side and to stay as far away from Jillian as possible—and Henri, if he shows.

I'm sitting in the back of the cab between Ryan and Devi chatting with Ryan about her law school classes. Devi is looking out the window, quiet. I can't tell if I underestimated her apprehension about this event or if it's my own nerves I'm feeling. I reach for her hand and hold it against my thigh as Ryan continues to talk. The cab stops in front of the Crown Dorchester building, and the valet opens the door and helps Ryan out. I reach for Devi as Jett settles up with the driver. She stands, and her hands smooth down her hips. She looks up at the building and lets out a low breath. I put my hand on her hip and lean into her ear.

"When you're ready to leave, we'll leave, okay?"

She pushes my chest. "Stop it, I'm fine. It'll be fine," she says, and starts to walk for the entrance, calling over her shoulder, "It's not as if Jillian doesn't know we're dating."

I rub my jaw and exchange a sideways glance with Jett. It's not what Jillian doesn't know that's scaring me; it's what Devi doesn't know.

Devi pauses and turns back. "Besides, if Jillian says one word to me I'll grab her by that stupid bun she always wears on top of her head and dunk her face in the punch bowl." Her hair bounces over her back as she climbs the steps for the entrance.

I feel Jett and Ryan at my shoulders. Ryan gives me a sympathetic look and squeezes my arm, "She's kidding," she says, but her smile melts into a contemplative frown watching Devi heading for the doors with a determined clip. "I think," she says, skipping to catch up with her.

Jett presses his lips together and grips my shoulder. "I'm thinking we should start this night with a couple of shots."

"Oh, yeah, 'cause that's what we need."

He smacks my back and pinches my shoulder as if he's warming me up to get in the ring as we head in. "I just hope you wore your cup so you'll be ready for the throw down. Remember, I can't fight when Ryan's with me. We'll be under the table."

"Thanks, Treb."

The Trotts are celebrating the renovation of the Crown Dorchester Building. Tonight's event marks the grand re-opening since their joint reconstruction project with the commercial construction company of Solomon Brothers.

What was once a run-down warehouse is now a multi-use building with retail shops on the main level and condominiums on the upper floors.

We spend the first hour of the night strolling through the wide marble corridors as black vested servers swing silver trays in front of our path, offering mini skewers of bacon wrapped shrimp, paté fois gras on toast points, and crab-stuffed mushroom caps. Jett and I follow Ryan and Devi at varying intervals as we stop to visit with other Trott employees wandering the shops.

We finish our conversation with two of the employees on Jett's team, and I look up to search for the girls. Nothing. I don't see them anywhere. We walk, and I'm searching the entire span of the hallway while Jett talks about the tense relationship between Robert Trott and the Chief Operating Officer of Solomon Brothers. The girls are still nowhere to be seen. "Where'd they go?" he asks.

"No clue." With every second that passes, I feel another nerve bursting. I am ready to be done with this night.

"There's Ryan," Jett says, and we steer left toward the shop she's coming out of. I want to ask her where Devi is, but as she approaches, Jett runs into another colleague and introduces her. I'm looking through the glass window into the floral shop Ryan came out of, but it's only the size of a small box, and I don't see Devi anywhere. Another nerve springs loose. I pan over the crowded corridor again and see a flash of glossy brown. She's standing at the end of the hallway laughing and talking with three Trott employees she knows from the entrepreneur competition. I swallow the breath that's been building and turn back to the conversation in front of me, intending to bow out and join Devi.

"Oh, Ben, Devi told me to tell you she was going to find a bathroom," Ryan says.

"Thanks. I just saw her at the end of the hall, excuse me." I nod out and start toward where I spotted her, but she's gone again. *Jesus, Devi.* Another nerve erupts. I do not want her to run into Jillian or Henri without me. Well, she couldn't have gone far. I make it to the end of the hallway and turn the corner. I stop short to avoid running into Mrs. Trott.

"Ben!" she says. "So nice to see you. So tell me, how everything's going?" She settles into a stance that tells me she wants to chat. Another nerve busted.

"Fine," I say, feeling the strain of the lie on my face.

"What do you think of the renovation?" she says, holding her hands out and looking at the painted mural on the ceiling.

"Very impressive. They've done a wonderful job."

"Jillian reported that your team has almost made it through the revisions to the employee manual. We're looking forward to the final report."

"Yes. We're on target to have it completed by next week."

"That's great. I just saw Devin. She looks beautiful and happy." She winks at me. "You two enjoy the evening."

"Thanks, Mrs. Trott. Thanks for including us. I was looking for Devi, did you see where—"

She turns her shoulders and points to a hallway. "Bathrooms, down there."

I stand waiting by the bathrooms. After ten minutes, I'm convinced she's not in there anymore. *C'mon, Devi.* I turn and start to walk away, breathing out a long breath.

After a few stalking paces, I hear her voice behind me.

I stop and turn as she's skipping to catch me. "I ran into Renee," she says with an enthusiastic lilt in her tone. "We were talking about—"

"I've been looking for you for the last twenty minutes." She blinks hard. I've interrupted her, and my voice is much too harsh. Her happy expression melts into confusion, and she searches my face as I try to pull it together.

I let out a breath and run my hand behind my neck. "Sorry," I say, shaking my head. She's still searching, and I see the hesitancy in her stare.

"No. My fault," she says in a soft tone. She loops her arm through mine and curls her fingers on my bicep. "Should we find Jett and Ryan?"

I nod and close my fingers over hers. "Have you seen Vaughn yet?" she asks, glancing casually at the windows of the retail shops as we walk.

"Not yet. He said he was going to be a little late though. He had to help his aunt with a shipment that arrived for their import business. Apparently it got stuck in customs. She needed someone that spoke better English to argue with the customs officers."

We find Jett and Ryan in a jewelry store and join them. As we're strolling slowly past the sparkling cases, a soft voice pipes down announcing dinner service in fifteen minutes. Ryan and Jett have stopped by one of the glass cases and are leaning over Ryan's finger, pressing against the glass. I feel Devi's hand slide into mine and we keep walking.

"Meet you in there," I say to Jett. I feel like I should apologize again for snapping at her, but I decide it might be better not to bring it up again. We move through the wide corridor with a loose crowd toward the Dorchester's grand ballroom.

We step into the vast space and Devi slows, panning her gaze over the massive gold chandeliers hovering above us like an invasion of spaceships. Floor-to-ceiling windows line the back wall revealing the Manhattan skyline. A podium stands empty at front of the room, framed by a series of red curving panels. We move with a short line to the front of a check-in table, where we're handed small rectangular cards. Our names are printed in scroll below, "Table #17".

"I hope Ryan and Jett are seated with us," Devi whispers.

"Me, too," I say, and I hope like hell Jillian and Henri are not.

We make our way to table seventeen, stopping to admire the display on the walls. The iron gates that used to surround the building have been repurposed as artwork and are attached to the walls. Each gate has a series of pictures showing the phases of the building's reconstruction. I lead Devi by the hand, admiring the shots as we cross the room.

We're the first to arrive at the eight-person table. We stand behind our seats and chat, waiting for the other six to fill in. Jett and Ryan step up beside us. Ryan's seat is next to mine, and Jett's is on the other side, leaving the four seats next to Devi open. I see Robert coming, drink in hand. He takes the seat next to Jett. Three more to go, and I can feel the perspiration gathering under my collar. I tilt my neck, stretching to loosen the collar biting my skin—and here they come. Jillian and Henri are making their way over to our table. My gaze shifts between them and Devi as she chats with Jett. Henri sees me, pans a gaze over Devi and steps next to the open seat beside her while Jillian moves beside him.

"Hey," I hear Vaughn's voice coming from behind. He slides next to Devi turning a shoulder to Henri, forcing Henri and Jillian to adjust right. I nod and wink, silently praising his smooth move.

Henri reaches across Vaughn and extends a hand to Devi. "You must be Devin. I've heard a lot about you." He shakes her hand, and his gaze meets my cold stare. His eyes are way too bloodshot for a business event. He cocks a smile and I lock my jaw, resisting the urge to grip the back of his neck and shake him until his teeth rattle. I glance at Jillian—who's looking as anxious as I feel—and Henri introduces himself to Ryan.

Vaughn and I manage to keep Devi engaged in casual conversation. By the time the entrées are set before us, Devi is laughing, and it seems she's forgotten Jillian's presence altogether. In the meantime, Henri has consumed two more bourbons, and Jillian's listlessly poking her fork into a filet of uneaten salmon with a sick expression on her face—I almost feel sorry for her.

The cadence of the voices in the hall softens as Mr. Trott steps to the podium along with Jonathan Solomon, owner of the partnering construction company. They make a short presentation, mostly thanking the crowd as dessert is served. "So," Henri's voice rises to a decibel that can't be ignored and addresses Devi. "How long have you and Ben been together, sweetheart?"

The table grows quiet, and Devi looks at him a long moment as he rolls the ice in his glass.

"Are you talking to me?" she says, scrunching her eyebrows.

"Well, I'm sure not talking to your boyfriend. He is your boyfriend, right? Or is it one of those open relationships?"

"Are you drunk?" she asks.

"Henri, please," Jillian says in an urgent whisper. He turns to stare at her and it looks as if he can barely focus.

"I'm just trying to figure out who all the players are in this little love triangle." I clench my jaw, staring hard at Henri, trying to warn him that I am about to come over this table and take him out.

"Love triangle?" Devi says.

Robert interrupts. "The only love triangle you've got going is in your drunken mind, Henri. Jillian, you need to take him home." Jett flashes a quick glance my way. Devi reaches for her water and the table withdraws to silence. Ryan is panning a slow speculative look over all of us, which I avoid.

The volume in the room rises and falls as Mr. Trott steps behind the podium again, a welcome distraction. "I wanted to take a moment to make an official announcement and congratulations. As some of you may know, our daughter, Jillian has recently become engaged to Mr. Henri Lindell." He unfolds a hand toward the "happy" couple. Jillian stands and Henri rises slowly. They wave to the crowd. "Please join me in raising your glasses to toast my daughter and soon to be son-in-law, and may I be so bold as to suggest the ballroom of the Crown Dorchester for the wedding reception?" A soft round of chuckling follows as he raises a champagne flute. "Cheers. To the happy couple." Crystal glasses chime and the happy couple drinks. A look of relief loosens Jillian's pinched features. She starts to sit back down but is interrupted by the tinkling sound of silverware tapping glasses.

"Kiss!" someone yells.

Henri pulls Jillian to him and kisses her a little too roughly. A deep blush seeps over her pale skin. Ryan and

Devi exchange eyebrow-raised looks. Jillian pulls back and sits, looking disgusted. But I'm watching Henri, and he's still standing. When he realizes he's lost the crowd's attention, he lifts his own knife and water glass and starts chiming.

Jillian is reaching up grabbing his arm, urgently saying his name, but it's too late. A slow silence has spread over the crowd and they're staring at Henri. This is not good.

"Mr. and Mrs. Trott, distinguished guests, thank you for your well wishes." His words slur at the end, and he pauses too long between starting his next sentence. "As this evening is about new beginnings, I can't resist sharing one more surprise." He reaches for Jillian and she looks completely mortified, but she's trying like hell to save face for both of them. She takes his hand and stands next to him, a bitter smile on her face. I hear her whisper, "Henri, please," in a broken voice. "Don't do this."

"My beautiful bride has recently informed me she's three months pregnant. Imagine my surprise," he narrows his gaze and speaks through clenched teeth, "and delight." Our entire table watches him with a suspect look. A rush of applause erupts from the clueless audience and Henri kisses Jillian's cheek. She clutches the back of her chair, lowers her head, and raises her eyes, staring across the table at me. Blood rushes to my head, and my vision tunnels. All I can see in Jillian's eyes is the answer to why she's been a complete bitch to me in the last month. I know why Henri blew up at her, and I know why he's done what he's done. Either they know for sure the child's mine, or they think there's a chance it might be. My head is about to explode and my heart feels like a boulder pounding in my chest.

Robert stands. He walks to Henri, grabs his elbow, and

leads him to the nearest door. Henri seems to know his time is up, because he doesn't bother to put up any kind of fight. Jillian looks stunned, pale, and sick. After a long moment of awkward silence, Ryan leans over and whispers, "Jillian, are you okay? Is there anything I can do to help?"

Jillian moves her head with such vehemence the tear glistening down her cheek shakes. "No," she says, and she looks at me.

"I'm sorry Ben. I was going to tell you."

Confirmation of my fear—she's telling me it might be mine. Holy fuck! My eyes widen, and I'm staring at Jillian. I lean an elbow on the table and cover my open mouth with my fingers.

Devi's looking at Jillian, and I feel her turn slowly to me. Her eyes tighten their focus into an intensity that burns through me. "Tell you what?" she asks, confusion distorting her voice. I put my hand on her arm and lean.

"I need a minute with Jillian." I stop there. I can't say anything else until I've talked to Jillian. She stiffens under my fingers and pulls back.

"Ben," her voice is cautious. "Does this concern you?" Her words trail off and her expression begins to shift.

I rise from my seat and drop my napkin in my plate. I look down at Devi's tortured face and feel the air leaving my lungs. My words come out in a hoarse whisper. "I need a minute."

"Ben," she says my name with shock and as much hurt as I've ever heard behind one syllable. Her mouth remains open as I stand and move to where Jillian is sitting. It kills me to leave Devi like this, but I've got to know what I'm in for here. I can't work off of guesses and innuendos, and

I won't be able to explain anything to her until I know the whole of it myself. I help Jillian up and escort her to the door.

We turn into the hallway and Jillian gasps out a sob. She's pressing her index fingers against her temples, shaking her head back and forth. "I didn't mean for him to do that," she moans.

"Jillian, are you pregnant?"

She takes a deep shuddering breath, trying to compose herself. She nods. "Yes."

"How many months?"

"A little over two months." I count back in my mind. We were here in early July, Then there was August and September. I blink hard and rub a hand over my forehead, feeling dizzy. Is she about to tell me I'm going to be a dad?

Words rasp over the dryness in my throat. "Is it mine?"

Chapter Twelve

Devin Grace

I hold my hands in my lap to keep them from shaking as I watch Ben walking Jillian out of the banquet room. He's leaning over her, talking in her ear as she nods. The exchange is too familiar. I swallow, trying to control the inner panic that's building. He slept with her. That's what Henri meant by love triangle. I feel the blood draining from my face, pulling my mouth into a tight line. I look at Ryan. Her face is set with shock. She's come to the same conclusion.

We turn to Jett. He must have known. He's running two fingers over his forehead. I turn to Vaughn. His angular features appear strained, and he shifts his focus to his side. Soft sounds of silverware touching plates and murmured voices float around us, but the atmosphere overall seems quieter. Two women at the next table are whispering behind cupped hands. I draw in a breath and try to swallow. The panic is swelling now, pushing up into my chest and I'm breathless. I've got to get out of here. I need air. I can't make a scene here, and I can't control myself with this. Ryan's hand reaches, gripping my forearm. She's trying to help me hold it together. I mouth out the words, "I'm leaving," and her brow furrows.

"Devi, do you want me to—" She starts to stand, but I shake my head.

"No. Stay right there."

I push my chair back, stand up, and exit through the door Ben and Jillian went out of. They're steps away, but Ben's back is turned, blocking my view of Jillian. I walk fast in the opposite direction to the front exit. All I want to do right now is get away from this—whatever this is.

I am three steps from the end of the hallway. I don't want to hear their conversation, but I do. Jillian is apologizing, and then I hear Ben's words. "Is it mine?" There's only one thing that could mean. I reach for the wall. He's talking about her baby. A stabbing pain shoots through my stomach. I resist the urge to double over. I blink hard, trying to clear the spots flashing in my peripheral vision—the after effect of the back hand that just swatted my dreams against the wall. My insides are crumbling, and I lean, straining my fingertips, resisting the urge to sink and slide slowly down. I wouldn't believe any of this could be true of Ben if I hadn't seen it and heard it. I push off the wall, turn the corner, and run.

I move past the line of cabs in front of the hotel, certain I don't have cab fare enough for a single-rider fare back to our building. The wind blows gently against my face, taking away the sting of the six-block walk to the subway in my best heels. I ride the train leaning against the pole, letting the vibrations sway and bounce my lifeless body. With zombie-like numbness, I walk another four blocks to the entrance of our building. Our doorman's face lights up when he recognizes me and then falls as he takes in my expression.

"How you doing tonight?" he says in a soft, concerned voice.

I try to smile. "I've had better nights," I say, pressing a weak smile and slipping through the open door.

The elevator is a haunting memory of Ben. He was holding my hand hours earlier, laughing with Jett and Ryan. I make my way down our hallway to my door. *Fuck*! I don't have a key. My clutch isn't big enough for my makeup and my keys, and of course I chose my makeup. I assumed we'd all be coming home together. I kick the bottom of the door and lean against the wall. Now what? Deep breath.

I walk to the end of the hallway, hoping the rooftop door is open. Another memory of Ben invades my senses as I step out onto the terrace. I walk to the sectional couch and flop. My head drops into my hands, and I stare at my feet. It all seems surreal. Ben and Jillian. Seriously? I still can't believe it. Were there signs I missed? Was I so caught up in the bliss of it all I ignored warnings? *God.* And when? Last spring? Over the summer? Last night?

I try to recall every moment I've seen Ben and Jillian together. She was their team leader during the competition. I know Jillian liked Ben, but I never thought there was anything between them. A dull thud interrupts my thoughts and then a muffled voice. I raise my head and listen to someone yelling in the distance. It's Ben. My stomach drops. The thud comes again, and I can barely make out the sound of my name. He's at my apartment door. Shit. Christ he's got to be waking up the whole damn floor. I push myself up — might as well get this over with now. I descend the stairs holding the rail and open the door to our floor.

His voice booms down the corridor. "Goddamn it, Devi, open the door." He slams the palm of his hand against the wood and drops his head. "I know you're in there, the doorman told me." He shakes his forehead back and forth against the door and tries to turn the knob again. I watch him step back and scowl. "If you don't open this fucking door, I'm coming through it." I ought to let him throw his shoulder out trying to bust it down. I have absolutely no sympathy for him right now. He steps back and levels his gaze.

"I'm not in there, you moron," I say in a flat tone.

He turns and I see a flash of relief cross his features. We stare at each other a beat, and I turn and head back to the upper deck. I hear him entering the stairwell as I'm pushing out the door onto the roof. I'm crossing the deck to the sectional, and I hear the soft swoosh of the door opening behind me.

"Devi." His voice carries in the low wind.

My pump slips on the concrete and I stop, steadying myself. I am so fucking sick of these heels. I turn around to face him. He's going to try to explain it all. I can hear it in his tone. A sickening pit of anger burns in my stomach. I reach down for the strap of my shoe, hook my finger in it, and flip it up into my hand. I bounce it in my fingers for a firmer grip, pull back, and whip it at his head. With a fighter's reflex, he turns a shoulder. It sails past him, hits the edge of a high-top table, and skips across the concrete.

"Jesus Christ, Devin," he says, as I'm loading up the other shoe. He's ready for this one and easily deflects it with a forearm.

I shake my head and a small huff of laughter escapes. "And to think I was worried about my dress, about picking up the wrong piece of silverware. Gosh," I slap my forehead. "It never occurred to me that my 'boyfriend,'" I make air quotes around the word, "was banging his supervisor at work."

"I'm not banging her. It happened last summer."

"Are you talking about last summer? The same summer you spent trying to talk me into starting a relationship with you?" I glare at him.

His face sets in a hard line. He lowers his chin and starts to step toward me. "I am talking about last summer, the same summer you spent telling me over and over that you weren't interested. The same summer that you showed up at Ryan's graduation party with your old boyfriend."

"Do you know what it felt like tonight to be sitting at that table and realize you and Jillian have this, this thing, you've been hiding from me?" My voice is a broken whisper, and I press my hand over my mouth.

"Jillian and I don't have a 'thing'. It was a one-night stand. It was a mistake. I had too much to drink. It happened when we came out for employee training, and I didn't talk to her again until we started work. I had no idea she was pregnant, until tonight."

I feel the burning in my eyes, and the tears start to spill. Long wet lines roll down my skin. No use in bothering to hold it in. "Of all the shitty things that have happened to me in my life, Ben, I honestly think this tops the list." I turn my back and walk to the sectional. I drop down and hang my head over my lap, letting my hair form a curtain over the sides of my face. I wish I could disappear.

I hear him coming to me, slowly. His feet stop in front of me. He crouches, laying his hands on the sides of my thighs. "Devi," he whispers. His voice is a loving, tender sound, and it makes me want to cry harder. "I'm sorry. I should have told you." His hand smoothes my hair back, and I look into his tortured expression, feeling the same pain in my heart.

He lets out a breath, and his hands spread over my thighs. "I swear sometimes I think my biggest mistakes are not being able to say no to the women in my life. Jillian was all over me that night. I should have said no. I should have walked away. It was just one night."

"It was one night with huge consequences," My fingers feel numb, and I wish he wasn't looking at me. I press my hands over my face.

"I'm sorry," he says again.

"I'm sorry, too." I put my hands on top of his and push them off my thighs. "I can't do this with you." My voice breaks from the pain of saying the words.

An instant of anger flashes over his features. He stands and lets out a half-breath, half-laugh, shaking his head. "What do you mean you can't do this with me? You can't date me if I have a child? How does that change us?"

I look up at him. "How does that change us? Seriously? You're going to have a baby—with Jillian."

"If I am the father of her child, Devi, that's all I'll ever be to her. She'll never have my heart."

"She won't need your heart, Ben. She'll have your child."

He stares hard for a moment as if he's shocked by what I said. "Now that I have a problem, you're done? Now that I need you more than ever, you're out?"

He waits for me to respond, but I just stare. He turns away exhaling a long breath. His hands rest on his hips as his head drops back. Moments of silence pass as he stares into the night sky. "You know what I think?" he says, turning around and looking at me. "I think you're not done making me prove myself. Now you have the excuse you needed. I've fucked up with Jillian, I've gotta start all over."

His words strike me as some sort of accusation. I stand up, fully ready to defend myself. "I told you for six months it wouldn't work, and you wouldn't believe me. Then, the minute I give in to you—you turn around and give me back everything I've never wanted."

"Everything you never wanted? Really?" He tilts his head and his tone mocks my words.

I point my finger at his chest. "Don't put words in my mouth. It's not you, it's your circumstances."

He lets out a frustrated laugh and pulls a hand through his hair. "*My* circumstances? What about your circumstances?" He pauses, and his expression hardens. He steps forward, and I know he's going to remind me of everything I have to be ashamed of. I squeeze my eyes closed wishing I could cover my ears.

"The girl who grew up dirt-poor doesn't like my circumstances?" I feel his words like a lash, whipping scars that have never completely healed. "The girl whose brother is an abusive drug addict." I stand in front of him silent and stone-faced, except for the tremor I can never control along my jaw. "The girl who grew up in not one broken home, but two…"

"Stop! Haven't I heard enough for one night?" I scream through a sobbing gasp. I turn away from him, crossing my arms over my chest.

He lets out a low breath, as if he's trying to calm himself. A moment passes and he steps close to me, so close I can feel the heat of his body at my back.

He speaks low over my ear. "I know all of this about you, and I have never thrown it up in your face."

"Except for now," I say. He touches the sides of my shoulders, and I let him turn my lifeless body. Warm hands close a firm grip around my arms, and he pulls me closer.

"Not now, either. I have always been able to see past your circumstances to who you are and what we can be together. I'm asking you to do the same for me. I have loved you from the moment I met you, but if the child's mine, Devi, I can't turn my back."

I shake my head and whisper. "I would never ask you to—never." My hands raise and brace against his forearms. "But I've waited my whole life to have a relationship where I matter. I know it sounds selfish, Ben, but I don't want to be the outsider. I don't want to come third." He drops my arms and steps back.

"I just want to be normal," I say.

We stare at each other a long silent beat, paused in the moment of impossible. Regret and exhaustion show in the redness of his eyes.

"This is real life, Devi. There is no normal." He lets out a long breath, turns and starts to walk away. My stomach falls. The sight of Ben walking away from me is physically painful. He stops and turns back.

"You know, if it was *you* that was pregnant—I would never leave you." His stare burns the truth of his words into my soul, but I say nothing. He turns and walks out. I feel myself collapsing against the stiff cushions. My brain is a tangled pile of weeds. I'm ashamed of myself for not being the person he wants me to be, and I'm ashamed of myself for being the person I think I want to be. Hot tears slip, spilling over the corners of my lashes and trailing into my hair. I try to convince myself that this is just another dump added to my bucket of disappointment. Eventually it will swirl with all the other bullshit and the impact will fade. I drape an arm over my forehead and stare at the ink black sky dotted with stars, a million miles away and as distant as happiness.

Chapter Thirteen

BEN

I'm walking up the steps of The Children's Center. I haven't seen Devi since our disastrous throw down after the Trott banquet. I've texted her a couple times and asked her how she was doing. She sent back short, dead-end answers. *"Peachy. You?"* And the second, *"Fine. You?"* My responses? *"Not Peachy."* and *"Managing."* That's been the extent of it. Now that I have the experience of those two weeks of happiness with her, when we were fully committed to each other, it makes it so much more difficult to live without her. But I'm trying to give her the space she needs.

When Mario called last night and asked if I could help them move some bigger items at the Center after I got off work, I was thrilled to have an excuse. The thought crossed my mind that Mario might be trying to throw me a bone, and I jumped on it like a shelter dog.

Devi told me her office is on the second floor, and I'm going to head there first to see if I can catch her before she leaves for the day. I open the door and walk into the wide hallway. I take the stairway to my right and hear children's voices arguing. I stop outside an office. She's there, holding the arm of a pudgy black boy whom I recognize from her descriptions as Gator. A long red scratch is running down his cheek, and he's staring bug-eyed, trying to dodge the small hand of a blonde as she swats air and lunges. Devi grabs the back of the blonde's hoodie and yanks her back.

"Stop that! What is wrong with you two?" Gator wipes the tip of his nose with a finger and draws a ragged breath. "This is the third time this week I have broken up a fight between you. You've gone from being the best of friends to the worst of enemies, and you're exhausting me," Devi says.

"She keep lyin' and sayin' my Daddy ain't comin' for me," Gator says, and his warm brown stare looks to Devi for confirmation.

"Well, he just pushed me," the blonde's head bobs, and her curls bounce with sass. She crosses her arms over her puffed up chest, looking every bit the seven-year-old diva in her pink velour track suit. She points a finger into the air. "And I ain't gonna be pushed by no man." I cover my mouth to keep from laughing. So far, they haven't seen me.

"Both of you know we don't handle our disagreements with physical violence, we use our words," Devi says, and she looks like she's wishing she could swat both of their elementary-school asses. Instead she gives their arms a sharp tug. "Right, Louisa?"

"He needs to apologize to me," Louisa says, wiping a curl off her cheek.

"You both need to apologize to each other," Devi says.

They raise their eyes in unison to the door, and I'm busted. I meet Devi's shocked look and smile. "Hi."

"Hi," Devi says, dropping their arms.

"Is that your boyfriend, Miss Devi?" Gator says.

"He's just my…" her words trail off.

"I'm Ben," I say, stepping forward and extending a hand to Gator. "Put 'er there, my friend."

"This your girlfriend?" I ask Gator, nodding to Louisa.

"Uh-uh." Gator says with conviction. "That's Louisa, she don't like boys." I smile and reach out to shake Louisa's hand.

"I bet Louisa's just waitin' for someone special," I say.

"Well, I'm glad I ain't nothin' special," Gator says.

"What are you doing here?" Devi asks.

"Mario called me, said they had some things they needed moved tonight. I'm going to help out for a few hours. I could use a little more muscle though. Gator, could I steel you away from these beautiful women?"

"Hell yeah," he says.

I raise a hand to my mouth and hide a smile under my palm.

"Gator, language, please. And I'm still waiting to hear you two apologize to each other."

"Sorry," Gator says to Louisa.

"You should be sorry." Louisa starts in again, and Devi interrupts her.

"Louisa! Apologize or go sit in my office. Those are your choices. You've got a little too much pride going on under that track suit, girlfriend."

Oh my God, this is precious, and I'm trying not to laugh my ass off. I don't know how she does this with a straight face all day. I'd be howling at the things these kids say.

"Sometimes you need to cut people a break," Devi says.

"Sorry," Louisa says begrudgingly.

I nod and put my hand on Gator's shoulder leading him away.

"Well, what do you think of that?" I hear Devi ask Louisa as we're walking away.

"I think your boyfriend's mighty fine, Miss Devi."

Gator and I make our way back downstairs and find Mario. She shows us the items she needs moved, and we get to work. The kitchen is first, and I move the refrigerator to the new designated spot while Gator holds the cord. Next we load three files cabinets onto a dolly and wheel them down the hallway and into a storage room.

"Be my eyes," I say to Gator. He jumps in front of the dolly and waves his arms.

"Comin' through, comin' through," he says, lowering his voice to affect authority. "Step aside, now, ain't nothing to concern yourselves with." He nods to the kids as we pass. After the file cabinets, we move two bookshelves and a desk. The last task is a stack of chairs going to the game room. I load them onto the dolly and let Gator climb on top. He laughs the whole way as I repeat his script. "Comin' through, step aside. Nothin' to see here." I help him down, and we unload the chairs next to a shelf of board games.

"Wow. You guys have the hookup here. What's your favorite game?" I ask him surveying the shelves. He scratches his head.

"Ooh, *Life*!" he exclaims, pointing to the top shelf. "The game of *Life*."

"Wanna play?" I ask, grabbing it with one hand.

He kicks out a leg and claps once. "Yes! Yes! You're goin' down, sucka!'"

"Care to place a small wager?" I ask.

He wipes a hand over the top of his flat hair, thinking. "Ooh, candy. Let's bet for candy," he says, jumping on one leg.

"All right. What do you like?"

"Snickers. Two Snickers?"

"Okay, you win, I got you down for two Snickers. And if I win, hmmm, I can't eat candy, all that sugar makes me crazy. Can you draw?"

"Yep."

"Okay, if I win, you draw me a picture of Miss Devi."

"Yeah," he says, dropping down on his knees and pulling the top off the game.

"She's gotta have a dress on. A white dress."

"Yeah," he says, flipping the game open. "What color car you wanna be?"

An hour later I'm getting my ass handed to me in the game of *Life* by an eight year old. Gator is sitting cross-legged, tossing a yellow plastic car piece into the air and contemplating his next move.

Devi walks in and stares down at us. "I thought you might need some water, since you're working so hard," she says. We take the bottles and I smile at her, running my gaze over her tight jeans and "Fight Like a Girl" T-shirt. I'd like to find a job where I can dress like that—minus the "Fight Like a Girl" shirt. I'm sitting on the floor with my back against the couch, legs stretched in front of me. She steps over me and sits on the couch beside Gator's shoulder. "Who's winning?" she asks, as Gator spins the wheel. It ticks out a low zinging noise.

"I'm winning," he says. "Ben doesn't have any money left because he got so many kids."

I raise a brow and exchange glances with Devi as Gator laughs. "They all girls, too. See?" He points to the blue car piece on the board, loaded with small pink plugs and one lonely blue plug.

"That's one busy daddy," Devi says, raising a single brow.

"Thank God he's got a mommy riding next to him. That's a good woman, right there," I say, nodding toward my overflowing car.

Devi purses her lips and leans forward. "Mmm, she looks tired to me."

"They look broke to me!" Gator says. "He got all those kids, and he's a hairstylist. You can't pay for all them kids cutting hair—least, not where I grew up." He holds his hand over his nose and laughs, and it's impossible not to join him.

"Hey, at least I live in a penthouse suite with my wife and four girls, and they all have great hair. What more could they want?"

The wheel stops on five and Gator moves his game piece forward and pumps his fist. "Yes!" he says, pulling into the "Retire" space on the board.

"I told you, you should'na skipped college," he says.

"You skipped college?" Devi asks, in the same tone she uses to ask someone if they're a moron. "Bad move."

"Good game." Gator laughs. He jumps to his feet and does a victory dance. "Two Snickers, Mr. Ben. I'm going to find Diego," he says, running out.

"Thanks for your help today, Gator."

"Anytime," Gator says, his voice echoing in the hall.

I smile at Devi, and we both stand. I have such an urge to grab her and wrap her in my arms, but I can feel her reserve.

"How you doing?" I ask.

"Fine. You?"

"I'll manage." I brush dirt off my hands and pick up the water bottle. Silence passes between us as we stare, both painfully aware of our circumstances. I can see the sadness in her eyes, and it kills me that I can't do anything about it. I glance away and drink the rest of the water from the bottle.

"Well, guess I'll head back," I say.

She nods, and I kneel down and start to clean up the board. She drops to her knees to help. I'm watching her face inches from mine as she leans forward, balancing on her palms and reaching for the stacks of paper money. Her arm crosses mine, and I can't take it anymore. I lock my hand around her wrist and pull it slowly to my mouth, kissing the pulse point. I turn her palm open and press my loaded car into her hand, closing her fingers around it.

"I miss you," I say. She stares with a conflicted look. I drop her hand and see a glimmer of emotion slip past the reserve. She returns to the task of closing up the board. I stand up and walk to the door, stopping under the frame. I let out a long breath.

"Paternity test is scheduled for Friday, three p.m." I walk out without waiting for her response.

Chapter Fourteen

DEVIN GRACE

My phone is ringing, tugging me out of the fog of a bad dream. I sit up, blink sleep out of my vision and look at the clock. It's Thursday, 3:18 a.m. Shit. Only bad news comes in the middle of the night. Numb fingers knock against the nightstand and fumble over my phone. I flip it up and my mom's name appears. My heart skips a beat.

"Mom, Mom." All I can hear is her panting into the phone. I can hear her lungs gasping. "Mom! What's wrong?"

"Devi. Oh my God, Devi, It's Josh — " I search the darkness, and the pause in her voice lasts an eternity. "He's overdosed. The ambulance is on its way." Her voice breaks. "I don't know if he's going to make it."

I throw back the covers and fall out of the bed onto my knees. "Jesus Christ!" I take a deep breath and then another. My mom's voice borders on hysteria and with every breathless syllable she speaks my heart skips.

My mom did everything she could to support me when I was growing up, but in the last year she's the one that's needed support, and never as much as now. There's nothing I can say over the phone that will be enough to help her. I have to be there for her. Regardless of my anger toward Josh, he's still my brother. I swallow and blink, trying to calm my racing heart enough to speak.

"He's going to make it, Mom. He's going to make it. I'm coming right now." I stretch my arm and feel in the dark for my jeans.

She gasps a loud sob into the phone that wrenches my heart. "I think they're here—the ambulance. I'll call you from the hospital." She hangs up.

"Shit." I say out loud. Stay calm. Stay calm. "Shit." I press my hand to my mouth, tears burning. Pull it together, Devi. I flip the light, and I'm running to the bathroom, grabbing my cosmetic bag, scraping the jars off the sink. Sweatshirt. Baseball cap. My fingers fumble. Clothes. I have to pack clothes.

What am I thinking? I don't have a car! *Ben.*

I stumble across our moonlit living room, yank open the front door and run down the hall. My fists pound on his door, and my voice is a pleading shout. "Ben! Ben!" He's not answering. A sob escapes, and I clasp my hand over my mouth. I need my phone. I know he sleeps with his phone by the bed, and he doesn't turn the ringer off in case his mom or sisters need him.

I start back for my apartment, and his door opens and he's in the hallway, blinking. He takes a giant step toward me. "What's wrong?" He's bare-chested, and his jeans are unzipped, hanging half off his hips. "Devi." I lunge at him and he grabs my shoulders. "What's wrong?" He looks into the hallway behind me and over his shoulder as I attempt to form the words. My hand is on my mouth, and I'm trying to calm down. Deep breath.

"Josh overdosed. They're taking him to the hospital, and I think my mom is going to have a breakdown. Can you take me home?"

He swallows. "I'll get dressed, go get your things." I nod and head back to my apartment as Jett is coming out to investigate the commotion.

In five minutes Ben's at my door, dressed in jeans, flannel shirt, and a ball cap, ready to go. Jett woke Ryan, and she's helped me pack and made us each a cup of coffee from our Keurig.

"Good luck," Jett says.

Ryan hands me two travel cups and tucks Splenda packets in the pocket of my hoodie. "We're here if you need anything."

I hug them both. "Thanks. I'll let you know as soon as we hear."

Ben takes my overflowing bag from my hand. "You got your phone?" he asks. I nod, and we head out.

I spend the first hour of the trip sobbing off and on and waiting for my mom to call. Ben holds his hand over mine and tries to calm me down, speaking low and reassuring words to counter the panic. I can hardly hear them. I flip the phone over and over in my hand, checking my texts, waiting for it to light up.

"Why hasn't she called? I feel like I'm going crazy. What if he dies, Ben?"

"Hey, look at me, Devi. He's not going to die. That's not

happening right now. Right now he's at the hospital, and they're helping him. Take a deep breath." I do as he says, breathing in until my lungs are full and exhaling slowly.

"Take another and tell yourself it's going to be okay."

I nod my head, take another breath, and whisper, "It's going to be okay."

"Why don't you tell me about Josh, growing up. What was he like?" Ben says.

"Shy. Awkward. We actually used to get along, before he started using." A small laugh escapes as I think about it. "Josh was everything I wasn't." I stare out at the strip of empty road in front of us, surrounded by darkness on both sides. It's as if we're driving through a tunnel, not knowing what waits on the other side.

"You know what my most vivid memory of Josh as a kid is?" I have to stop to control my breath, I can feel the emotion waving up again. I take a deep breath and continue. "We used to walk home from school every day. I remember the puffy down coat he used to wear. It was green. And every day he had a piece of paper, folded in half and pinned to his back with one straight pin at the top. It was a note from his teacher to my mom. I used to stare at that paper as he walked in front of me. God, I was so mad at him, because I knew when my mom saw it she'd be sad. Every night she would sit at the kitchen table, trying to figure out what was going on with him as he stared at his feet. I think that's part of the reason I've always done so well in school, to make up for all that." I let out a low breath and look at Ben. He rubs his thumb over the back of my hand, and I am so thankful that he's here with me right now. If our relationship never gets back on track, at least I know our friendship can.

"Josh was always the kid that was in trouble, and I was constantly sticking up for him. With every bad thing that happened to us, it seems like he survived it all by sinking a level lower into himself. I was the exact opposite. I over-extroverted myself. I needed the distraction—anything to get away from the worrying. It's funny how two people who grow up in the same house can be so different."

My phone rings and I jump. It juggles in my hands. "Mom, Mom—"

My brain feels blank waiting for the answer to the question I haven't asked. *Did he make it?* Her voice is strained, but I hear her words clear enough.

"They think he's going to pull through. They've pumped his stomach, and he's regained consciousness. Heroin and Xanax," she says and her voice, although still weak and shaky, has lost the edge of hysteria I heard earlier.

The boulder that had been pressing over my heart lifts, and I release a full breath.

"Good God. Are you okay, Mom?" I look over at Ben and take the hand he's holding out to me. I grip his hand as my mom fills me in on all the gory details. Justin, my brother's junkie friend, had been over yesterday afternoon according to the neighbors, and that tells me all I need to know.

"We're crossing the Pennsylvania border, Mom, we should be there by noon."

I hang up the phone and look at Ben. A flood of relief rushes through me sending my emotions into an upward spiral.

"He's going to be okay. They think he's going to be okay."

He pulls my hand to his lips and kisses my white knuckles, and I realize how much I need him here with me right now.

"Thank you for taking care of me, Ben."

"Always," he says. I don't bother to say I didn't have any choice. But as I think about it, I did have a choice, Mario or Robyn or even Vaughn. But I needed Ben. I wanted Ben. I even went to him before I woke up Ryan.

At eleven forty-five a.m. Thursday morning, we're walking into Sparrow Hospital. The brunette behind the information station looks up Josh Dalton and directs us to his floor. I hear my mom's voice as we're turning into the room. Josh is sitting up in bed. His complexion is gray and his frame looks skeletal, but he's alive.

The smell of my mom's fruity hairspray stings my nose with welcome familiarity as she hugs me close. My mom usually looks a little bedraggled but even more so now. Gray roots spread from the part of her brown hair, and the soft skin under her eyes looks darker. Despite that, she's still pretty, but nowhere near what she could be if she didn't have the strain of Josh and the financial troubles in her life. I hear Ben introduce himself to my mom as I'm moving to the side of the bed.

"Hey," I say to Josh. I lean in and kiss him on the cheek, which seems completely foreign to me. I pause and stare down. The reality of not having touched or talked to him—at least in any kind way—for the last two years beats through me.

"How you feeling?" I ask him as I'm moving back to my mom's side.

"Like shit, but they say I can go home tomorrow."

"He has to see the hospital psychiatrist first," my mom says. Josh's gaze moves to her and then settles on Ben. I turn to introduce Ben, but Josh interrupts me.

"Hey, Ben."

Ben steps to the other side of the bed and holds a hand out. "How you doin', man?" They grip, palm to palm and thumbs up, as if they're reunited homeboys.

"Doin' all right," he says, letting a small laugh escape. "My source gave me some messed-up shit." His voice is a mix of regret and blame as he rubs his fingers over his forehead.

"Yeah, your source gave it to you and you took it," Ben says.

Josh stops rubbing and smiles at Ben, "Yeah, I took it," he says with a guilty look. I'm watching the two of them talk, wondering if they somehow know each other. Ben's the type of person that connects so easily with everyone, as if he's never met a stranger—but Josh is the type of person that connects with no one.

"We're gonna break some ground here, get you some help," Ben says to him.

"Yeah," Josh says, letting out low breath. "Yeah."

Hmmph. Usually when we say things like this to Josh, he acts as if we don't exist. I glance at my mom and see a glimmer of relief on her features. She's still wearing her work clothes, and it strikes me she must have come straight home from the night shift to find Josh passed out on the kitchen floor. I should take her home, put her to bed, and clean up the house while she sleeps.

I cross my arms over my chest and study Ben's face as he and Josh talk. What is it about him that makes everyone he meets instantly comfortable? Even though Josh is sorely in need of a male role model, I don't think it's the fact that Ben's another guy. It's more than that. Maybe it's the aura of unspoken authority that's apparent from one glance at Ben. He's an imposing force to stand next to, always the biggest man in the room, and yet I've never seen Ben look threatening to anyone. Well, except me when I got in the cage fight. I watch him looking at Josh. He's present and connected—open and accepting.

I let myself think about the possibility of Ben—of us. I know he'd be a good dad, I'm just not so sure about me. I'd be dating a guy who has a child with another woman. And if we continued to get serious, I'd have a title with the word "step" in front of it again, as in one step outside the family. Every time my stepdad introduced me as his stepdaughter, it felt to me like he was saying a bad word. Do I really want to be in that position again? I resisted Ben for so long feeling like his family would never accept me, and we'd have problems with that. I finally put that aside, and now I have to worry I'll feel like an outsider in my immediate family. If the baby is his, Jillian will always be that baby's mommy, and where does that leave me? I shouldn't think about it right now. It's all still too much.

Ben's phone rings. "It's my mom," he says, "I'm going to step out to the lounge." I nod my head, and he leaves the room as a nurse comes in to check on Josh. Mom and I move to the peach vinyl couch under the windows and sit. We talk in low tones, and I try to reassure her. She's quiet. Her eyelids flutter, as if she's fighting sleep. I stop talking and scoot closer, propping my shoulder close to her drooping chin. Within minutes I feel the heaviness of my eyelids and give in, leaning on my mom.

Minutes pass and my mind is suspended in a half conscious state. Through the haze of my exhaustion I hear an unfamiliar voice in the room. It's a man's voice, speaking to Josh—not Ben, but they're laughing together. I'm half dreaming—riding in Ben's truck with my face in the sun, his hand on my leg. The voices echo in my ears like words spoken underwater.

"You gotta get me out of here...I can't pay you if I'm stuck..."

"I'll get you out, dude, you owe me another two hundred dollars...you think I'm gonna let that go?"

My eyes fly open. The truck in my dreams has plunged into a cold lake. I'm staring at my brother's drug dealer, Justin, sitting beside the bed. He's quite likely the guy that stole my money or at least the guy that took my money after Josh stole it. He pulls the black stocking cap off revealing a scruffy mat of red hair. The two of them are laughing—fucking laughing, like it's a big joke. In the span of a ten-minute nap, Josh has slid back into the world of an addict. I bolt upright, and my mom gasps as her head jerks off my shoulder.

Josh and Justin turn to me. The laughter disappears, and Justin stares warily. His faded red hoodie sags over his six-foot frame as he stands and wipes his hands on dirty jeans. This isn't the first confrontation I've had with him. He's three years older than me, but he's been Josh's friend since his freshmen year in high school. He's a local kid who works with a moving company during the day and sells drugs at night, and I can't fucking stand him.

"What the fuck are you doing here, you junkie predator?" I clench my fists and nudge my mom's restraining hand off my arm.

"Hey," he dips his knees and spreads his fingers up into the air as if he's showing me his rings. "I came here to pay my respects."

Three quick steps and I'm in his face, my finger inches from his nose. "Get the fuck out and stay away from my brother."

"Devi, Devi," my mom is raising her voice in a panicked tone. I'm out of control and I know it.

Justin knocks my finger away and leans into my face. His sour breath hits me as he sneers, "I'll stay away from him as soon as he pays me back the money." I bring my hands up between us and shove him as hard as I can. The back of his hand swipes my face, and he grabs a handful of my hair and it strains against my scalp as he stumbles. I clutch his hand to keep him from pulling it out at the roots. My knee draws back and I thrust into his balls as hard as I can. I hear my mom scream my name as Justin makes a gurgling sound and falls into a hunched stance, cupping his balls with one hand. In the background Josh and my mom are yelling, but the only thing I can concentrate on is Justin's grip on my hair. I bite my lip, clasp my hands and pull back, ready to drop him with the hardest punch I can exert but a solid force stops my forward movement.

Arms circle my waist, and I'm weightless. Ben's behind me, lifting me and moving his body between our scuffle. He raises a leg and kicks Justin with a swift jab. The pressure against my hair releases at the same time Justin wheezes, trying to catch the breath Ben just knocked out of him. He lands on his knees with a cracking sound. I kick out aiming for one last shot. Ben swings me around and carries me to the couch. He sets me down and holds his spread fingers against my chest as I start to get up.

"Sit!" he yells.

I push my tangled hair off of my face and yell at him. "That's my brother's drug dealer."

Justin is recovering, rising slowly with a hand against the wall. "I was just leaving." He coughs.

Ben crosses to him and grips a big hand around the back of his neck. "I'll walk you out." He holds an arm out and points a finger at me as I'm standing. "You stay there." I feel my mom's arms circle my waist.

"I'm fine, Mom."

"That wasn't necessary," Josh says. "I just gotta get him his money, and then he's out of my life." I rub my fingers over my burning cheek, feeling the sting of the puffy welts.

"You should stop trying to fight my battles for me."

"If I could fight the drug monkey you've got on your back, you know I would, Josh, but I can't, I've tried. You have got to do this for yourself. You're killing Mom." I wipe a tear from my cheek and repeat in an adamant tone. "You have to, Josh."

"I know. I will." He turns a cheek to rest on the pillow. "I'm glad you hit him."

A soft knocking interrupts us. We look up to see Jade standing in the doorway. "Is this a good time?" she says.

"It's never a good time with this family," I say, laughing and crossing to her.

Next to Ryan, Jade is my closest friend, and she competed with us in New York against Team Jett. She stayed in Michigan after graduation and took a job with Ford.

I throw my arms around her and kiss her on the cheek. She smiles, and I see her inspecting the red welts on my cheeks. We exchange a quick glance, but she doesn't ask. She hugs my mom and steps beside Josh's hospital bed. She shakes his hand with both of hers. Josh smiles softly, and his pale complexion rises to a faint blush. He's never admitted it, but I think he developed a crush on Jade when we were in high school and she used to come over with Ryan. She's asking him how he's feeling and talking to him in a calm voice, as if she understands what he's going through—probably because she grew up living with an alcoholic father. She's a welcome connection to the real world for all of us, beyond the sterile and stressful environment of a hospital room.

"Hey, Jade," Ben says, coming back into the room. He wraps her in a big hug, and I see he's carrying an alcohol swab and a tube of some kind of ointment.

"Is that stuff for Josh, need me to move?" Jade asks.

Ben looks at me and smiles. "Oh no, it's for Devi." He rips the square alcohol packet with his teeth and moves to stand in front of me. He holds my chin in one hand and starts to drag the cool, wet wipe over my cheek. I flinch at the burn and grab his hand with both of mine.

"Ouch."

He raises his eyebrows. "Might not hurt so much if you tried using your words instead of your fists." I drop his hand, smirking and he begins to dab again. "What would that be like? Hmm?"

"I did use my words. I told him he could fuck right off. Then I kicked him in the balls."

"Mmhmm. You got an awful lot of pride goin' on under that track suit," he says, repeating the words I used on Louisa when she and Gator were fighting. The corner of my mouth lifts and my mom weighs in.

"Well, that is just the truth, Ben. Devin's always had her pride. No one's gonna tell her what to do."

"God forbid you tell her she's wrong," Jade says.

"Oh, stop. I'm too tired to defend myself against all of you."

With Jade's arrival, the mood in the room has lightened. We visit for most of the afternoon, taking turns running to the cafeteria for coffee or snacks, while Josh sleeps intermittently. Ben watches football and dozes in the chair while we make a run to Jimmy John's for subs. At seven p.m. Ben volunteers to stay the night with Josh and encourages us to go home. I contemplate his suggestion. I don't want my mom to be alone, and she's had no sleep. I am exhausted, too, but I feel bad leaving him here.

"It will give you a little time to help your mom and get a good night's sleep," Ben says.

"I'll come with you and help you get the house cleaned up," Jade offers. "I'm probably the only one in this room that actually got a full night's sleep last night."

"Are you sure, Ben?" He reaches two hands out and pulls Jade and me up off the couch.

"Go," he says, nodding to the TV hanging in the corner. "I want to watch the game anyway. You might as well stay the night in your bed. I'll crash here. Josh is probably out for the night."

We watch my mom lean over and kiss Josh's forehead.

"Thank you, Ben," she says. "I'm going to the nurse's station to talk to them about the plan for tomorrow." She grabs her purse and heads out. Jade hugs Ben good-bye and leaves the room with my mom.

"Was everything okay with your mom?" I ask,

remembering the call he took earlier.

"Hmmph. Yeah. I almost forgot. She saw Jett's Facebook post wishing me safe travels back to Michigan. She knows I'm in town. She's traveling this weekend and wants me to check in on my sisters."

"We can do that."

"I'd love for you to meet them, but we'll see how tomorrow goes for Josh."

I let out a small breath, and it strikes me that Ben's paternity test was scheduled for tomorrow. He's dropped everything to be here with me. "I'm sorry you're going to miss your appointment."

"Well, as much as I'd like to get it over with, family is more important right now. I'll call Jillian a little later and tell her I need to reschedule."

"I'm sure she'll be thrilled about that." He smiles and the awkwardness of discussing the subject catches up with us.

"Can I bring you anything from the cafeteria before we go?" I ask.

"I'm fine. I'll go down later if I get hungry. Go."

"Thank you, Ben, for helping me." I glance at Josh sleeping peacefully, "For helping us." Ben steps closer and kisses my cheek. I close my eyes and feel the warmth of his skin against mine — wishing the moment could last.

"Go get some sleep. I'll be right here."

Chapter Fifteen

BEN

I open the door of the truck for Devi. It's Friday evening, and we have just dropped Josh off at his inpatient rehab facility and said our good-byes. Devi's mom left earlier to make it to her night shift. Despite the teary good-byes, everybody had a better day today. Josh is committed to his program, and Devi and her mom seemed less fragile, speaking positively and feeling good about Josh's first steps toward recovery.

"Are you sure you feel up to heading to my house? I have seen a couple posts on Facebook that make me think my sisters are having a party," I say to Devi.

"A party sounds like what we need. Might just take the edge off," she says. We stop at Anita's Kitchen, the restaurant at Nine Mile Road and Woodward that we met at earlier this summer. We sit on the patio eating pita pizzas, talking about the uphill battle that Josh faces and then about my mom and sisters. The part of us that behaved so well together as "just friends" seems back on track, and for now, I'll settle for that. I want Devi to come back to me on her own—not because I pushed her.

It's close to nine p.m. by the time we pull into my neighborhood, and from the looks of things, the party at the Winslow house is in full swing. There are so many cars lining the drive and the street, I have to park halfway up the block.

I'm leading Devi up the sidewalk and over the lawn. She hesitates a step. "Geez, Ben, is this your house?"

"Yep, and this is what it looks like when my mom's out of town." The front door is open and music beats out, mixed with the sounds of loud voices and laughter. All the lights in the house are on, and behind every window of the four-story brick colonial bodies are bobbing against each other.

"How many bedrooms?" she says with a stunned expression.

"Nine." I say, and immediately change the subject. "You ready to have some fun?" I ask, pulling her up onto the porch next to me. "The Facebook post I saw said something about an A-B-C theme party."

"I like these things," she says, running her finger along the scalloped edge of the planted urns that have sat at the base of our front porch for as long as I can remember. "And hell yes, I am ready to have some fun. What's an A-B-C party?" she asks, as I hold a hand against the open door.

"I don't know but I have a feeling we're about to find out." I told Devi I had read something on my sister Priscilla's Facebook page about an A-B-C costume. I'm assuming it was code for tonight's festivities.

We step into the wide front hallway, which is lined with a colorful array of people standing shoulder to shoulder, red cups in hand, wearing anything but clothes. The guy closest to the door turns to us. He's wearing a Scooby Doo mask and a grass skirt, smoking a cigarette. He steps in front of me and mumbles out high pitched syllables that end in a questioning tone.

"Hey, Scoob, how's it going?" I pat his shoulder and start to move past him. He holds out an open palms and growls at me. A guy plastered in Campbell soup labels turns around.

"Cover," he says. "He wants you to pay cover. It's five bucks." Scooby growls and pokes a fist into Devi's arm. I knock it away and pull the cigarette out of his mouth.

"I live here," I say. "If you want to smoke, take it outside, and keep your paws off my girl." I smash the butt of the cigarette against his furry forehead. He covers the spot with two hands, stumbles, and moans.

"Awww, Ben, you hurt him," Devi says with a tone of amusement.

"Good," I say, grabbing her hand. She flicks her thumbnail over her index finger as we pass. "Here's a Scooby snack," she calls. He snaps his snout into the air and chomps down the imaginary biscuit.

"Ben!" My sister Cate's blond curls bob as she pushes through the bodies. She dodges a guy covered in Monopoly money and lands in front of us wrapped in layers of white feather boas, wearing red cowboy boots. She hugs me and her expression looks torn between excitement and all-out worry as feathers billow around her heart-shaped face. "What are you doing here? Did you come home for the party?"

"Was I invited?" I ask, and she hesitates a beat.

"Well, Priscilla said she wanted to have fun." She stops abruptly, and her green eyes widen, as if she's just realized she's said too much.

"Hmm. Where is Priscilla?"

She casts a guilty look toward the game room at the end of the hallway and shrugs. "I don't know."

"You're such a bad liar, Cate. Seriously, you've got to work on that." Her red lips pout making her look like a glammed up Kewpie doll.

"Ben!" I hear Chloe's voice from across the room. She's dodging bodies and coming our way. I kiss her cheek and return her hug. My hands slide over the yellow crime scene tape she's wrapped in. Her brow lifts, and the crime scene headband she's fashioned raises an inch. "We didn't know you were coming home this weekend."

"That's pretty obvious," I say glancing around the foyer. "When does Mom get home?"

"Tomorrow night." As if on cue they both turn a bright smile to Devi.

"Devi, these are my sisters, Cate and Chloe."

"Nice to meet you," Devi says, admiring their costumes. "We didn't know what an A-B-C party was."

"Anything but clothes," Cate answers and looks at me. "Priscilla's idea."

"I feel really overdressed," Devi says, grinning.

Cate hooks her arm in Devi's. "Well, we can fix that," she says, looking delighted at the prospect of playing stylist. "Follow me." I watch Devi climbing the stairway, laughing with my sisters. They disappear around the spiral, and I head for the game room.

I shoulder my way through the crowd, exchanging home-boy handshakes with the guys I recognize as my sister's classmates. As I draw closer I can hear shouts and laughter rising from the room.

"Hey, Ben." I'm face to face with Priscilla's friend Dan.

"Hey, bud, put 'er there," I say, shaking hands. "How's life?"

"All's good here. For you? How's New York?"

"No complaints. I'm looking for Priscilla."

He smiles and nods to the game room. "She's holding court." I detect a note of melancholy in his voice. Dan used to date Priscilla, but it didn't last that long. He's such a good guy but Priscilla doesn't "do dating," as she explained to me. Dan is bare-chested, and around his waist he's taped squares of condom packages to form a kilt.

"Great costume."

"Thanks," he says holding his hands out, "You can never be too prepared or safe."

"Tell me about it." I pat his upper arm and move past him as another hooting rush erupts from the game room. I step in and survey the commotion. There are around forty people crammed into the room, standing against the walls. They've cleared a space and put down black garbage bags for the players. At each end of the room a girl is sitting on top of a guy's shoulders, holding a bucket. The teams are throwing orange Nerf balls at the girls, which they are trying to catch in their buckets. A roar of laughter bursts from the crowd as the foam ball hits one of the girl's heads, splashes beer all over, and drops into the bucket. She reaches into the bucket pulls out the beer soaked ball and rings it out first into her mouth and then into the upturned mouth of her partner. She soaks the ball and then whips it at the opposing team.

Across the room, I see Priscilla. She's standing on a table

next to a giant chalkboard marked with columns and white lines. The costume she's wearing is a design of strategically placed hockey pads, including a cup. Her honey blond hair streams from the Red Wings baseball cap that she's turned backward, and like any well respecting bookie, she's holding a fistful of cash and smoking a cigar.

My first instinct is to grab that cigar out of her mouth and drop the curtain on this show, but my sisters have seen me throw at least a dozen parties like this and they are all in college now. By the time I was a high school senior, I was on a first-name basis with the Grosse Pointe police force. For the most part, I'm going to let them handle their own shit. But I'm glad I can be here, watching from the sidelines just in case. I move into the room and lean against the wall, surveying the action for a minute. The spectators roar as blue scores again and team red empties her last sponge full of beer into the mouth of her partner. He steps and sways, steps and sways, and his friends rush in to rescue the winning team.

"Team Cross and Team O'Neill, you're up," Priscilla calls over the noise. "Bets are open." I reach for my wallet and move to the line in front of her.

The guy covered in ping-pong balls hands Priscilla a five-dollar bill, and she turns to write down his wager. I step up as she's licking her thumb and counting the cash in her hand. "What'll it be?" she asks, still counting.

I move my cash into her sightline. "I got fifty bucks that says you'll never be able to clean up this shit show before Mom gets home." She stops thumbing and looks up. Her cigar droops against her bottom lip as she gapes at me.

I reach down, pull it out of her mouth, and hit it.

She smiles. "Double or nothing I'll have the whole house clean by noon and not lift a finger."

"Skimming enough off the pot to pay for a cleaning lady, eh?"

She flashes a raised brow and smiles. "I learned from the best."

"Nice costume." She's wearing my old hockey gear. "I'd hug you, 'Sil, but I wouldn't know where to put my hands."

Someone rings a bell, and I look for the source. I take the bell from the guy wearing a duck-faced inner tube around his waist, hold it up, and swirl it above my head like a lasso.

"There will be a short intermission while we gather in the front hall to discuss party etiquette at the Winslow house," I shout over them.

"Please tell me you're not doing this every weekend now that I'm gone," I say, handing her back her cigar.

She smiles as she takes it from me. "Oh no, this is my first time," she says, motioning the stogie at me and faking a cough.

I kill the music and make another announcement in the hall. The crowd gathers and the gabbing and laughter sinks to hushed whispers and nervous laughs. I jump onto the third stair of the spiral staircase.

"Thank you all for coming to my sister's 'Let's rock this bitch because my brother moved out of the house' party." The partiers starts to hoot and cheer, and I pause waiting for them to settle down. As I'm surveying the crowd I see their gazes shift to the stairs above me. I turn and see Devi coming down, laughing with my sisters. Her hair is piled on top of her head at the sides, spilling long flowing curls over her bare shoulders. There's something silver pinned to the top of her head like a crown. She's wearing a toga that crosses over her chest and plunges to her waist, revealing her stunning figure. For a moment I'm lost in the fantasy that is Devi, pulling that sheet off her, lifting it up her legs, bending her. I brush my thumb over the sweat forming on my upper lip and turn back to the crowd.

Dan hands me a beer, and I resume my sermon. "Just to make sure my sisters are carrying on the Winslow tradition of responsible partying, I'm gonna go over the house rules. Number one: no drugs. Number two: you puke, you're back at nine a.m. working the chain gang with the cleanup crew. Number three: Condom-Dan here will be collecting keys from anyone deemed unfit to drive. Number four: unless your last name is Winslow, your feet don't touch the upper floors of this house. And number five to stay alive: keep your hands off my sisters." I turn back and look at Devi. She's leaning against the bannister with her arms crossed, one hand gripping a long neck. "And my girl. Have fun, kids." The crowd cheers and starts to disperse. I turn to stare at Devi, smiling down at me. I crook a finger at her, and she laughs and steps down, hips swaying, pressed tight against the sheet.

She stops on the step above me so that we're eye to eye. "Turn." She raises a seductive brow and pivots slowly. I pan my gaze down her curves and realize my sisters have wrapped her in the sheet from my bed. It's light gray with a wide pattern of white stars, purchased during my astronomy phase. I catch the light from the chain sparkling against her dark hair. Weaved into the tresses piled on top of her head is my all-state champion MMA medal. Nice touch.

"You know, I'm going to need that sheet back at the end

of the night," I say measuring her expression. She lifts the corner of her mouth and lets out a little laugh.

"We'll see about that, but for right now," she reaches for my waist, "you're seriously overdressed." I reach back, grab a handful of T-shirt and help her pull my shirt off. "That's better," she says moving her hands up the bare skin at my sides. I'm watching her face, wondering if she's starting to come back to me, but I think she really just wants to have a good time. I can't blame her after the last few days we've had. I sure as hell am ready for a throwback to my college days. She grabs my hand. "Come on, I want to see the human beer pong game your sisters were telling me about."

Two hours later Devi's twisting a beer-soaked Nerf ball above my face, while my hands hold her thighs over my shoulders. She raises her arms in the air and starts to scream out our victory. I reach up for her, and she slides down the side of my body while the crowd cheers.

"Oh my God, I'm dizzy," she says, laughing and clutching my forearms. She drops the red bucket, and I hold her waist while she tries to get her balance. Between catching a beer soaked Nerf ball a dozen times and squeezing it down her throat and then mine, the front of her sheet is completely drenched. No wonder they were cheering.

"Come on," I say, taking her hand and leading her to the kitchen.

"That was so much fun," she says, laughing. I open the fridge, pull out two bottles of water, and head for the back stairway off the kitchen.

"I can't believe you grew up in a house that has two staircases." She grabs my arm and pulls me back. "Wait! I am not a Winslow." She sways and leans back against the wall.

"I can't set foot above this floor. House rules, remember?" I hand her the water bottles, and she takes them with a confused look. I bend and scoop her up over my shoulder. She screams and laughs as I carry her to the second floor and down the hallway to my room. I push the door open with my foot and drop her on the sheetless bed.

I close the door and she smiles, not bothering to get up. "I love your sisters, and Ben, this house is amazing." Her fingers graze her forehead, and she rolls over on her side, laying her head on her arm.

"Did you have fun?" I ask.

"Too much fun," she says, rubbing her hands up her ribs and scrunching her face as she sits up. "I'm sticky." I watch her reach behind her neck and fumble with the sheet. "Can you help me," she says, standing and turning. She holds her hair to the side and tilts her neck. For a moment I'm mesmerized by the curve of her neck, beautiful and sensuous, like every other curve on her body.

She casts a questioning look over her shoulder, waiting for me. I step forward and run my knuckles over the skin on the back of her neck, certain I am not qualified to undo the contraption my sisters have secured. After a bit of fumbling I crack the code and find the line of safety pins, unclipping one by one. The sheet slides down her body. She turns around and hands it to me. "You said you wanted this back." I take the sheet, transfixed by the view of her naked body in front of me. She reaches into her hair to start unpinning the MMA medal. I'm staring at her damp skin and tight nipples. "Can I borrow a T-shirt, or something to sleep in?" I pull myself out of my trance, cross to the dresser, and find a white V-neck. I hand it to her, a little reluctant to provide the source intended to cover my living, breathing fantasy.

"Thanks," she says, taking it from me and tossing it on the bed. "I'll put it on after we're done fucking." I cock a brow, wondering if the alcohol I've consumed is affecting my hearing. She raises her hands to the side of my face and pulls me in. I kiss her soft full lips as her bare skin presses into my equally sticky chest. She tilts her head and starts to trail kisses down my neck.

As much as I don't want to do anything to put the brakes on this, I have to ask. I tilt my head back and try to ignore the feeling of her nipples grazing my chest as she moves. "Devi," I whisper.

"Mmm…"

"How drunk are you, babe?"

"Mmm," she purrs, gripping my sides and kissing lower. I know where she's going with this, and I have to make sure. I grip her shoulders and pull her back. She tilts her head to move her hair off of her cheek. Her lips are parted, and I'm trying to determine for myself.

"Talk to me, babe," I whisper.

She drops her forehead on my chest. "I'm sober enough to feel the ache of not knowing what's going to happen between us." She rocks back and forth. I thread my hands through her hair and lift her face to mine. "And I'm sober enough to know that right now is not the time to figure it out." Her eyes narrow into a pleading look. "I just want to feel you love me, Ben, and I want you so bad it hurts."

Every word she speaks stings and soothes at the same time. I hold her gaze and she returns the intensity I feel, burning between us. "I swear to God, Devi, ever since I met you I feel like every fiber of my soul has been unraveling.

Everything I used to hold in my heart is gone and nothing fills it anymore except you." I bend, scoop her up in my arms and carry her to the bed.

I lay her on top of the soft white mattress cover and let my senses absorb the vision of her naked body. She raises her arms above her head and into the tangle of rich brown hair, stretching, arching, and smiling. I unbutton my jeans slowly, hook my thumbs on my boxers, and pull them off. Her eyes travel the length of me, and she holds her arms out as I roll on the condom. I kneel on the bed, reach my hands behind her bent knees, and pull her body down with one swift movement. My hands drop, parting her thighs. I guide myself into her, slowly leaning my weight. She arches and moans, and I'm watching the sensual expression of sex on her face. Her eyelids are pressed closed, mouth open. I lean over her, pausing to strengthen my own resolve. Her body moves in slow waves underneath me. I'm still, letting her set the rhythm until I have to move. I drive deeper with full strokes and feel myself approaching the edge. I pull slowly away and lean back, resting my hands on her knees, breathing hard. Her eyes open, and she searches my face. Her brows pinch together, and she whispers my name. "Ben," she says, raising up.

"Shhh," I say, catching my breath. "Not yet. Lay back down, babe." She swallows a breath and reclines. My hands push her knees open slowly and move down her thighs. My mouth follows the same path, nipping at the tender skin of her inner thighs, as low as she'll allow, until she's gasping and pushing my shoulders. She sits up, and the flush on her face casts a soft glow against her pale skin in the moonlight. She's the most sensual thing I have ever seen. Dark waves cascade over her shoulders, eyes sparkling with intensity, lips parted.

She reaches her hands to me, and the expression on her face looks fragile. "Ben—please." I circle her wrists with my hands and pull them to my mouth, kissing the insides. I lower my body on top of hers, kissing her deeply. She presses tight against me and wraps her legs around my waist, moving until I'm inside of her again.

She gasps, and I drop my mouth on hers. We're eye to eye, connected on a level that exists beyond our bodies. I raise my hand to her face and speak low, stroking between her legs until we are wound so tightly around each other we explode. I feel her body pulsing with the last of her release underneath me and kiss her deeply.

Chapter Sixteen

Devin Grace

The sun streams in through the window, warming my cheek. I nestle deeper into the pillow. Muffled sounds are coming from the floor below. I arch and stare at the indentation left in the bed from Ben's large frame. The memory of last night fills my senses. Ben's touch, his taste, his words. I have to get up. I swing my legs out from under the comforter and scan the floor.

My overnight bag is in Cate's room. I left it there when she was helping me get dressed in my A-B-C costume. I reach for Ben's T-shirt lying on the floor and slip it over my head. I tiptoe into the hall, intending to find Cate's room. I try three doors—none of which are right. Shit. I'm going to have to do the walk of shame downstairs to find Ben or one of his sisters. I step lightly, seriously hoping I can find a Winslow before meeting up with one of the cleaning crew that Ben talked about.

The main hall is deserted except for a middle-aged woman in jeans and a cardigan leaning over an oversized black bag on the floor. She looks harmless enough.

"Hi," I say and she jumps at the sound of my voice. With her palm pressed to her chest she turns and stares up at me. "I'm sorry, I didn't mean to scare you. I was just wondering if you might be able to find Ben or one of his sisters for me?" She trails a wide-eyed gaze down my T-shirt and bare legs, with a confused look on her face. "Ben's the tall one. He's probably on the main floor somewhere helping."

She crosses her hands in front of her waist and closes her mouth. "Helping with what, dear?" she asks in a tone that sounds way too snooty for a cleaning lady.

"Your crew, the cleaners—from the A-B-C party last night." A feeling of unease stirs inside of me—something about the way she's looking at me—but before I have another second to ponder it, Cate bursts into the hallway holding a bottle of Windex. She looks as if she's seeing a ghost, staring at the cleaning lady who nods at her.

"Hello, Cate."

"Mom!" She says in a tone mixed with horror and surprise. Ben appears and stops in his tracks.

"Ben," his mom says, "so nice that you made it home. I guess that explains the party." He moves forward and kisses her cheek.

"Mom," he says, "you're home early."

"We came home last night. Aunt Polly's gout was acting up. I stayed the night with her so I wouldn't have to drive in the dark, and it sounds like it's a good thing I did." Ben starts to move but she holds his arm and nods toward me on the steps. "I was just about to introduce myself to your friend. I assume she's your friend, as she's wearing your underwear."

Ben's entire body stops moving for a beat. He turns his head up to me standing in the middle of the stairway. It takes every ounce of willpower I have to stand there as they all look up at me—a living, breathing, disastrous picture of everything that went down in this house last night. I caught a glimpse of myself in the hallway mirror upstairs, and I know what they're seeing. My hair looks like a rat's nest, I have black streaks of makeup smudged on my cheeks from the pallet of robin's-egg blue Cate applied, and the makeup covering the red scratches on my face has worn off. I look like a three-dollar prostitute, and overpriced at that. I cross my arms and shrink back.

"Mom, this is Devin," Ben says.

It strikes me that he doesn't introduce me as his girlfriend. He always introduces me as his girlfriend—to everyone—even over all of my objections. Heat washes up my face. I start walking back up the stairs, and by the time I'm turning into his room he's steps behind me.

"Hey," he says.

"I need my clothes," I pin him with a death stare, "and I can't find them in this house with eighty fucking doors."

"Calm down," he says, and I want to scream at him. *I just called your mom the cleaning lady and asked her to help me find my clothes that I lost at a drunken bash in her house last night when I was fucking her son.* My mind is growling with frustration.

"Cate's room," I say in a shaky voice. He lets out a breath and holds a hand toward the door. I exit and follow him. Cate's room is at the end of the hall. He opens the door and

I walk past him and grab my bag. "Bathroom, please," I say, hugging it to my chest. He's looking at me like he wants to help, and I know when I come out of the shock that's fogging my brain right now, I will likely feel bad for taking it out on him. But right now, I feel like shit. Absolute shit.

"Do you want me to wait for you?" he asks.

"No." I close the door in his face and let out a shaky breath.

I wash my face and clean myself up. By the time I come out, I'm feeling a smidge better. At least I look like myself and have my lipstick on. Fearless Red, I remind myself as I descend the stairs with my bag. I set it by the front door, hoping we are leaving soon.

"I was just coming to check on you," Cate says. "Ben asked me to see if you needed anything."

"Oh, no, I'm fine, thanks, Cate," I say, feeling anything but fine.

"Mom brought us lunch, we're just waiting for you. Are you hungry?" she asks, nodding to the dining room.

"Sure," I say, lying. I follow her into the formal dining room and Ben stands. I walk to his mom and hold my hand out. "Devin Dalton," I say. "So sorry about my earlier entrance." She stands and shakes my hand. Her bobbed blond hair waves back from her face, and her almond-shaped blue eyes barely move as she forces a smile.

"I can't wait to tell my friends at the club you thought I was the cleaning lady."

I let out a small laugh and start for the empty seat next to Ben. "I'm sorry about that."

She flips her napkin into the air and lays it on her lap, sitting back down. "That's okay, I thought you were a stripper."

I skip a step but keep walking. I don't laugh. I don't smile. I know I should try to fake it for Ben's sake, but I can't. I walk to the seat he's holding and my insides flinch at the murderous look he's directing toward his mother. This ought to be interesting.

Chapter Seventeen

Ben

I settle into my seat at the end of the table. Devi is on my left, and I'm facing off with my mom, who's seated at the other end. My mom is not usually a vicious person, but every once in a while she feels the need to circle her nest, baring her fangs and flashing her talons. Unfortunately, every once in a while just became today. We stare at each other, and I can feel the momentum gaining in her eyes, blinking faster and harder like wings beating in the wind.

"Well, now that we're all here," she says, "let's say grace, shall we?" My sisters and Devi bow their heads over the table, but I know what she's about to serve, and I am done bowing my head for that. Her eyes narrow to blue lasers, beaming across the table and landing on Devi. I follow her inspection over the exposed skin at the back of Devi's neck.

Her voice is low and controlled. "Bless this food for the

sake of our bodies and the nourishment we are about to receive." After a few more generic prayer lines, she pauses. Devi straightens and starts to mouth an "amen." She pauses, seeing my sisters' heads still bowed and resumes the position. The Winslow kids know the show is just getting started.

"Now, for my children's blessings," my mom says, assuming her "Dean of the Winslows" tone. "Lord, please help Priscilla to realize that no matter how much she tries to hide her beauty behind Carharts and overalls, she's not fooling anyone, and if she expects to find a husband that can support her in the lifestyle to which she has grown accustomed, she'll have to remind herself she really is a female and try and adopt one or two traits common to the softer gender." With her head still bowed, Priscilla reaches for a celery stick sitting in a glass of water in front of her plate and snaps it with her teeth. My mom moves on.

"And please help Chloe to realize that just because she has an artist's talent, she doesn't have to live the life of an artist, smoking and swearing." Chloe raises her eyes, and her mouth opens as if she's going to protest, but my mom continues. "Don't think I don't know. We all know."

"Well, you all know now," Chloe murmurs bowing her head back over her lap.

My mom turns to Cate who is already, scrunching her nose, anticipating the tongue lashing. "Help Cate to be strong and independent and realize she doesn't need to be dating a construction worker from the other side of the tracks just to make her mother angry. I have plenty of other things to be angry about—like the fact that she failed her chemistry class. With a face like yours, Cate, no one will ever expect brilliance, but we all know what you're capable of."

Devi raises her head high enough to see Cate frowning.

"And Ben," my mom says, casting a mannequin smile. "Lord, please help him to know how very much we miss him and *need* him. Don't we, girls?"

A community "mmhmm" rises, and my sisters turn their faces toward me and make various twisted, cross-eyed, nostril-flared expressions, which my mom can't see.

"Very touching. Amen," I say in a definitive tone.

"Oh, wait. I have a prayer for Deveen," she says, feasting her eyes on Devi.

"It's Devin, Mom."

"Of course. Now, let's see. Please help Devin to know that we are a loving and accepting family." I relax my stare a bit as she continues. "We will be accepting of her no matter how she got those scratches on her face or that bruise."

"Really none of your business, Mom."

"I thought it was a nice thing to say. I just want her to know she doesn't have to hide anything. It all comes out eventually."

"Saying grace before a meal is really not the time to preach to your kids," I say, reaching for a bagel.

"Well, I disagree, Ben. It's the only time I have all your attention, and I want you to know what's going on here so that you can help. That's all. We can eat now."

"Good because I'm frickin' starving," Chloe says, lunging for the tray of pastries.

"Ben, can you help Chloe and me change rooms after breakfast?" Cate asks.

"I just did that before I left in August."

"I know, but we want to change back. Chloe's room doesn't get enough natural light, and I like to put my makeup on in my bedroom, but I have to have natural light."

My mom is next. "And I need you to talk to the gardener again, Ben. It's the end of September, and he hasn't started the fall fertilization. You know he barely listens to me." He doesn't listen to her because most of what she wants him to do will kill all of the grass on our lawn. But what does he know? He's only a master gardener. I keep eating.

"So Devin, tell us a little about yourself," my mom says, a setup for sure.

Devi directs a tight smile down the table toward my mom and takes a moment to wipe her hands on the linen napkin. In a low, controlled tone, she tells my mom where she's from and how we met.

"Holt, Michigan. Hmmm, I don't know Holt. Is there a country club in Holt?"

"Not that I'm aware of," Devi says, sipping her water and narrowing her eyes.

"I don't know what I'd do without my club. That's where I do all of my charity work. Does your family do any charity work? Your mom?"

"I'm pretty sure we are the charity work," Devi mumbles under her breath and Chloe laughs.

"I'm sorry, what was that?" My mom counters.

Devi lays her forearms on the table and snaps, "No. We don't do any charity work." Her lips tighten as if she's trying to hold onto the last ounce of restraint she has. A faint blush rises over her cheeks, heightening the deep wine color of the scratches.

I drop my bagel. I was famished when I sat down at this table. Now all I feel is sick. My mom is purposely goading Devi as some sort of passive-aggressive way to get back at me. But for what? It can't be just the party that she's mad about. I can feel the sweat beading at my temple, and my stomach is swirling with dread. This is going to get worse before it gets better.

"Those scratches on your face look red, dear. Can I get you anything for them?"

"No, no, I'm fine really," Devi says, with clipped words that fall flat.

"Where did you say you got—"

I'm about to interrupt my mom, but Devi beats me to it. "I didn't say, but if you really want to know, I was in the process of beating the *shit* out of my brother's drug dealer, and he scratched me." Priscilla raises a curious gaze, Chloe stifles a laugh and Cate looks startled. *Great.*

"Charming," my mother says, sipping from a hand painted teacup. This conversation is spiraling downhill so fast I don't know which way to turn first to stop it. If I could get Devi to make eye contact with me I think I could help, but she's determined to ignore me, determined to engage and determined to prove to me that she doesn't fit in to my world. My mom is certainly doing everything she can to accommodate her.

"Oh, and I just remembered." Devi says, and I see the slight trembling of her jaw, the first crack in the concrete wall of defense she's been trying to maintain. Her hand is resting on the table, and I reach over to cover it with mine. She pulls away and keeps talking. "Charity work. My mom runs the cow-pile plop at the Eaton County Fair every year. I think that's charity work, it raises money for the food bank."

"And what exactly is the cow-pile plop?" my mom asks, more than willing to nudge Devi further out onto the ledge of "you don't fit into this family of snobs." I throw my napkin on my plate and steeple my hands in front of me—a sick feeling spins in my stomach.

"Well, you section off squares in a corral—like a check-erboard, giving each square a number. Then you sell the numbers to the people at the fair. After the squares are all sold, you let the cow into the corral. If you have the number that the cow shits on, you're a winner!" Cate and Chloe start to laugh, and I cast them a warning glare. They stifle giggles behind their napkins, and Devi continues.

"We used to do an art auction, but the cow-pile plop ended up being a better moneymaker. So that's what my mom does for charity work," she says, biting into a bagel spread with cream cheese.

"I'm afraid to ask what your dad does," my mom says.

"He's dead," Devi replies. She wipes her mouth with her napkin and silence billows around us. I see the tremble working its way up her jaw again. She blinks hard and it disappears. I'm certain she's not lying, but she never told me that.

I lean toward her, saying her name in a firm, low voice, trying to stop this rant that's hurting her more than anyone else, but she continues to ignore me. My mom is silent a long beat, pursing her lips, trying to work up enough humility to say something nice. "Well, I'm sorry to hear that."

Devi reaches for her water glass and drinks. "Oh, don't be sorry, he was beating the hell out of my mom. She shot him." She sets the crystal glass down but her fingers remain gripped around the stem. "I was five so I don't really remember much. Other than stepping over the body to get out of the house." I lean forward staring at her. I have got to get her out of here.

She lifts a brow and raises a rigid smile. "That's why it's so nice to be welcomed into your family. I've always dreamed of having a big family to love and be loved by. I never had that." Her gaze moves over the gold and red striped silk curtains that match the linen tablecloth, around the marble fireplace and massive gilded mirror above it, up to the mural painted on the ceiling. "I dreamed of having enough money so that my mom didn't have to worry about whether or not our heat was going to be shut off in the dead of winter, too." She shrugs her shoulders. "Most of all I dreamed of a family that would accept me for who I am, not judge me for what I'm not," she says, staring down the silent table to my mom.

My mom and sisters resemble one another in looks—blonde with light eyes and delicate features—but the resemblance is most prominent in their expressions, and right now their expressions are a mirror of shame. I get it now. I know what's set my mom off. She's feeling the effects of my absence. Without me, there's no one here to cater to her whims, and Devi's presence is another threat to her loss of control. I've always realized my mom needed more help from me in my dad's absence, but until now I've never realized how far over the boundary line into my personal space she's been willing to step. I feel like shit. I love my mom and my sisters, but I should have backed them all down a long time ago—just as Devi's doing right now.

I reach for my glass and raise it over the table, staring intensely at my mother. "Here's to the Winslows," I say. Slowly my sisters lift their glasses and turn to my mom. With as minimal effort as possible she raises her teacup and lowers her head to sip. I chug the rest of my water and push back from the table. "Well, I wish I could say we hate to eat and run, but I can't. Let's bounce," I say, to Devi. I pull out her winged-back chair, and she attempts to smile, but all I see is pain. Behind the touché soliloquy she's just delivered is the sting of a painful childhood. Devi was worried about not fitting into this family. Despite the fact that she goaded them into it, this family could not have made a worse showing today.

"Ben!" My mom says my name in an admonishing tone and turns in her seat. Years of carrying too much of the load for this family has just come crushing down on me and on Devi. I stop in the wide archway, pause for a moment and turn back.

My mom starts to speak but I raise my hand, interrupting her. I hold it over their heads as if I'm casting a spell. "I am done over serving this family. Everyone's grown up now. From here on out you handle your own shit. Get your act together, bitches."

I grab Devi's hand and cross to the front door. She swings her bag onto her shoulder and stumbles, trying to keep up with my mad-as-hell stride. I grip her elbow, skipping every other porch step. She reaches a steadying hand toward the scalloped edge of the urn but I pull back, stopping short at the sight of a dried white foamy substance coating the soil and spilling over the scalloped rim. A fleeting vision of Scooby Doo returns to me—gripping the sides of the urn, hunched and yacking.

"Ewww," Devi moans.

"Leave it. They can deal with it." We cross the yard and load into the truck. I slam my door and stare over the dashboard for a moment. Disastrous. I let out a long breath and turn to Devi, staring straight ahead.

"Great job using your words," I say to her.

She glares at me, an accusatory look in her eyes. "Likewise, Ben." I shake my head start the truck and roll out.

We drive in silence for an hour. As hard as I try to keep the scene at brunch this morning from playing over in my mind, I can't loosen the reel. I know we both have more to say, and I'm hoping we've calmed down enough to have a civil conversation.

"Do you want to tell me about your dad?" I ask.

She turns a flat stare my way. "No," she says, looking annoyed.

"Do you want to tell me why you didn't introduce me as your girlfriend?"

"What?" My brow tightens with confusion.

"When I was on the steps, with your mom. You said, 'this is Devin.' Not 'this is my girlfriend.'" Her bottom lip tightens and she stops talking.

I'm speechless for a moment—I've been waiting patiently, trying to calm the burning fury twisting in my stomach, hoping she might say she was sorry. "Are you serious right now?" I say, not bothering to keep the anger out of my tone. She returns my hard stare. "For six months you tell me you're not my girlfriend, you give in for two weeks, then I'm out again. If I didn't call you my girlfriend this morning it's probably because I can't fucking keep it straight anymore."

"Do you need some help?" Her voice raises. "Here's where we're at. My 'boyfriend,'" she says, speaking about me as if I'm not in the conversation, "has quite likely fathered a child with another woman—making me the odd woman out in my own relationship, and his mom will likely hate me the rest of my life. And I think he expects me to feel good about all this."

"I am not going to be your whipping boy over the child issue. I've apologized for not telling you sooner and given you all the assurances that I can. And as for my mom, well, I couldn't help but think as I was watching the two of you — if either of you had thought about how I felt, maybe one of you would've shut up. Did that thought ever cross your mind? I've been sitting here for the last hour waiting to hear something that sounds like an apology."

"You think it's *my* fault?" Her mouth remains open, and the tips of her fingers press into her chest. Her eyes hollow into an expression of pain and misunderstanding. "My fault that your mom insults me and thinks I'm poor white trash?"

"It is your fault!" I slam the butt of my palm on the steering wheel. "It's your fault for believing it!" She winces at my outburst, and I fist my hand to ward off the tingling sensation. "My mom sat down at the table ready for a fight, and you couldn't keep your smart mouth shut. You offered her a case of ammunition and ask to be shot down — with all of the stuff that hurts you most!"

She lowers her chin and speaks through clenched teeth. "I have always known your family wouldn't accept me." she pauses and her mouth rests open, words lost, buried in something she can't escape.

"You've always known it because you were determined to make it happen."

She turns to me and the expression on her face is as much pain as anger. "It's who I am, Ben."

"You didn't show them who *you* are. You showed them a bunch of jaw-dropping shit that happened in your past," I shout.

She crosses her arms and squeezes her eyes shut, tightening until the tiny creases are red, trying to block me and the tears, but I am too worked up to settle down and my voice comes out in an angry growl.

"I swear to God, Devi, I feel like I'm hanging on as hard as I can to this relationship while you throw side kicks to my ribs. Maybe I should just let you beat the shit out of me—I honestly think you'd feel better, and it'd be quicker."

She snaps a rage-filled glare my way. "I would feel better," she yells, thrusting her chin forward. "I would!"

When I turn back to the road, my neck jerks and my entire body stiffens. We are way too close to the back of a semi that's going way too slow. In my worked-up lather, I've been accelerating. The back doors of the truck are coming closer with every millisecond, small letters—BLUE SKY SEAFOOD—enlarging. Devi gasps in a terrified breath, and every worked up nerve in my body drops into my stomach. I slam my foot onto the brake pedal as she screams. The high-pitched sound slices my stomach. We're fishtailing—careening toward the back of the semi. I tighten my grip on the steering wheel until my knuckles bulge. My arm moves instinctively across to her, pressing a palm against her chest, as if it will do any good when we hit. Her fingers clench around my forearm and I feel the life-threatening bite of her fingernails sinking into my skin like the hook of an anchor. I'm pleading with every ounce of energy I have. *Please let us stop before we hit.* The wheels of the truck bump and lift off the road adding to the weightless feeling in my stomach. My guts have left my stomach and are stuck in my throat. We're inches from connecting when miraculously the truck starts to pull away. I heave out a breath and Devi's scream converts to an open-mouthed sob.

The sickening realization that I just about killed us with my rage melts over me, coating my nerves with disgust. Devi is sobbing. "It's all right. We're all right." I'm trying to reassure her, panting to pump air back into my lungs at the same time. I exit into a rest stop and pull into the first open spot. Crossing to her side of the truck, I grip her shoulders and pull her out. She's stopped sobbing, at least, and is drawing in deep breaths as we cross to a picnic table and lean against the end. I wrap my arms around her, and she buries her face in my chest.

"I'm sorry. I'm sorry," I say, speaking against her temple. "We're okay. It's okay." I feel her body sinking, and I lower her onto the seat and sit beside her. We're silent for a long time, both reflecting on how close we came to true disaster and our argument. I lean my elbows onto my knees and stare at my hands. I'm disgusted with myself for getting so worked up, yelling at her, and not paying attention to the road. I'm disgusted with Devi for not being able to figure her shit out either.

"It's my fault Ben. I…it's my fault," she says and her eyes look tortured. "You've been so good to me this weekend. You've helped me, and I repay you by making you fucking crazy. I've never seen you get mad at anyone until today because of me." She raises the back of her hand to her mouth and shakes her head. "I'm sorry." I put my arm around her shoulder and pull her against me. With the exception of the intermittent deep breaths we are taking turns exhaling every few minutes, we sit in silence.

She leans her head and I speak against her hair. "We're both exhausted." She nods her head and wipes the tears, casting me a quick glance.

"If you're tired, I can drive," she offers, but her voice is weak and her eyes barely meet mine before returning to the ground.

"I'm not tired. I've got so much adrenaline in my veins after that, I think I'll be awake for another week." We walk back to the truck. She's a pace in front of me, and it feels like she's miles away. We didn't hit the back of that truck, but my emotions did. I can't do this anymore — to myself or to Devi.

Since the day we met, she's been torn between wanting me but not wanting who I am or what my life is. I've tried everything I know to fix it for her. I'm not going to raise my hand over her head and preach as I did with my mom and sisters, but I'm done over serving Devi, too.

We resume our journey and eventually our conversation. Each of us takes turns asking surface level questions and staring out the window. We avoid topics remotely close to Jillian and the baby, her family, or my family — neither of us wanting to hit a nerve the last conversation has left raw. I feel the distance between us in what we're not saying, and I know she feels it, too. Eventually she dozes off, and I let my mind adjust to the thought of life without Devi and the possibility of fatherhood. I never dreamed my life would come to a screeching halt months after graduation. I try to convince myself it's not a halt, just a hard right turn, but all I can feel is that clenching feeling in my stomach — the same I felt an hour ago when we were seconds away from colliding.

At nine p.m. we pull into the parking garage. I help Devi out as she's gathering her things, holding her hand as she steps down.

"Hey," I say, pulling her toward me. She looks up, and

there's a reserved sadness in her eyes. She's pale and looks exhausted, and I wish I hadn't come to the conclusion that I needed to do this now—it seems like such a bad time to add to her stress. Then again, maybe it will be a relief. She's staring, waiting for me to say something.

I swallow and step closer, raising my hand to the side of her face.

"I wish so badly we were in a different place with each other but I just can't seem to get us there." Her eyes narrow with uncertainty and she studies my face. "I'm going to pull back for a while."

She draws in a quick breath, and for a second I think she's going to argue with me. "Ben, I'm sorry." She lowers her gaze to the ground and touches her forehead with the backs of her fingers. The expression on her face and the echo of my words strike a pang in my chest. "It was my fault," she says again.

In her eyes, I am drawn to everything I want so badly and yet also the agony of what she's never been willing to give me completely. I've seen flashes of it, when she's let down her guard, but the reserve always returns. Like now, as I watch her press her lips together and nod, the protest she was about to make fades as fast as it erupted. I'm left with a deflated, sinking feeling.

She's not willing to fight for us, and I can't keep swimming upstream, locked in constant battle with an alter ego that wants me gone. I've been existing in no man's land where I'm neither fully loved nor fully out. If I am going to have a baby, I don't want my own life to be out of balance. I want my child to have more than I did from a dad—and from a mom, or in my case, a stepmom. I know nothing about being a father, except what I can draw from my own experience. Kids need stability. I can't keep teetering at the edge of commitment, trying to keep balance for both of us while Devi jumps on and off.

I draw in a breath and watch a tear run a jagged path down her cheek, mimicking the crack in my heart. I pull her into me, crushing her against my chest.

"I'm sorry, Ben," she says and I hear the acceptance in her voice. It's an "I'm sorry it didn't work out," not an "I'm sorry, please don't leave me."

I pull back and kiss her forehead, and we walk into the garage elevator. I lean against the back wall, watching her stare straight ahead while wet streaks trail down her skin. Absolute torture. My hands curl around the back rail of the elevator, forcing myself to hold on to this nightmare until the end. The doors open. I let out a breath and walk her to her door. She leans up and presses her wet cheek against mine.

"Thank you for taking me."

I look down into her hazel eyes. Pain and defeat mark the turned-down edges of her mouth. There's nothing left to say. Every second I remain threatens my resolve. If I stand here any longer, I'll end up on my knees.

I nod and turn.

"Ben," she calls to me as I'm steps away. I stop and look back. "We'll still be friends, right?"

"Hmph." My smile is as weak as sadness and as real as irony.

"Yeah, just friends."

Chapter Eighteen

DEVIN GRACE

I hardly slept last night—tossing and turning Ben's words over in my mind—but I finally dragged my ass out of bed an hour early and got in to my office at eight a.m. Sunday morning. I wanted to get caught up after taking two days off, and I wanted to avoid seeing him.

I woke up this morning with such a thick feeling in my head. For a moment I thought it was just a dream until the fog of sleep burned off and the memory of losing Ben rose up like the sun—all around me, impossible to block. I fled to the shelter of my office and began working. At least here I have something to focus on other than Ben.

My phone chirps. I reach for it, irritated that my mind immediately jumps to thinking about him. It's Ryan.

"Where are you? What time will you be back? I have a test tomorrow, leaving for a study session at three."

I heard Ryan come in late last night. I was still up but I wasn't ready to rehash the disastrous weekend with her.

I text back. *"I'm working to catch up. I'll probably miss you."* My head aches at the thought of sitting down and telling her about everything—barfing it all up to the surface again.

She responds. *"Okay, not sure when I'll be back, wait up if you can. Everything go okay with the rest of your weekend? Josh still doing well?"*

I bite my lip and contemplate my answer. *"Yes, Josh doing well. I probably won't wait up—still exhausted from the weekend. Let's do dinner tomorrow or Tuesday if you're free."*

At one I decide to take a break. I haven't been out of my office since I arrived. I'm going to try to find Robyn to ask her a couple questions about the budget plan for Halloween next month, but before I do that, I'm going to find Gator and sneak a big hug. A cool breeze wafts down the hallway as the big blue door to the back yard play area swishes open. I see Louisa's blond curls bob across the hallway with three others, but no Gator.

"Louisa," I shout to her. She stops and runs to me, wrapping her arms around my waist.

"Miss Devi, we missed you."

"I missed you, too. What have you been up to?"

"Oh, we're just playin'. I lost a tooth though." She smiles and points to a pink gummy gap just beside her front teeth. I hold my thumb against her chin, bend down and peer into her mouth.

"Wow! I can see straight through to all your shiny brains."

"Uh-huh," she says.

"Have you seen Gator?"

"Well, he gone, Miss Devi."

"Gone? Where?"

"His daddy picked him up."

Panic and confusion seize my mind. "What? What daddy? When?"

"Yesterday."

I force a dry swallow down my throat and thank Louisa. How can he be gone—just like that? Did they screen his father? Did someone do a site visit? It's possible Louisa misunderstood something...she must have. I walk with anxious steps feeling the breath coming harder in my throat.

Mario is sitting in Robyn's office with half a sandwich spread out before her on a square wax wrapper while Robyn types on her PC. "Hey!" they say in unison.

"Did Gator leave?" I ask, trying to keep the distress out of my voice. There's a silent beat and they exchange a quick look.

"He did," Robyn says, pulling her glasses off her face and folding them. "His father came for him yesterday."

I hold my elbow in one hand and give up trying to conceal my distress. "But how? Why so quick?"

"Have a seat, honey," Robyn says in a tender voice. I step in and flop down into the open seat. Mario moves behind me and closes the door.

"We'd been trying to contact his father from various leads the neighbors had given us. We found Gator's bag in the yard on Thursday. I decided to go through it when it was brought to me. There was a bible in that bag that had a couple more names I was able to track. One of them thought they knew Gator's father. They reached out to him and he called in. We were able to verify everything through Gator's mom on Friday. She was in favor of the temporary custody and arrangements were made for the pickup on Saturday, yesterday."

"I just can't believe it." I shift my gaze between them. "Did you check everything out with his dad? Do we know for sure?" They're looking at me with sympathetic expressions. I'm sure they've been through this plenty of times, but it doesn't make me feel any better right now.

"We did a very thorough check, and Gator was thrilled. I know it's hard. We all love these kids, and it's so easy to get attached, but the family unit is always the best thing."

Mario rubs my back and I nod. "I know. It just seems so abrupt." Robyn reaches into her desk. "Gator left this for you," she says, handing me a piece of paper that's been folded into a puffy rectangular shape. "He asked his dad if they could come back and see you. They wrote their phone number on the back." I stare at the crooked block letters of my name etched in pencil and lined with purple marker feeling sick.

"Okay," I say, standing up. "Did he seem like a good guy?" I watch Robyn's face for any kind of hesitation, but she answers without blinking.

"He really did." I stare at her. I can hardly believe this is the truth. What kind of dad goes missing for years and then miraculously shows up? I wonder if this number he wrote down even works. If it does, I'm going to meet this man and see for myself, and if I see one thing that I don't like, God help him.

"Want part of a sandwich?" Mario asks thrusting a wedge toward me.

"No. I'm not hungry."

I walk back to my office fingering the soft folded paper. I flop down, pull the phone in front of me and stare at the digits written in neat block numbers. I peel open the note. In the center of the page Gator has drawn a picture of a brown-haired girl wearing a long white dress and holding a bouquet of purple flowers. Standing beside her with his arm hooked through hers is a short stocky boy with a flat top haircut. Tears cloud my vision, and I read the blurry words he's written. "Family are people that—heart—you." I bite my lip and reach for the phone.

A deep voice answers on the third ring.

"Hi, I'm Devin Dalton calling from The Children's Center. Is this Gator's dad?"

"Yes, yes," I hear enthusiasm in his voice. "Gator's told me…"

"I'd like to set a time to pay a visit," I say, interrupting.

He pauses a beat. "Sure, we'd love to."

"What works for you?"

He pauses another beat. I know I'm being short, but I have every intention of letting him know I'm watching him.

"Well, he has a half day next Friday. How would noon be? We're at the Looking Glass Apartments in Queens, Apt 333."

Friday after next. Two weeks. That seems like an eternity to wait. "Fine." I pause and clear my throat. "Could I talk to him?"

"He's out with his Grandma, she took him shopping for some new clothes."

Grandma? He has a Grandma now, too, and where the hell has she been? "All right. Well, tell him I called to check on him, and I'll see him soon."

"I will, Miss Devin. Oh, and my name's Sam."

"See you Friday after next." I hang up the phone and let out a long sigh. In the course of the last twenty-four hours, I have lost both Ben and Gator. I drop my forehead on the edge of my desk and stare at my shoes. Life sucks.

Chapter Nineteen

BEN

"I took the blood test this morning. The doctor said he'd call us to come in as soon as the results are back," I say to Jillian. It's Tuesday, and I'm in the atrium cafeteria of the Trott Building with her. She asked me to lunch to talk about where things stand.

"God, I wish we didn't have to wait so long," Jillian snaps and lets out a long breath. She hesitates a beat and looks back at me with a pained expression. "Henri left me this weekend," she says.

I set down the turkey sandwich I was about to take a whopping bite from and wipe my hands on my napkin. I watch her crunch down on a chip and chew slowly, trying to gauge how she's feeling about this news. She looks pale and sick, but truthfully, she's looked pale and sick for the last month.

"As in left for good?" I ask.

"I don't know." She gives me a guarded look—like she's not sure she wants to tell me, but I'm thinking she's got to talk to someone. She's already told me she's not going to tell her mom and dad about the possibility that the baby isn't Henri's. She lets out a breath and her expression shifts to one of defeat. "He thinks I set him up."

I watch her expression, and clench my jaw, suppressing the urge I have to ask, "Well did you? And did you set me up, too?" It's really a question I don't want to know the answer to. If I believe she's gotten us all into this mess on purpose, it'll be impossible to forgive her. I have no idea what I'm doing here, but I keep telling myself to think about what would be best for a baby. That seems to be so much easier to figure out than what's best for me.

Jillian nods to three employees carrying brown plastic trays. She watches them until they pass and leans closer to the shield of a large tropical plant potted next to our table. The split green leaves dangle above her auburn hair as she speaks. "When I told Henri I was pregnant at the end of the summer, he offered to marry me. I should have told him then that there had been someone else back in the summer, about the possibility." Her small green eyes look elfish as they narrow in thought. "He was the first guy that really seemed interested in me—I just didn't want to admit to anything that could ruin that, now I've really ruined it." She sets an elbow on the table and presses two fingers against her temple. Despite the topic, it's actually nice to see her show some emotion. She's usually all business, tucked neatly behind a high-buttoned collar.

"Well, I made the same mistake with Devi. I should have

told her it happened sooner. Is Henri calling off the engage-ment?" I ask, not wanting to shift the focus of the conversa-tion to Devi and me. It's hard enough to have the "baby" conversation with her without admitting things with Devi didn't work out.

"He just packed a bag and left. You're a guy, what do you think? Should I assume it's over?"

I don't want to be the one to tell her, but hell yes, she should assume it's over. I imagine Jillian can be quite the handful in a relationship. She sees things pretty black and white, but still, I can't help but feel like leaving her right now is an incredibly shitty thing to do. He's not out of the running here unless he knows something we don't. Which brings me to the question I've wanted to ask her since she dropped the maybe-baby bomb.

I shake my head and raise my brow. "I don't know," I say in answer to her Henri question, but I have a question of my own. I clear my throat. "Jillian, I don't know how to ask you this but how close—"

She gives me a flat look. "I was with both of you the same week. I fucked you on—" I hold up my hands and shake my head.

"Same week. That's enough. I don't need the details."

She presses a fake smile on her face, responding to the greeting of a passing employee, turns back to me, and lets out a long breath. "I was taking an antibiotic, and the doctor said it probably knocked out the effectiveness of my birth control." She pops another chip in her mouth, looking dis-gusted with herself.

"Well, after the results come back we will all know what we have to work with. I can't speak for what happens if the baby is Henri's, but if it's mine, we're going to need to help each other, to work together."

"Agreed," she says.

We finish lunch and walk to the elevators in contemplative silence. The thought of having a baby seems so surreal, I haven't let myself start thinking about it in real-life terms. I never pictured myself moving permanently away from Michigan and my sisters, but I might be stuck in New York for the rest of my life. And what about my living circumstances? Jett's been my best man since grade school, but it might be asking a bit much of him to live with me and a baby. A screenshot flashes in my mind—me holding up a screaming, red-faced, leg-dangling infant in the middle of the night—Jett and I staring at each other with "I don't know what the fuck to do" looks. I scrub my face with one hand. I don't need to think about all this yet.

"You all right?" Jillian asks.

"Fine. Yep. I'm fine. You?"

She snorts out a laugh and shakes her head. "I'm screwed."

It's a little after five and I'm standing in the sunshine, waiting outside the Trott Building to walk home with Jett. I see his reflection pushing through the revolving glass door and nod out a greeting.

"How was your day?" he asks.

"Oh, just ducky. Blood test this morning, lunch with Jillian." My cell rings and I lift it in front of us. It's a Face Time request from Priscilla, which means more than one of my sisters is likely to appear on the screen. "Ha! And now Face

Time with the crazies." I roll my eyes and hit accept.

Jett grabs the phone from me and holds it in front of his face, angling it so I can still see the action. "Jett!" I hear Priscilla's voice. "I feel like I just won the Bingo grand prize at Mom's club," she says to him, and he laughs.

"Well, I'll try to live up to that," he says.

I hear Cate's voice in the background and see a swish of blond hair whip across the screen. "Is that Jett?" she says, her green eyes peering way too close to the camera. "Hi Jett."

Priscilla's hand shoves the side of her face. "Quit crowding me," she says.

Chloe dips her face in from behind Priscilla's shoulder. "Hi, Jett," she says jumping back to avoid Priscilla's shoulder bump. My sisters each went through a stage of having a mad crush on Jett. He and Priscilla settled into the closest friendship, he and Chloe like to exchange bad jokes, and as for Cate, well, I'm not sure Cate ever really got over him. When we were home from college two summers ago, I saw a flicker of interest on Jett's part, but thank God nothing ever developed. I'm sure he restrained himself out of respect for me.

"Hello, ladies," Jett says, a smooth smile on his face. "How's everything back in Michigan? Had any parties lately?" Priscilla face dimples and she tilts her head. "My invitation must have gotten lost," he says.

"Always an open invitation from the Winslow sisters for you," Priscilla replies. "Probably a good one to miss if you had to miss one though. It ended with Mom busting us and Ben calling us all bitches," she says.

"What?" he says, in mock offense. "How in the world could anyone look at those three beautiful, innocent faces and see anything other than the glow of halos over your heads?"

"I know, right?" Priscilla says, raising her eyebrows and turning a palm up.

"Especially me," Cate says, bobbing her head in, and flashing a playful smile.

Priscilla shoves her again, and she snaps, "Stop that, just because there's a camera rolling doesn't mean it's your show, Cate." Priscilla turns back to the screen. "Anyhow, we called because we have realized the error of our ways. We've taken an oath, put on our big girl pants, and are ready to officially put an apology to our big brother on the Winslow record."

"Well, let me see if he's available to take your call, ladies." Jett cocks a brow and holds the phone to me.

"They probably need something," I murmur, taking the phone and holding it face level.

"Awwww, Ben," Chloe moans.

"We're sorry," Cate says. "We love you."

"Seriously, do you hate us right now?" Priscilla asks, turning her Tigers baseball cap to the side.

"Hate's a strong word, Sil. I wouldn't say hate, exactly." I exaggerate a grimace and flinch. "Feels more like a tic on the side of my face when I think of the three of you." Jett pulls a hand over his mouth to muffle his laughter.

"Well, we are sorry. It was our party, and we didn't mean for you to have to take the brunt of Mom's nastiness."

"And we're not going to bug you as much," Chloe says.

"So what can we do to make it up to you?" Priscilla asks.

"We could come to New York for a weekend visit?" Cate suggests.

"No—God no," I say, "And before you get anymore

bright ideas on how you can make it up to me, apology accepted."

"I really do want to come visit though," Cate whines.

"Don't bug him, Cate. This isn't about you. He's got enough going on," Priscilla says.

Hmmph. That's an understatement. "How's Mom?" I ask. "Did she have heart palpitations after I called her a bitch?"

"No, but Chloe heard her talking to her doctor about increasing her medication, and telling him she's fighting with her kids too much." Well, I suppose that might be as close as an admission of guilt as I will ever get from my mother.

"Will you send me Devi's email or number, Ben? We were going to apologize to her, too, and tell her not to be scared off by the big bad blonde," Chloe says.

Too late for that, I think to myself, but I guess it can't hurt. "That'd be a nice gesture. Despite the way the weekend ended, she had a blast at the party."

"We were thinking you could bring her home for my band's competition." Cate says, a note of enthusiasm in her voice. "Mom said that'd be okay."

I pause a beat. I had told Cate I would come home to see her perform. I decide to give up the pretense of status quo with Devi and update them. "I'll be there, but Devi and I broke up."

"Oh, Ben," Cate gasps and then her eyes widen. "Why? She seemed so perfect for you. She gasps. "Oh my God, it was because of us, wasn't it?" Priscilla shoves her out of the way again.

"Send us her email, Ben."

"Will do, and thanks for the call, kids."

"We love you, Ben," Chloe yells in the background, and Cate makes fish lips at the screen.

"Love you, too," I say "Oh, and Priscilla, you owe me fifty bucks."

She smiles and flips the rim of her baseball cap over her eyes. "Check's in the mail, big brother. Peace out."

I hang up and look at Jett. "You're lucky to have them, you know?" he says shaking his head and smiling.

I laugh. "Lucky in a pain-in-the-ass sort of way."

"Ah, Ben, it may be harder for you to see, but they adore you. All those years you've spent having their back will pay off for you someday. You watch. Come on, I'll buy you a beer," he says, clutching my shoulder.

Chapter Twenty

DEVIN GRACE

Ryan and I are walking to our favorite sushi restaurant, Samurai. I ended up staying over at the Center last night to help Mario paint the front doors and this is the first chance we've had to catch up since the weekend. I did call her and tell her Ben and I broke up—mainly because I knew Jett probably knew—but I didn't go into the gory details until we had a chance to be alone.

My cell rings and I pull it out of my pocket. "I gotta take this, it's my mom, probably with a Josh update," I say to Ryan.

"Go ahead," she whispers, walking silently beside me as I chat with my mom.

"How's Josh, Mom?" Her voice comes through low and smooth.

"He's doing really well. I can't have any contact with

him but the counselors email with daily updates. They say he's had a couple rough days, but he's making friends and adjusting."

"I hope they're the right kind of friends."

"Me, too," she says, and I hear a pause in her voice as if her thoughts are already gone in another direction. "I hate to burden you with this, honey, but we have a problem. Our health insurance deductible is $1200. I've used the mortgage money to buy a little time."

I close my eyes and shake my head. "Twelve hundred dollars, Mom, seriously? Why even have insurance?" Ryan turns a concerned look to me. "Do you have any of it?" I ask her.

"Well, I think I can come up with about three hundred." I let out a breath. That leaves the other nine hundred to me. Ryan loops her arm through mine.

"You know I don't expect you to come up with all that, honey, but if you have any extra money in your budget this month. Once I get my tax refund I can pay you back."

Two men pass around us on the sidewalk and one of them turns back and runs an appreciative gaze over us. "How you doin'," he says to Ryan.

"Just fine," she says in a dismissive tone that's not enough to turn him back around. He's walking backward, looking at us smiling.

"Where you ladies off to tonight?" he asks as his buddy turns around and joins in.

"Just out for a walk," Ryan says in a flat tone.

"Well, we like to walk." He spreads his hands out as if he's offering himself up to us and sways sideways.

"That's nice," she says in an "anything other than nice"

tone.

"I gotta go, Mom. I'll get the money, don't worry about it." I press my phone to disconnect, annoyed as all shit and pin the clown in front of us with a glare. "Beat it, Romeo."

"Hey, now. You can't blame a guy for trying to get some action." He stops and his blood shot eyes focus on our linked arms. "Oh, I get it, you two's together. She's your girlfriend." His full lips puff with smugness.

"Well, if drunk and rude are my alternative, hell yes, she's my girlfriend," Ryan says.

"I don't mind that, don't mind that one bit. You can bring her." His buddy throws an arm over his neck and turns him around, urging him to leave us alone. We turn down the next block and lose them.

The chimes ring a raindrop melody against the door as we step into Samurai. The soft gold light and pale wood decor cast a Zen-like feel. We pull off our boots and sit on black padded circles, clutching miso soup bowls with our fingertips. I fill Ryan in on my weekend with Mom and Josh and my fight with Justin, lifting my hair off my cheek to show her my battle wounds that have faded to dotted pink lines. "I am so thankful to Ben for taking me. I honestly don't think I could have made it home without him. Sitting there waiting for my mom to call and tell me whether or not my brother's dead…" I close my eyes and shake my head.

"Thank God Josh is all right and getting some help." We lean back as the waiter sets a curving roll of sushi in front of us, layered and decorated with spikes of avocado and ginger, resembling a small dragon.

"Yeah," I say, seizing a rounded rice paw with my chopsticks. "I'm going to go back to the cage fight place and see if I can get in the ring with Helga again—my mom needs money for our health insurance deductible."

Her eyes widen and she drops her chin a notch. "Are you serious?" I nod my head and chew. "Well, I know I can't talk you out of it. If you go down there at least let me come with you. I don't know what good it'll be, but you should have someone with you. So tell me what happened with Ben," she says, pulling at a piece of the dragon's tail.

I sigh and pour tea into the oversized thimble cup. "I don't even know where to start," I say, motioning the small black pot her way. "Want more?" She nods and holds her cup out as I pour. "We went to his house in Grosse Pointe on Friday night. His mom was out of town, and his sisters were having a huge party. We had a blast, an absolute blast, and then spent the night in his room, but the next morning..." I lean an elbow on the table and drop my forehead against my fingers recalling the scene. I direct my eyes up to Ryan's questioning expression.

"His mom came home early." Her mouth gapes.

"I was coming downstairs, and she saw me." She closes her mouth and her eyes pop wide. "I thought she was the cleaning lady, helping to clean up from the party." Her hands rises to her mouth, and she leans back.

"So, as I was standing on the stairway, wearing nothing but Ben's T-shirt and his underwear." I put my hand over my face and talk to her through split fingers, "I asked her if she could go find Ben for me and told her he was probably working with the rest of her 'crew' to help clean up from the party."

"Oh my God," she says.

"Yeah. Oh my God is right. And then she had us all sit

down for lunch and proceeded to twist the knife of shame I already had hanging out of my back—as if it was all my fault that her kids like to party their asses off." I cross my arms and my defense instincts start to fall. "Then I got so pissed I totally went off on her."

"Oh, no, Devi, you didn't."

"Oh, I did."

"What was Ben doing?"

"Oh, he was pissed. Pissed at his mom. Pissed at me. You know, Ryan, even without the Jillian mess, I knew I wouldn't fit in with his family. He lives in a fucking mansion. Do you know what his mom does for a living?" She raises a brow. "Charity work—that's her profession. From the moment I realized who she was, and she realized who I was, I could not have felt more out of place."

"Well, maybe Ben feels out of place, too, Dev. Maybe all her kids do, and that's why they party their asses off when she's gone."

"I just hate that feeling. It makes me anxious, and it makes me feel like I have to defend myself. That's how I felt the whole time my mom was married to my stepdad—like part of the family didn't want me around."

"Yeah, but Devi, no matter who you're with, you're always going to have things that happen. Some circumstances in life you can't avoid, like Josh. The best you can do is find someone that will stand by you, someone that will get up in the middle of the night and drive nine hours holding your white-knuckled hands while you're waiting for the call." I bite my lip and think about her words.

"So then what happened?"

"We drove in silence for about an hour and then totally

exploded on each other. When we got back to New York, he basically told me I wasn't committed enough. I was too unstable." A wave of sadness moves through me, stopping in my chest and expanding. She reaches over and grips my forearm as I try to suppress the growing sting in my eyes.

"It makes me feel bad," I say, in a tight whisper. "Because I know he's right." I brush a tear away. When I'm with him, I'm worried about my place in his life and when I'm not with him I feel like life sucks. Everything around me is completely "blah." I shrug and raise the corner of my mouth. "Doesn't matter now anyways. I finally did it—convinced him I wasn't right for him, offended him and his whole family. I'm such an ass." I shake my head and stare at my hands resting on my napkin.

"Hmmph," I let out a soft laugh. "And the final kicker to my weekend—I went into work Sunday to try to catch up. I'm looking all over for Gator. Well, his dad came and picked him up Saturday. And just like that," I snap my fingers, "he's gone."

I reach into my purse for the folded piece of paper and hand it to her. "Oh, Devi, I'm sorry." She unfolds the paper, tilts her head right and left and reads aloud. "Family are people who—heart—you." She shakes her head and whispers, "That is so sweet. I'm gonna cry." She raises a white napkin from her lap and dabs the inner corners of her eyes. She looks at the paper again, squints and turns her head. "I think you're in a wedding dress."

"Seriously?" She flashes me the picture and I look closer. "Hmmm." She turns it back and reads the bottom.

"I never thought his dad would actually come. I mean who leaves their kid for three years and then magically appears?"

"Whose number?" she says, pointing to the digits written across the back.

"His dad's. I called him and I'm going to see them next Friday."

"I know it doesn't seem like it right now, but things will get better eventually. 'This too shall pass', right?"

I drop my face in my hands and run my fingertips up my forehead, emitting a low growl. "I think the only thing that just passed was my future with Ben."

Chapter Twenty-One

Ben

I reach for the longnecks the bartender is handing my way and distribute the second round of Friday happy hour to Jett and Vaughn. We compare notes on our week as we tip brews and watch sports highlights on the big screen behind the bar.

"How's Jillian doing?" Vaughn asks.

"Sick as a dog and still no sign of Henri."

"Nice guy," Jett says in a sarcastic tone.

"I'm beginning to think she's better off without him in her life anyhow, but she's pretty broken up over it."

"Is Ryan coming out?" Vaughn asks.

"She has class late tonight. I met her for lunch earlier." He pauses as if he's going to say something more and looks at me. "Supposedly, Devi's going to try to get in the cage with Helga again."

"What? Why?"

"To help her mom pay for Josh's medical expenses."

I stare at him for a bewildered second and shake my head. "Well, that's not going to happen. " I down the rest of my beer and set it on the bar.

"What are you going to do?" Vaughn asks.

"I'm going to talk to whoever it is that runs that shit show. Helga's a guy, and they've been promoting that whole clown show as a girl-on-girl thing." Devi and I may not be an item anymore, but my feelings for her haven't diminished. I have stepped back from trying to "fix" things in her mind, but I'm not going to step back from fixing things that are outright dangerous for her. "They're not putting her in that cage again, even if I have to take Helga out myself." I pat Vaughn's shoulder and start moving past them.

"Hey, wait," Jett says. "We should go with you, I mean, you probably shouldn't be making threats to MMA guys without a little backup."

We take the subway to the Sovereign Mixed Martial Arts Studio in Queens and walk through the side door like we own the place. It leads into the back of the warehouse where Sovereign runs training classes. A dozen shirtless, tattooed guys are scattered in pairs around the black mat sparring. They stop for a second and stare at the trio of suits that have just appeared. They probably think we're from the State here to shut them down. We bow in and one of the guys in the back yells. "You just missed her." He tags his partner with a high five and heads our way. It's the guy that helped me when Devi went down in the ring with Helga.

"Actually, I was looking for you," I say. "I'm Ben Winslow, and I wanted to talk to you about your amateur Helga round."

"I'm Juan Gutierrez, and it's my boss you want to talk to. He's not in right now, but you can talk to our assistant manager. He's the one that was dealing with your girl." His gaze assesses the three of us and he jerks his head to the back of the room. "Follow me." He crosses to an open metal stairway against the wall, and we climb in single file our feet echoing a hollow drumbeat.

"Can't say I'm surprised to see you," he says. "I take it she doesn't know you're here?"

"No," I say, trying to keep the annoyed tone out of my voice. I'm annoyed Devi would walk into this place by herself thinking she was going to fight again and not tell me about it.

The hallway that Juan leads us down is open at the top. Black, snake-like ducts from the ventilation system run above us as we draw closer to the baritone sound of a man's voice. We follow Juan into the last office on the right and wait for the square-jawed man to end his phone conversation. His thin brown hair is combed forward—an effort to enhance what's left of the hairline. He ends his call and stands, adjusting black track pants on his waist. "What can I do for you, gentlemen?"

I step up and extend a hand. "Ben Winslow, and these are my friends, Jett Trebuchet and Vaughn Jung."

"I'm Orlo," he says.

"I wanted to talk to you about your amateur cage fight this week—particularly the promotional stunt you run with Helga."

"He's the Red girl's boyfriend," Juan says.

"Ah, have a seat, guys, please." He motions to the seat in front of his desk, and I take one. Jett takes the other, and

Vaughn and Juan stand against the back wall.

"I wasn't in favor of her getting in the cage for that last round, and if she's signed herself up for the round this Thursday, I'm here to talk you out of it."

He leans back in his swivel chair and crosses his arms over his chest. He lets out a small laugh. "Talented fighting women who are willing to get in the ring are a hot commodity right now. The Rousey-Zingano fight drew thousands of new spectators to the sport. Your girl's got some real potential, and she's beautiful. These one hundred-second promos we've been running are a huge draw. Last Thursday we had Spiderman and Batman going at it. The crowd loved it. We tried to talk her into a permanent spot and her little blond friend, too."

Jett flinches in his seat and sits forward. "Ryan?" he says with a trace of disbelief in his voice.

"Rose," Juan says, "She said her name was Rose."

"Must be her fighting name," I say to Jett, winking at him.

"Anyways, your girl said she was only interested in the Helga stunt. You know, we haven't had another volunteer since she stepped in, and every Thursday someone asks me when we're gonna bring her back."

"Well, I've got a problem with that Helga stunt," I say. He leans back in his chair, crossing his arms. "Actually, I've got a problem with your entire operation."

He raises a brow and his tone changes, "And what would that be?"

"Respectfully, I wouldn't even know where to start. You had no medical personnel on sight, you put my girl in the ring with a guy nowhere near her weight class and tried to pass him off as a woman. You left the cage door open."

"That was my fault," Juan says as Orlo stares at me for a long beat. "Amateur cage fighting in New York is the real deal, son. We don't have the kinds of regulations other states do. We're self-regulated at the amateur level."

"And that's exactly why my girlfriend won't be getting in the ring on Thursday."

"That's too bad, because she's a draw for our crowd. I was under the impression she needed the money." He leans forward, picks up a piece of paper from his desk, and hands it to me. "Since she signed the pre-engagement contract, there's a $500.00 penalty for backing out. That covers our promotional expenses. I just placed an order for the flyers and posted the ad."

I expected it wouldn't be easy to talk him out of it if Devi had already gotten to him. "I'm prepared to make you a counter offer," I say.

He lets out a long breath. "I don't have the authority to break a contract. You'll have to talk to the big man." He opens the desk drawer, pulls out a business card, and hands it to me. "I'll tell him to expect your call. Mornings are best."

I stand up and thank him for his time, shaking his hand. Now that I know they have no license and no real guidelines they have to follow, there's no way I want Devi in this fight. If she was the first girl to survive the Helga round—Helga will be revenge-ready. I may have reached a dead end tonight, but this fight is not over. I just have to figure out how to stop it before it starts.

We walk out following Juan down the steps in single file. "Hey, the guy that plays your Helga, is he here tonight?"

"You mean Chuck. Yeah, I think so."

"Thought I might say hello, introduce myself," I say, trying to sound friendly.

We step onto the floor and he shrugs, "Sure, follow me." I cast a smiling gaze over my shoulder at Jett, which he returns, shaking his head. I may have just found a way around that dead end.

Chapter Twenty-Two

DEVIN GRACE

I'm sitting in my office staring at the string of emails on my computer screen: There are four of them, all ending in Winslow. I open them one at a time. The first three are from Ben's sisters, telling me they're bummed that we broke up and apologizing for the scene at their house.

The last one is from his mom. I hold my breath, open it, and read. "Devin, I wanted to offer you an apology for the way I acted when we met. I was not feeling well that day, and I am afraid that I directed more anger at you than I should have. Clearly, you did not organize the party. I hope you will accept my apologies. You are welcome at our home anytime."

I lean an elbow on my desk and rest my fingers over my mouth. Wow. I'm amazed. I wonder if Ben made them. It doesn't matter. Even if he did, they still had to agree and write it. I smile, feeling a little weight lifting. If he had asked me if I wanted an apology from his mom, I would have said no way. But now that I have it, something inside of me feels redeemed. I'll return the olive branch they've extended and write them back tomorrow.

"Hey," Mario steps into my office doorway, "you're still here. I thought you were leaving an hour ago." I look at my watch.

"Shit!" I say, standing up. "I got sucked in by my emails. Thanks for the reminder."

"Have a good night," I call to her over my shoulder and head for the subway.

I flip the lock to our apartment and walk in. I have to be at Sovereign by six thirty. I open my mouth to yell for Ryan.

"Surprise!" I look up and see Jade standing next to her in our living room. They are both wearing black baseball caps embroidered with the word "Fearless", standing with their hands on their hips. "Ta-dum!" they say, shifting their heads left and right.

"Oh my God!"

"I came to see Fearless Red," Jade says, holding fisted hands straight up in the air.

I start laughing and hug them both. "You guys are so awesome. I have to tell you, I'm not feeling so fearless right now," I say.

"You just need a pep talk," Jade says.

"And some lipstick," Ryan adds.

"I'm so glad you're here," I say to Jade. "Does Vaughn know you're coming?"

"No, I was going to surprise him, too."

Two hours later, the three of us are standing shoulder

to shoulder at the top of the aisle, waiting to be announced. "Ready?" Ryan asks.

"Go Green!" I say.

"Go White!" Ryan and Jade echo.

I'm dressed in yoga pants and my red T-shirt and the crowd hushes to a low murmur. The announcer opens the cage door and walks in with the microphone. Juan is in front of us, ready to serve as my bouncer and walk us down the aisle.

"Back for a one-time special appearance, ladies and gentleman, turn your eyes east for the Beauty ready to take on our Beast, the one, the only: Fearless Red." I jump into the aisle waving to the crowd, clasping my hands, and flexing my muscles. Ryan and Jade are strutting behind me clapping their hands above their heads. The guard at the cage door checks me over and I survey the perimeter. I look to the spot where Ben was standing last time I got in the cage. It's empty and a wave of sadness washes over me. I wish he was here so badly—I hope I can do this without him. The man in front of me gives me the all clear and I step in. I dance around the octagon, stopping to throw practice punches at the air after every lap.

The lights flash, and the spotlight moves to the top of the opposite aisle. "Our Beauty is ready. Now let's bring on the one and only, our very own Beast, Helga the Horrible." I glide around the ring with my thumbs pointed down, joining the boos and hisses coming from crowd.

"All right, all right," Juan says. "Get over here and let me tape your gloves, would you?" I stand in front of him with my fingers raised. "Now remember, they've upped the game here, you gotta score some points to win this time. Strike and move out of her zone as fast as you can. You don't want her to get her hands on you. When you throw, throw hard."

"I got it," I say, watching Helga's back. Her braids fall higher on her shoulders and her shirt looks tighter on the muscles moving in her back. "She looks bigger," I say to Juan.

"He is bigger," he says smiling. My stomach drops. I slap the muscles of my arms to warm them up and shake my legs. Juan nods to me and follows the announcer out of the ring. "Good luck, beauty," he says, and the cage door closes with a loud crack.

Along with being physically bigger, this Helga has a bigger ego, too—she's still working the crowd. If they blow the horn I'm going to be able to run over there and kick the oaf in the ass before she even turns to face me. The horn blows a shrill shriek, and I fly across the cage, slamming my thigh hard into her side. I connect with solid muscle, and she barely flinches. Shit. She straightens as I'm bouncing back. I try to remember the advice Ben was giving me when I was in the cage last time. Strike and get out of her zone.

Helga is turning as I move in for another shot. I swing for her face and feel my arm twist against her side. She pulls me in slowly as I throw two knee jabs. My chest hits hers, and I swing for her face with my free arm. She blocks the shot and locks her arms around me. I feel weightless and dizzy as she spins me onto her shoulder. I squeeze my eyes shut waiting for the force of the drop, but instead, she eases me down. My back touches the mat and I immediately arch and roll, escaping the hold. She gave me that one, and I'm going to have to step it up if I'm going to win the money this time.

The crowd is roaring, their taunts and jeers so loud, it's

making the blood in my head pound. I wish I had one voice I could focus on, I wish Ben was here.

Helga is slow to rise up off the mat, untwisting her red cape. I bounce and lunge, taking position to throw another knee jab to her chin as she's rising. Something stops me. I see her profile, and in an instant everything looks familiar. I blink hard as my mind tries to make sense of what I'm seeing. I drop my hands, narrow my gaze, and step closer. I start to say his name, but before the word escapes, he side-kicks my thigh more gently than any fighter ever would.

I stumble and widen my eyes. "Ben! What are you doing?" I shout.

He wipes his chin with a gloved hand and bounces in front of me. He kicks again and moves in, locking his arms around me. I hear him over my ear as he takes me down.

"I kicked Helga's ass and won the right to fight you," he says, a challenging tone in his voice. He's really going to fight me. His eyes are inches from mine, and I'm arching my back, twisting and squirming to avoid getting pinned.

"Get off of me!" I gasp, breathless from the weight of his arm. "You're ruining my fight!" He rolls off and I stand and stare at him with my hands on my hips. "I can't fight you, Ben." He kicks my thigh again, before I've even finished speaking. "Ow! Stop it!" I grit out. "Why are you doing this?"

He lunges toward me and his arms circle my body. He speaks close to my ear but I'm hardly resisting.

"I'm doing this for two reasons." He swings me in the air and takes me down. "I know you're still pissed at me, and this is your chance. This is it Devi—this is where it starts and ends. We're leaving it all on the mat." His hand smacks hard beside my head and I flinch. "Get it out, and we're moving on." He leans right, giving me the opportunity to get back on my feet and I take it, landing a hard shot to his ribs on the way up. He flashes a surprised look and raises a brow.

"Nice one," he says, and I throw the same shot.

I shake my head. "This is ridiculous. I can't fight you, Ben." I raise my wrist and tug a glove with my teeth. I'm done.

He stands bouncing in front of me and lands another shot to my other thigh. I stumble. Anger flares, and I glare at him. His smile deepens. "You feelin' me?" he taunts. "C'mon, Devi. I'm every man that ever did anything bad to you, your dad…"

I swing at him, and my fist connects with his shoulder. "Josh," he says, and I swing harder. His abs ripple as he tightens. He moves sideways as I connect and he keeps talking. "Stepdad." I run at him and land a flying kick. He barely manages to stay up, but when he stabilizes, he narrows an intense stare at me.

"Okay, now me," he says. I hesitate, glaring at him, and he lunges. I jump back and we're staring each other down. "C'mon!" he says, "You scared of me, Fearless?" I feel the anger rising and he continues. "You are scared of me?" he taunts. He springs forward at the same time my last tic of patience snaps. I let loose, landing a hard shot to the side of his face. He stumbles, and I take advantage of the momentary fog, landing another shot in the same spot. He drops to one knee. I move in and hit him again and I see him smile, right before he falls over. Shit! The big idiot didn't even raise his hands. He didn't duck or block or try to resist in any way. He's either dizzy or he's faking it.

I jump on top of him, but he's not moving. Holy shit. I knocked him out. The referee is pulling me off, raising my arm up, and Ben is still lying on the mat. I shove the ref and he releases me. I drop beside Ben and try to shake his shoulders. Panic and shame fill my stomach. I should not have hit him that hard. He was holding back and I should have been, too. His head turns on the mat. I lean over his face and hold his cheeks, calling his name. "Ben!" Jesus. I really knocked him out. His eyes open and blink several times before settling into a squint. I let out a breath as his focus sharpens. "Nice shot," he raises half a smile and blinks.

"Kiss me, Ben," and it's all I can think about. He rises up on his elbows and kisses me. The crowd releases a roar mixed with laughter and objections. Ben reaches up and tugs a braid until his wig slides off. He drops it and threads a hand through my hair, deepening our kiss as the crowd hoots and cheers.

"God, I'm sorry," I say, pressing my cheek against his.

"Forgiven."

I stand and hold a hand out, pulling him up. My hands hold his sides, feeling warm skin and smooth muscle. "Are you okay?" I ask, watching him shake his head.

"Of course I'm okay." His palm covers my hand and he raises my arm into the air, turning us toward the cheering crowd. I look under our raised arms and watch him flash a showman's smile at the audience.

"You know you're going straight to the doctor after this," I say. He smirks and turns us to the other side of the arena. "And that is not the right lipstick shade for you."

An hour later we are in Dr. Oscar's office, and Ben is sitting on the exam table while a tiny dot of white light moves over his eyes. "So tell me again how this happened," the doctor asks, clicking the light off.

"He got a little lippy with me, and I knocked him out," I respond. The doctor pauses and looks between us as Ben shrugs.

He steps back and puts his hands in the pocket of his white coat. "Has this kind of thing happened between the two of you before?"

"No," we answer in unison.

"Think there's any risk of it happening again?" Ben raises a brow to me, and I tilt my head, thinking about it.

"Maybe," I say, and Ben interrupts.

"No way." The doctor scratches the back of his head and smiles, moving to the keyboard of a lap top.

"I'll write you a script for a higher dose of ibuprofen, and you can take it if you need to. No concussion this time." I let out a breath. Thank God. I feel bad enough as it is. The doctor stands, crossing an arm and holding his chin in one hand, "Mr. Winslow, I have to ask, do you feel safe around Ms. Dalton?"

Ben bursts into a fit of laughter that fills the small exam room. "Hell no," he says. "I haven't felt safe since the day I met her."

"Well," Doctor Oscar says moving to the door, "I've been married twenty-two years, and my wife still scares the hell out of me." He looks at Ben. "I suspect that's how you know she's the right woman for you." He winks at me as he's walking out.

Chapter Twenty-Three

BEN

I open the door of the Monkey Kick for Devi and wipe my hand over my mouth. "Are you sure you got all the lipstick off?"

She stops and raises her hands to my cheeks, angling my face into the light. She wipes her thumb across my lips and smiles. "What? Are you afraid someone's gonna hit on you?"

"Yeah. The wrong kind of someone."

"Don't worry, baby," she holds up her arms and flexes. "Two tickets to the gun show right here." She kisses her biceps and winks. "I got your back."

I grab her wrists and pull her arms down. "Stop that. No more fighting."

I watch the crowd turn and the guys smile as Devi passes. If I stay close enough to Devi no one's going to be looking at my lips, that's for sure.

"Hey!" Devi says, stopping in front of two attractive young women. "Ben, this is Dena and Maria. They are friends of Ryan's from law school." I shake their hands, and we chat with them. In the background buzz I hear Jett. He's calling my name and raising a beer. That's what I want to be talking about. "Nice to meet you, ladies," I say, slipping past Devi. "I'll be at the bar with Jett and Vaughn."

Jett hands me the longneck and pats my shoulder as he and Vaughn laugh and shake their heads. There were so many people around Devi and me when we made it out of the cage, we didn't have time to talk other than to shout, "Meet you at the Kick."

"Well, I never thought I'd see the day," Jett says. "You finally got your ass kicked by a girl. Cheers." We click longnecks, and he and Vaughn laugh.

"You were the first to go down, Treb. Ryan kicked your ass last spring, and we all watched it happen."

"I may have been the first, but you win the prize for falling with the most flair. The bigger they are the more ridiculous they look on the way down," Jett says.

"You looked like a cross between the Swiss Miss Cocoa girl and Hulk Hogan," Vaughn says. "You have got to be crazy in love."

"Well, I really didn't see I had a choice. If the real Helga had gotten another shot at Devi, I'm sure it would have been so much worse. Being part of the freak show is better than watching someone throw shots at her from the sidelines."

"Devi got in some hard hits. You're going to be sore tomorrow."

I take another drink and feel a small twist in my stomach at the mention of tomorrow. "Being sore is the least of my concerns. Test results will be back tomorrow afternoon, and I'll know whether I'm entering the wonderful world of parenthood—from tearing through my college years on two wheels to minivan nation." I shake my head.

"That'd be a hard right turn," Vaughn says, feeling my pain.

Jett raises a hand to my back. "It is what it is, brother."

"We'll see. I'm torn between wanting to get tomorrow over with and not wanting it to come."

"You'll get through it. And hey, at least you know that Vaughn knows how to braid hair if you need help in that department." He's talking about the scene between the three of us earlier in the locker room when I was putting my Helga costume on. The braids on the wig were loose and the guys were standing on either side of me trying to put them back together—Vaughn doing a much better job than Jett—as I was trying to put on lipstick.

"I feel like we should have a pillow fight later," I say to them and we all crack up.

"Where's Ryan?" I ask.

"She's in the bathroom with Jade. Jade came in for the fight."

"They *were* in the bathroom. Now they're talking with Devi," Vaughn says, pointing his beer down the bar to where the girls are standing. We watch them laugh at something Devi says. Her hands are moving as fast as her mouth, and her hair bounces around her shoulders. The immediate circle they're talking to is girls, but the outer ring is starting to thicken with clearly interested guys.

"We'd better go stake out our territory," Jett says, "before we have to fight our way in. Hey, I've got a prank I want to pull on the girls when we get back to the apartments," Jett says.

"I hope this doesn't end with me getting my ass kicked twice in one night."

"Just make sure you wear your running shoes," Vaughn says, following Jett.

We spend the rest of the night laughing and drinking, and when the girls decide they're ready to head home, we stroll behind them, hugging them all good night in the hallway. We open the door to our apartment and sitting on the kitchen table is a life-size blowup alligator. Beside that sits three red plastic beer cups filled with powder paint.

"Okay, here's the plan," Jett says, calling the play like a quarterback on game day. Ten minutes later we're opening the door and stepping lightly down the hall. Vaughn lays a trail of sheets out in the hallway and Jett balances the plastic inflatable gator on their door. We move to our spots—Jett just behind the gator, Vaughn and I at his side, each holding a cup of paint. I stare down at the orange powder, shaking the cup gently. "Are you sure this stuff will come out if we get it on the walls?"

"Since when are you the voice of reason?" Jett says.

"Since now."

"It's totally washable, now pipe down while I make the distress call." He walks a few steps and raises his phone to his ear.

"Hey babe, do you have any Advil? Would you mind bringing it over? I'm in boxers...I know you can't stay the night...yeah, just two." He presses end call and gives us an evil grin. "Go Blue!" he says.

Within seconds the lock is clicking, and I'm watching the

round handle jiggle, feeling a flutter of pre-play anxiousness in my stomach. The door opens and the six-foot gator swoops down on Ryan's head. She releases a blood-curdling scream, and her small frame starts to thrash back and forth, arms flailing, legs kicking, still shrieking. In her panic, one of the gator's claws has entangled in her long blond hair. Devi and Jade appear in the doorway with startled expressions and Jett says, "Payback's a bitch, girls." That's our signal. Vaughn and I step in and the three of us toss the cups full of powder paint into the air. It sails above their heads, billowing into a plume of rainbow colors, shrouding their upturned faces in a mix of neon. They sputter and Ryan's shrieks turn into sobs from the trauma of being attacked by a plastic green monster. Devi and Jade are standing with mouths and arms gaping, trying to figure out what just happened. Devi moves in and closes her arms around Ryan. Her face is coated in pylon orange powder and her teeth gleam white as she lets lose a slew of swear words.

"You assholes! Jett, how could you do that to Ryan?" Ryan's shoulders are shaking, hands pressed to her face. Jade scowls, wiping the back of her arm over her face and smearing the neon pink stripe running from the tip of her nose up and across the top of her head like a skunk's stripe.

"You guys are so immature," she says, spitting paint out and rubbing Ryan's back. Ryan continues to gasp and sob in Devi's arms, and I'm guessing Ryan had a little too much to drink tonight at the Monkey Kick. Being attacked by a six-foot gator has pushed her over the edge. The smile on Jett's face is melting.

"Aww, shit," he says, moving forward. Devi and Jade step back, and he wraps his arms around Ryan. "It was a joke, baby," he says rubbing her back. Devi holds a fist up at me. I flinch and start walking backward to our apartment door with my palms up. Vaughn follows with small steps, and we watch Jade coming out of the apartment with two of the plastic cups we threw at them. Judging by the look on her face the cups are still loaded. She hands one to Devi and they break into a run after us. *Shit!*

Vaughn and I reach for one another—failing in our attempt to use each other as a shield. Devi and Jade let loose at the same time, and powder flies through the air and settles over us in shades of lime green and baby blue.

"Aww, man," Vaughn says. I look at him and shake my head.

"There's only one person left who's not doused in powder paint," I say, and we all turn on the quarterback.

Jett sees us coming. "Hey," he says, "Ryan's injured here."

Ryan puts her head up, shoves him at us and disappears into the apartment. We dive on Jett. Devi and I put our arms around him and pull him down. Jade and Vaughn join us on the floor, pinning his arms while we smear him with paint. The blowup gator comes soaring out of the apartment door, followed by Ryan, clutching a steak knife. She casts an evil stare over our piled bodies and Jett's eyes widen. He stops laughing and sits up, pushing us off with an alarmed look.

She drops to her knees on top of the overturned alligator, raises her arm above her head and plunges the knife. A loud pop fills the hallway and she grunts with the effort of a serial killer, gutting the green monster. Something flashes behind her as she stands up. She's moving toward Jett with a crazed look in her eyes. She raises the knife above her head, holding it in two hands. "I should have done this a long time ago. You're next, you evil bastard." she sneers, advancing slowly.

"Ryan, calm down!" Jett says in a firm voice raising a halting palm.

"Don't tell me to calm down!"

"Ryan, wait!" He presses his palm to the floor and starts to raise himself, but she dives at him. He shifts and focuses on grabbing the knife she's holding as she lands in a straddle position, sitting on top of his legs. He locks his grip on her descending wrist and holds her arms up, staring at her with a distressed, enraged look—as if she's completely lost her mind. She leans down and sneers into his face.

"I could cut your heart out." Her fingers open and the knife drops onto his head and bounces to the floor. "If I didn't have a plastic knife." She leans over and kisses his cheek as he grimaces and exhales a loud breath.

"Jesus, Ryan…" he says. She stands and slaps pink paint off her hands. She rests her hands on her hips and stares down at him still breathing hard on the floor.

"You about gave me a fucking heart attack," he says.

"Awww, baby," she says, dipping her knees. Her eyebrows pinch together and she twists her lips. "It was a joke, it was just a joke," she says, moving her head side to side and imitating his voice. She raises her hands to her hips and pans a disapproving gaze over him.

"Come on, girls," she says. She takes two steps and stops abruptly turning back to Jett. "I almost forgot." She pulls out a fisted hand and swings. Two tiny red pellets pelt his chest and bounce into the mix of neon powder.

"Here's your Ad-fucking-vil," she says. Devi and Jade stand and follow her in. Devi peeks her face through the crack just before the door shuts.

"Night-night, losers," she says, smiling.

Jett rubs a hand over the back of his neck and cocks a brow. "Well, that didn't go quite according to my plan." We bust up laughing. I sink onto my side and roll on the floor, rewinding the pictures of Devi's orange neon face, white teeth, and Ryan's half-yellow, half-pink murderous glare. Jett stands, kicks my hip with the side of his foot, and offers a hand. It's a good thing the apartment between ours and the girls' is vacant right now.

"You should have seen the look on your face when Ryan lunged at you with that knife," I say to Jett. Ryan Rose is the only woman I've ever known who has the ability to bring my buddy to his knees. She's his perfect match. I shake my head laughing harder while Vaughn smacks paint off of his jeans.

I may be going home covered in a rainbow of neon, but I think I made progress with Devi tonight. The doctor called today and the test results will be back tomorrow. I'm ready. I think.

Chapter Twenty-Four

DEVIN GRACE

I press the doorbell and step back, double-checking the address I wrote down, 84B North Wilson. This should be it. I hear fast footsteps and muffled voices of excitement on the other side of the door. It opens, and Gator jumps out. I drop down and hug him, kissing him on the cheek. "Hey, my friend. I've missed you," I say, trying to control the lump in my throat.

"Come on in, Miss Devi, come on in." He takes my hand and pulls me up. Standing just at the door is a large handsome man with warm brown skin and dark eyes. He extends a hand. "You must be Devi," he says, "I'm Sam."

"This is my dad," Gator says with enthusiasm in his voice, staring at Sam with a look of adoration.

"Nice to meet you," I say, stepping in.

"I can take your coat," Sam says. He's a few inches taller

than me and his muscular physique is obvious under the black polo shirt he's wearing. His eyes are striking, light in color and wide set. I hand him my coat, and he smiles.

"When Gator told me how beautiful you were, I thought he was exaggerating. I see I was wrong."

I force a smile. *When he told me you were coming for him I thought he was wrong too, and you can flatter me all you want, buddy, you've got a long way to go before you'll see a real smile from me.*

I hear giggling as Gator reaches behind the archway leading to the next room and pulls a struggling little boy to his side. "And this is my cousin, Charles."

"Well, hi there, Charles," I say, beaming a smile at him. I see Sam looking at me from the corner of my eye as a heavy-set woman comes around the arch holding a dishtowel.

"Hi, Miss Devi, I'm Grandma Sara."

"Nice to meet you," I say, and I'm wondering where all these people have been for the last three years of Gator's life.

"I was just turning off the chili. I hope you can have lunch with us."

"Sounds wonderful. Is there anything I can do to help?"

"Oh, no, you visit with the boys, I'll call you when it's ready."

"I want to show you my room, Miss Devi," Gator says. He holds a stiff arm against his cousin and with a tone of authority says, "Step aside, Charlie."

"Please." Sam and I say at the same time. Our eyes meet, and he smiles again. I let Gator pull me through the living room, past the dining room table, down a short hallway, and into a bedroom.

"This is my bed," he says pointing to the top of a bunk bed and jumping onto the ladder. "This is how I get up there." Charles dives into the lower bunk and buries his head under an Olaf pillow.

"Wow, Gator, this is awesome," I say. He jumps off the ladder and spins across the room.

"Let me show you our backyard." I follow him out to the small yard, and he and Charles disappear in a wooden playhouse. They take turns opening and closing the shutters and popping their heads out of the window frames. Charles exits the playhouse and crosses to a sandbox. He falls to his knees, pulls up a blue shovel and starts to dig.

"Come swing with me, Miss Devi." I hop on the seat next to Gator's and we push, pull, and pump until we're soaring so high we bump off of our seats, catching air and laughing until we're breathless. When our pace slows, I lean my head back and feel the flow of air in my hair, staring at the blue sky.

Gator imitates my move. "Do you like my new home, Miss Devi?"

"I love it, Gator, do you like it?"

"Yeah, but my daddy says we're gonna get a place of our own soon as he can find one. He just got out, so he hasn't had time…"

"Gator lunch is ready. You and Charles come on in and wash your hands," Sara calls from the screen door.

I sit up. Just got out—that's it. He's been in jail. Gator was about to say he just got out of jail. I look back to the doorframe at Sam and I catch part of a tattoo plastered over a large bicep, half-covered by sleeve. I wonder what he did, and if Robyn pulled his criminal record. I watch him step into the backyard. He doesn't seem like the kind of guy that would commit a serious crime. He has an ease about him, and a pleasant demeanor—unless it's all a show—but I'm usually pretty good at reading people.

Gator jumps off his swing and heads for the door with Charles. Sam has his hands in his pockets, and I think he's noticed by now that I've smiled at everyone else, except him. I walk to where he's standing waiting for me, brushing sand off my hands. I guess this is the opportunity I've been waiting for.

"So, Gator tells me you just got out. Is that the reason you lost contact with him? What were you in for?" He stares at me with a blank look.

"You think I've been in jail?" His eyes widen with surprise and then narrow. "Because I'm black?"

Now it's my turn to be surprised. "Your son is blacker than you, and I love him like family. I don't think you've been in jail because you're black. I think you've been in jail because it's the only possible excuse you could have for losing track of him for three years." We stare at each other for a hard beat. "And because Gator told me you just got out."

His mouth shifts and a slow smile creeps into the corners. "Fair enough," he says. "I see that Gator loves you right back." He shakes his head, and emotion changes his expression. "I have to be thankful for those who came to his rescue and led him to us."

"Sam, Miss Devi, lunch is ready," Sara beckons to us holding the screen door open. We stand and I stare at him. He holds his hand out for me to lead the way. Okay, so I guess that means he wasn't in jail, but where's he been? Did his mom kidnap Gator from Sam?

Gator pulls out my chair and Charles giggles. We sit and Sara asks me about my background, where I'm from and how I came to New York and The Children's Center. Gator chirps in, telling them how we both arrived at the center on the same day and it was our job to clean the fish tank every Friday.

"Can we get a fish tank, Dad?" he asks Sam.

"I think we could do that, soon as we get ourselves re-settled." Sam stands and carries his bowl back to the crock-pot. "This is wonderful, Ma." He sets his bowl on the table. "Devi, can I get you some more?"

"No, thanks," I say. I draw in a breath and ask Sam the other question I've been avoiding. "Will you be resettling in the area?" He gives me a soft smile and nods his head.

"Well, didn't you tell her?" Sara asks. "Sam just returned from a tour of duty in Afghanistan." I just about choke on my chili as it's going down, pulling my napkin off my lap and coughing. I turn to Sam and stare at him. "My son's always been a bit modest. He's a Captain in the Army. He'll be hearing from Garrison Headquarters any day now with his new housing assignment for Fort Hamilton. Fort Hamilton is in Queens, and we are just so thrilled."

"You must be very proud," I say, feeling like a complete idiot.

"My Sam has always made me proud," she says with a tear in her eye. Sam leans back, drumming his fingers on the table and smiling at her.

"Can we go get ice cream, Dad?" Gator says, tipping his empty bowl toward Sam. "I finished it all."

"I suppose we can do that," Sam says. "There's a party store around the block that sells ice cream, Devi, want to walk the kids there with me?"

"That sounds nice. Will you join us, Sara?"

"Oh no, I don't need any more ice cream, you all go ahead and I'll clean up."

Gator and Charlie run ahead of us, and Sam and I walk side by side in silence for several minutes. His pace is slow and easy beside me, and I feel no indication from him that he's holding a grudge against me for assuming he's been in jail. I'm holding a grudge against myself, though. I've been so focused on my own hurt feelings for losing Gator, and I've let that taint my judgment.

I let out a breath and turn to Sam. "I have one more question for you, and once you answer it I'll know how big of an apology I need to give you."

"You want to know how I lost touch with my son?" I nod my head. He stares hard into the distance at Gator and Charles.

"Until around a week ago, I didn't know he existed." My mouth drops open and I make a conscious effort to close it as he continues. "I knew his mom from high school, knew her family. I had a relationship with her the summer after I graduated from college—just before I started basic training, but it didn't last. I had heard her life took a turn for the worse and that she'd gotten into drugs, but I didn't know she had a baby. I found out some time later that she had married. It must have been shortly after our fling, and I assume they just raised Gator as their own. When they got divorced, Gator's stepdad pulled out of his life, and it left him with no one but an addict mom. I haven't seen her yet. She's in rehab, but when I do, I suspect that's what she'll tell me, based on what Gator's said. I don't want to push him too hard for details. He's been through a lot. I'm hoping his mom will be willing to grant me custody if I give her my assurances we'll not block her from his life."

"And you shouldn't. I don't think it would be good for him."

"I know. And I also know it wouldn't be good for him to lose touch with you. I hope you'll stay in our lives."

"Of course. I'd love that," I say.

"I imagine you've been his silver lining these last few months. I have always thought that having a strong family was the most important thing in life, but now I see that doesn't matter half as much as having someone who loves you. I thank you for being that for my son these last few months."

"He's been that for me, too."

Gator and Charlie are ahead of us running to the corner. Sam yells up to them. "Wait there for us before you cross the street, please, and hold Charlie's hand."

We step up to the single cooler holding six flavors of ice cream and place our orders with the teenage girl. Sam insists on buying the ice cream and helps Charlie wrap his cone in a napkin while Gator and I step out.

I walk back to the house beside Gator, spinning my sugar cone in my hand and swirling ribbons of strawberry ice cream over my tongue. "Your Dad seems super cool, my friend."

"Yep," Gator says, licking drips of blue moon from between his thumb and index finger.

"I almost forgot," I say, reaching into my purse. "I brought this for you from Michigan." I hold the Michigan State baseball hat by the bill and hand it to him.

"Aww, cool!" he says, pulling it over his head.

"Your dad said I could come back and help you get your new fish tank set up when you move into your new place. Sound good?"

"Yep."

When we get back to the house I hug them all good-bye and walk out with a feeling of joy in my heart. My life may be a mess of tangled loose ends right now, but Gator's world is right. It makes me feel great about the work I'm doing at the Center. For five weeks, I've made a difference in that child's life, and he's made a difference in mine. I think about the words that Gator and I shared. "Family are people that love you." It's not about being able to present a biologically correct family tree—it's about love. If I can form a meaningful bond with an eight-year-old with whom I have very little in common, I can certainly do that with a baby—Ben's baby.

I check my watch. It's 2:35 p.m. I need to be there for Ben—in his corner—and I need to be there *before* he gets the results. I want him to know I'm all in—and there for him even if we remain just friends. I pick up my pace and catch the Manhattan bound train. I fidget the entire ride, tapping my fingers on the window until the doors open. I run up the stairs and cross the street into the Trott Building. It's 2:55 p.m., and Ben's appointment is at three. I think I've made it. I pull the door of the office open and a bell pings as I step in. Ben is sitting in a chair against the wall, leaning forward with his forearms resting on his thighs, staring at his feet. He's wearing his casual Friday jeans and T-shirt but he looks anything but casual. He looks every bit the vision of a man waiting for life-altering test results. Jillian and Henri are sitting on the other side of the room, whispering softly to each other. I nod at Jillian and move to stand in front of Ben's down cast eyes. He sees my shoes and tilts his head. He stares a moment and the corners of his eyes narrow, as if he needs to be certain. I reach my hand out for his. "I came to sit in your corner." He takes my hand, and I sit down next to him.

"Thank you," he says. The tension in his voice matches the look on his face, and my stomach hollows. His usual golden tone looks sallow and the tiny lines at the corner of his eyes are drawn tight. I have never seen Ben look like this, and it's hard to keep myself calm staring into the face of his anxiousness. I take a breath, put my hand on his back, and rub slowly back and forth. Right now, even if I don't feel calm, I have to fake it for him.

"No matter what happens, it's going to be all right, Ben." The corner of his mouth rises but doesn't quite make it to a smile, and he doesn't say anything.

The waiting room door pushes open, and a young male dressed in pale gray scrubs looks at his clipboard and calls Jillian's name. "Dr. Oscar is ready for you now." Jillian and Henri stand and stare at him.

Ben raises his eyebrows. "This is it," he says.

"I'll be right here," I say, squeezing his hand. "No matter what happens, I'll be here." His fingers touch my cheek, and he moves to follow Jillian and Henri. The door clicks shut and I let out a breath. Ugh. Now all I have to do is wait.

I pull out my phone and text Ryan. *"I am at the doctor's office with Ben, in the waiting room…"*

"Wow! I'm proud of you for being there, Dev."

"I'm proud of me too. I feel like I'm going to pass out…"

"Head between your knees, deep breaths. You got this."

"Met Gator's dad, all is right in his world. We might need a drink when Ben comes out. I will text you if Ben wants to go out."

"We're here if you need us. Just say the word."

What now? I have got to keep my mind occupied or I'm going to go crazy. I text my mom and get the update on Josh. He's had a rough week, but he's holding his own and still in rehab so that's good news. The interior door of the waiting room swings open, and Ben walks out. I stand and stare anxiously at him. He lets out a long breath and drops into the seat beside mine. I lean forward, watching him. He's staring straight ahead, thinking. He leans an elbow on the arm of the chair and presses a hand over his mouth. I have no idea what he's going to say.

"Ben…"

He tilts his head and raises his brow. "It's a girl…and she's mine," he says, letting out a breath.

Jillian and Henri step into the waiting room, looking like they hate each other, and us. "Can we talk to the two of you?" Jillian asks, but it's not really a question. She's said it as if it's a directive. "We can use the conference room on the ninth floor. Give us ten minutes and meet us there." Ben continues to stare at the door with a distant expression.

He stands and reaches to help me up. We walk to the conference room, and I see the hold of the initial shock on his emotions loosening, replaced by a look of cautious uncertainty.

We enter the boardroom, and the air around us seems to thicken. Jillian is sitting at the table looking sick. With the exception of the red around her eyes she looks as pale as paste. Henri is staring out the glass window with his arms crossed over his thin chest. He turns and stares us down as we walk in. I feel like flipping him off. I get the distinct feeling he's trying to intimidate us. It makes me want to laugh. Ben pulls a chair for me, and we both sit.

"We have a proposal for you, Ben." Henri says, taking a step toward us. Jillian's hand is covering her mouth, and I can't tell if she's nervous, sick, or possibly both.

"We want to ask you to give up your parental rights."

I grip Ben's forearm and shake my head. "Absolutely not."

"I was talking to Ben, not his 'good time girl,'" Henri sneers. I feel Ben's arm moving, as if he's going to get up and confront Henri, but I hold him in place.

"Actually, I think it's your fiancée that's the 'good time girl', seeing as she's the one that had the one-night stand and until an hour ago didn't know who fathered her child." Silence expands in the room, and Henri's nostrils flare. Under the hair gel, and one too many spritzes of cologne, he's nothing but a bully. I don't know how Jillian can stand this toad. I glance at her, staring into her lap with a distressed look, and her pitiful state takes the edge off my anger.

Henri refocuses on Ben. "We're prepared to pay you."

"No," Ben says.

"You haven't heard the offer yet." Henri says.

"I heard your offer, and the answer is no," Ben says.

"We're talking about more money than you'll ever make in your—"

Ben points a finger, interrupting him, barely containing his rage as he speaks. "You must think I'm an idiot. You've insulted me, and you've insulted my girl. Since you're two for two, I suggest you keep your mouth shut for the rest of this discussion or I'll come over there and shut it for you."

Henri's thin lips mold into a scowl, and he crosses his arms over his chest.

"Jillian," Ben says. "This isn't what I would consider working together, and it's not doing what's best for the baby. Was this your idea, or his?" Jillian eyes droop at the corners, and she looks lost. I can't believe I am about to come to her defense, but I feel the urge to help her. She presses her fingers to her mouth, and her cheeks puff. Oh my God. She's going to barf. Yellow liquid erupts through her fingers, and she spews all over the conference table.

"Holy fuck!" Henri says. Ben stiffens and freezes, as if he has no idea what to do. Jillian drops her head in her lap and starts making a noise somewhere between coughing and sobbing.

"Get!" I say, pointing Ben and Henri to the door. "Get out, I'll help her." Their expressions change from shocked disgust to relief and they scramble for the exit. "And find me some paper towels and water, please!" I dig through my purse for the pack of Kleenex and wet wipes I've learned to carry with me from working at the Center. I manage to clean up her face by the time Ben comes back to the door with the towels and water.

"Anything else?" he says.

"Just wait out there for a few minutes." I hold my breath against the sour smell that waves over me as I mop up the barf. Henri's face appears in the glass window beside the door, and I walk to him with the plastic garbage can full of puke sopped paper towels. I open the door and shove it in his hands.

"Make yourself useful and get rid of this." I close the

door in his face and catch the faintest hint of a smile on Jillian's face as I twist open the water bottle and hold it out to her. I sit beside her, and she stares at me.

"You sure are being nice to me," she says, taking the water bottle. "Considering the circumstances, I can't imagine you like me more now." The note of sarcasm in her voice is distinct and her mouth settles into a grim line.

I let out a short breath. "We should probably try to get to know each other a little better."

She takes another drink and casts a sideways glance. "Well, since it looks like I've messed up your life too, I owe you at least that much," she says.

I pull out the chair beside her and try not to look conspicuous checking the cushion for puke. I sit and give her a sympathetic look. "You know, after we all get over the initial shock of having a baby, I don't believe it's ever a bad thing. We have jobs, we're healthy, we're all adults here, right?"

"Well, three of us are," Jillian says, glancing to the door. I sit beside her in silence. A phone pings, and her eyes turn toward her purse. She lets out a small huffing noise staring at the oversized bag. "I bet that's Henri texting me that he's out, now that he knows." I struggle to contain my horrified response.

"If you think that's the kind of guy he is, Jillian…"

"I know that's the kind of guy he is."

"Do you really think he's right for you and the baby?" I ask in as non-threatening a voice as I can manage.

She wipes a tear. "The thought of what my parents will think and going through all of it alone." Ben knocks softly and pokes his head in.

"Need anything else?"

"You can come back in now," Jillian says. She looks at Ben. "Did he leave?"

He hesitates and nods. "I didn't touch him, I swear. I wanted to. But he just stood there for a minute then said, 'I'm out of here.' Sorry, Jillian."

She wipes a tear and sniffles. "It's all right. I'll be all right. It's just scary to think of telling my parents and having a baby, alone."

"You're not alone, Jillian. You might be a single mom, but the baby will always have a dad," Ben says.

"I'm sorry I asked you to give up your rights. I'll try to be more respectful of your role, and you too, Devi. It's the least I can do."

"Do you want me to go with you to tell your parents?" Ben asks.

She thinks about it for a minute. "No, I can do it. I think I'll tell Robert first and he'll help me. God knows he's screwed up enough, he'll know the best approach."

We're all silent for a moment. Ben braces a hand against the sill of the window and stares out. His shoulder raises and then lowers from his exhale, and I have the urge to move behind him, wrap my arms around him and lay my cheek on his back. My heart aches. I can't imagine what it would feel like to be pregnant right now. As bad as it would feel to be in Jillian's position, I think it must feel worse for Ben. He has so little control over what's going to happen. He's smart to try to lay a foundation of cooperation with Jillian.

Ben lets out a long breath and turns back to Jillian. "So, what's next then?" he asks in a level tone.

"Well, I have another doctor's appointment in a month. I guess we'll need to talk about a schedule, and a name, and how we feel about religion and stuff like that."

"Maybe you could have lunch every week and start thinking about things," I suggest.

"Yeah, that'd be a good idea," Jillian says, beginning to stand. "And Devi, you are welcome to join us if that's how the two of you want it." I exchange a quick glance with Ben as I reach for my purse but the connection I usually feel when we look at each other is either buried under the gravity what's just fallen on his shoulders or it's gone.

We cross to the elevators and Jillian interrupts my anxious thoughts. "I should probably warn both of you, I've never changed a diaper in my entire life," she says. "The thought of it makes me gag."

"Well, that makes two of us," Ben says.

"Didn't you guys ever babysit?" They stare at me with blank looks. Of course not. Palm to the forehead. How silly of me.

Jillian shakes her head and Ben shrugs. "We always had nannies," he says.

We say good-bye to Jillian and watch her walk down the wide sidewalk alone. "I can't believe I'm going to say this, but I feel sorry for her," I say.

"She's Jillian Trott," Ben says. "I gotta believe, even on her worst day, she'll be all right. She'll feel better after her family knows, and she has more support." I look back and Jillian has disappeared into the crowd of pedestrians.

"Do you want me to text Jett and Ryan and tell them?" I ask.

"No. Not yet, I want to let it sink in before I share it with the world." His fingers rest in the front pockets of his jeans, and he pauses a beat. "And I just want to be with you.

I have some stuff I need to talk to you about," he says. His eyes hold a melancholy reflection and the reserve in his tone sends a nervous ripple into my stomach. "Do you have anywhere you need to be?" he asks. "Will you walk with me for a while—maybe grab some dinner and talk?"

"Sounds good," I say, trying to mask my worries. "I'll follow you." I lower my aviator glasses from the top of my head and angle my face to the sun, shifting my focus between him and the flow of pedestrians as we walk. He's quiet, withdrawn with his thoughts. Ben is always so openly warm with me, his silence rattles me. The distance seems to be expanding between us with each step. I'm telling myself to stay calm but the dread in my heart is growing with alarming speed at the thought that he's moved on without me.

He suggests Italian for dinner, and we board the train heading to the Bleecker Street Station, pressed tight against the mass of Friday rush hour bodies. Ben grips the pole behind my back with two hands, and I feel the familiar heat of his body as he shields me from the jostle of the other riders. I close my eyes and draw in the deep scent of him, trying to relax my nerves as the train sways.

I want so badly to tell him that I know what I want now—that I want *him* and I'm ready. Last night at the Helga match he said the word "forgiven" but I can't take that to mean forgiven for everything—more likely he meant forgiven for knocking him out.

We rise out of the station and follow behind the flowing crowd. Brass instruments strain "My Country 'Tis of Thee" in the distance as we turn onto Mulberry Street. Arches span the buildings, decorated with fringe that flickers tiny spots of green, white and red over the crowd. "Looks like there's a street fair in Little Italy tonight," Ben says, pointing to a banner that announces the festival of San Gennaro. Cheerful greetings of "ciao" and "benvenuto" echo as we trek deeper. Despite the energetic buzz, all I can focus on is Ben—or the lack of Ben.

We walk a few blocks from the fair and find a small restaurant for dinner. The door of Mamma Mia's closes behind us, dousing the distant sounds of the street fair, and we follow the hostess through the dimly lit restaurant. She seats us in a small alcove, and we order drinks and dinner.

"Here's to new beginnings," Ben says, a note of forced acceptance in his voice. I raise my glass and toast, watching him from behind my bellini. "Devi," he leans forward. I swallow and brace myself. The fizzy drink expands in my throat, dumps into my stomach and mixes with the nerves that have been swarming for the last hour.

"When we got back to New York, after our trip to Michigan…" He's going there, back to that disastrous night."

I nod my head feeling the tremor at my jaw. I have no idea where he's going with this. I am certain Ben's life is moving on. I can feel it.

He levels his gaze on me. "I can't take any more steps backward. You know that," he says and I feel an instant chill from his calm, determined tone. I drop my gaze to my lap, and he stops talking. I'm a coward. The least I can do is hear him out. I take a breath and raise my head. He hesitates a beat. I'm certain he's reacting to the tears I can feel starting. "I told you I needed to step back for a while." His brow lifts, as if he's waiting for some kind of acknowledgement from me.

What does he want me to say? "I heard you. I know," I

say.

"No, you haven't heard me yet, Devi. I have a feeling you don't want to hear it but I'm going to say it. I have to." He shakes his head as if he's frustrated with me. "I took a step back because I wanted life to move in a different direction—a direction you weren't ready for—but I can't move forward without you. There is no forward without you." My breath hitches at his words. "There's only—" he pauses mid-sentence, searching.

"Pain," I say, "there's only pain." He nods slowly.

"And emptiness," I say.

"And emptiness," he repeats, letting out a small laughing breath. "You've been there too?"

I shake my head. "Ever since you said the words, 'step back', that's where I've been." It's my turn to talk now. I have to say what I should have said last Saturday. "I have been confused about us for too long. I spent so much time second-guessing my feelings. But I know now, Ben." He reaches across the table and holds my hands.

"You set me straight," I say. "The pieces of my mind—that normally twist and turn—gather together when I'm with you. As bad as that moment was last Saturday night—when we were driving home and our lives felt like they were fishtailing—careening out of control, in that moment of forever, I knew you were the only one I ever wanted beside me."

His fingers thread between mine, drawing me closer and I lean against the table. "That first day we met, when I climbed in the limo on the way to the competition, and you moved to sit next to me...do you remember?"

"Umhmm," I respond.

"In that moment, the thought flashed through my mind:

I could sit next to this girl for the rest of my life. From that day on, I have never wanted anything else than to have you beside me."

I cup his face and kiss his mouth, reveling in the words we've spoken. Moments of quiet relief and celebration pass between us until we're interrupted by a deep sound coming from our waiter. He's clearing his throat holding two steaming plates of lasagna, waiting for us to lean back. We allow him the space he needs and eat dinner holding hands off and on under the table.

Ben's arm circles my shoulder as we step out of Mamma Mia's. He pulls me close and kisses my temple, and we start back for the subway. We're passing a block lined with carnival games when Ben redirects our route, drawn in by the bells, whistles and flashing lights.

The game operators beckon to us as we pass, 'five dollars to climb, wins your choice' and we stop to watch two teenage boys preparing in front of rope ladders. The thick lines are strung on an upward angle, hanging over a red moonwalk floor. The object is to climb eight rungs up and ring the bell without losing balance and falling. "It looks simple enough," Ben says, as the guys flip furiously and hang from the rungs. "It can't be as hard as they're making it look." The attendant demonstrates the proper technique, skipping up the rungs as if he's dancing. "All right, I gotta do it," Ben says, moving forward.

I put my hand on his arm. "Wait for me." I lift my cross strap purse off my shoulder. "If you're doing it, you know I'm doing it."

He casts a challenging look my way. "Care to make a small wager?"

"What do you have in mind?"

"Loser owes a favor to the winner."

"Game on."

Ben pays the attendant, and we stand in front of our ladders. He cracks his knuckles and stretches his neck to both sides, murmuring to me, "You're goin' down, Fearless."

"Don't count on it, Helga." I take a split foot stance in front of my ladder.

The bell rings, and I step with my left foot, lean my right hand and walk up the eight rungs with the expertise of a girl who worked three years for her uncle's concession trailer at the state fair—truly there's not a game here whose code I don't know how to crack. I grip the bell cord and strike the ball with gusto. Ben watches from his spread eagle position on the mat as I tip-toe gracefully down. His large form is sunken and pressing a huge indent as his ladder swings frantically above him.

"I'll take the green snake," I say to the attendant, hopping off the last rung and brushing my hands. I reach a hand to help Ben. "You're right. It wasn't as hard as they were making it look," I say, smiling.

"You State girls always have something up your sleeve," he says, standing up.

"Yeah, it's called skill." I drape my five-foot snake around him and pat his cheek. "Calling in that favor."

He holds the ends of the snake around his neck like a locker room towel, smiling at me as we walk. "I might regret asking, but how exactly did Devin Grace become a carnie huckster?"

I laugh and give in. "During my high school summers I worked for my uncle's concession trailer at the state fair to earn money. As the cotton candy girl, I made friends with lots of carnies and they told me all their secrets."

"Cotton candy girl?" he says, holding his hand over his heart and stumbling back, as if he's so impressed. "The story just keeps getting better," he laughs.

I put my hand on my hip and twirl my wrist, demonstrating technique.

"Impressive," he says, smiling.

"Yeah, well it was a lot more profitable than searching for quarters in the couch and watching soap operas all summer. We never had the kind of couch you could find quarters in anyways." We laugh and I am instantly warmed at the realization that we feel like us again—laughing, joking, betting—pushing ourselves with physical challenges and happy just wandering together.

I notice a small grin lingering on Ben's face as we approach the subway station and I bump his hip with mine.

"What? What's so funny?"

He looks at me, still grinning. "You know, as soon as Dr. Oscar told us the baby was a girl, I knew she was mine."

"How?"

"Taking care of girls is what I do. My mom, my sisters." He hesitates. "And then there's you."

"Me? You don't have to take care of me. I can take care of myself."

He shakes his head. "Well, you're a completely different kind of 'take care of.'" Our laughter subsides but I'm still watching his face.

"Are you scared of having the baby, Ben?"

"I'm scared I don't know what I'm doing. There's so much about babies that I don't know. But I'll get through it.

I have to."

His fingers reach for my waist, and he stops walking and pulls me close. He's staring at me with the most loving look anyone has ever bestowed on me. He kisses my forehead and his expression grows serious. "How about you? Is there anything else you're scared of? Anything you want to talk about?"

His words are familiar. They're the same words Robyn asked Gator when he came to start life at the Center. Ben wants to know that I'm okay with the baby too, not just life with him. I recall Gator's answer. He was frightened that his daddy wouldn't be able to find him—frightened that he wouldn't find love. That's what I've been afraid of all this time too.

I reach in my pocket and feel the Game of Life car, loaded with one blue peg surrounded by tiny pink pegs. I've been carrying it ever since he gave it to me that night at the Children's Center, running my fingers over the smooth plastic bubble heads on my walks to and from the subway.

"Now that we know the baby's mine, Dev, how are you feeling?"

I pull the car out of my pocket, place it in his palm and curl his fingers. My toes press up, and I kiss his mouth.

"I'm fearless."

Acknowledgments

Thank you to my fearless editor, Candace Havens. I have such respect and admiration for your talent. Your enthusiasm and energy are a constant inspiration. My pretty smart girls and their friends are so lucky to have landed on your desk!

Thank you to the talented and dynamic team at Entangled Publishing who work so hard to help their authors succeed including Liz Pelletier, Curtis Svehlak, Debbie Suzuki, Heather Riccio and Jessica Turner.

To my family, Mark, Kirstin, Kailey and Jack, and to my friends. I am eternally grateful for all of the love and support you share with me everyday.

About the Author

Shae Ross grew up in the suburbs of Detroit, Michigan. She discovered a passion for romance novels while on summer vacations, reading by the shores of Lake Huron. Shae attended Michigan State University and Detroit College of Law and spent the majority of her career practicing corporate law and running a title insurance business. She now writes romance full time and lives with her husband and three children in the greater Lansing area.